To Persis, from whom I get
my words and my silences.

PART I

Ekamishe - Vishnuthva - Anvethu

With this first vow of Saptapadi, as your husband, I promise you Isha, to take care of your material needs and bring you prosperity.

Urmila

Recapturing the mythical
journey of love and longing
in contemporary India

PERVIN SAKET

JAICO PUBLISHING HOUSE

Ahmedabad Bangalore Bhopal Bhubaneswar Chennai
Delhi Hyderabad Kolkata Lucknow Mumbai

Published by Jaico Publishing House
A-2 Jash Chambers, 7-A Sir Phirozshah Mehta Road
Fort, Mumbai - 400 001
jaicopub@jaicobooks.com
www.jaicobooks.com

URMILA
ISBN 978-81-8495-666-5

First Jaico Impression: 2016

Page design and layout: Inosoft Systems, Delhi

Printed by

If my husband switches on the TV now, he will disapprove. Not because the whole thing is dangerous. No. He would simply find it distasteful that I am in the vortex of this controversy. My mother-in-law is anxiously fending calls from relatives and stealing glimpses at the mob outside. She paces around the living room as she speaks, clutching the end of her sari, beads of sweat erupting on her forehead.

A jostling group of dissenters has gathered outside the gate, hockey sticks, stones and banners in hand. Behind them, a larger group of media persons shout into glaring cameras, betraying excitement through their monotone.

"Protesters have lined up since morning…"

"Not sure if it's politically motivated."

"Scandal caused by the painting simply titled S, recently displayed at…"

"…now removed and locked up in an undisclosed location."

"…demand that it be burned and destroyed immediately."

"Urmila Karmarkar has refused to comment on what is clearly the most controversial piece of art since Husain's infamous *Mother India.*"

The group carries digital reproductions of the painting. A man strikes a match. He holds it to one corner of the sheet. Several others, standing a few feet apart, repeat the process. The thin sheets vaporize into ash within seconds; the orange glow fizzles out too soon. Their faces fall, but their voices rise. I sense that the protesters have been looking forward to a more dramatic demonstration, a slower, stretched-out, symbolic obliteration.

I turn my back to the TV and face the windows. The news reverberates with an unpleasant stereo effect.

"Draw that curtain!" Ma cries.

A heavy clang punctures the chaos.

I run into the bedroom, expecting something to have landed against the windows. Before I can reach it, another jangle shakes the windows, then another and another. Pebbles and stones rain against the grill of the window, rattling the frame.

"Ma!" I cry out. "Ma!"

What if the grills give way? Or if they start using smaller pebbles that can escape the bars of the grills? Or if they force themselves past the police officers and jump the gate?

Ma comes running into the room and huddles beside me. "Sarita was saying we should come to her house," she offers, trembling.

"How will we get past this mob?" My voice is several tones too loud and Ma pulls her face away.

"Sarita's car has dark, tinted windows. We could cover up, take someone else along and hope they don't recognize us."

"We won't get away! No car has left the complex since morning! Even if they don't attack us, they will ruin the car, break the windshield, the headlights…"

I can hear the dogs upstairs barking furiously and the rush of water from the tap that Ma has forgotten to close. She has washed her face a dozen times this morning, either to wipe away perspiration or camouflage her tears. The clanging, the screams, the embers, the commentary, all beat against my head, louder, more urgent.

I stride into the living room and back, into the kitchen and back. I circle my bed. "No, no, we can't leave! I won't let them make me! What have I done?"

"This is not the time for grand stands!"

"If not now, when? Oh Ma, if only *you* hadn't been dragged in the middle of all…"

"Here, put this around your head! Pack a bag and lock your cupboards. I'm calling Sarita."

She thrusts a dupatta in my hand and I promptly throw it on the bed. "They won't let us pass, Ma! What if they break the car windows, what if the glass hits the…"

Ma holds my shoulders in a trembling grip and shakes me twice. "Think straight, Umi. We have to take a chance!"

Exhausted, I begin to nod when suddenly the onslaught dies out. Maybe they have calmed down. Or perhaps they have realized that most of the stones were just falling into the innocent balcony below.

"They'll go, Ma. Just wait." I whisper. "Please."

She falls on the sofa and hides her face in her hands.

"It's fading away, see?"

I check all the windows again and then sit beside her. On TV it appears that the crowd has thinned out a little. The flares of burning plastic have died out. Occasionally, a neighbour steps out to run some errands, seemingly unaware of the action outside the building. Reporters scramble for a byte. The neighbour puts on a surprised expression and throws light on living in the same building as the controversial Urmila Karmarkar.

"She has always been the quiet sort. Who would have thought a simple woman from such a good family would paint something so outrageous?"

A different reporter thrusts the mike at his mouth. "Have you seen any more of her work? How would you describe it?"

"No, no. I have only seen this one, that too on TV, on yesterday's news."

Just then, Mrs Ogale casually walks out of the lift. Immediately, all microphones and cameras follow her.

She speaks through painted lips, tucking an imaginary strand of hair behind her ear every few seconds. "Some people say that after her husband left… He's in Dubai since many years. You see, after that some people say that maybe, I don't know…"

"Are you saying that she might be, hmm… mentally unstable?"

"I'm sorry. I can't make any comments."

"What?" Ma cries, pointing to the TV. "This is ridiculous!"

"It's funny," I say, forcing a grin. I shake my head and hook my fingers close to her face, whispering in a deep, broken tone: "Urmila Karmarkar, the woman who went mad!"

"Umi, it's not funny!" She first pushes my hands away and then clutches them in hers.

We lean against each other, taking in the commentary and the new faces of our old neighbours. Most of them guard their speech more than Mrs Ogale did, but their eyes light up as they boldly face the camera. I can't help but notice the unusually neat hair and freshly pressed clothes of every resident who steps out.

The Patoles are particularly frequent in their excursions, and within an hour, every member of the household has visited either a grocer, a mall, a parlour or the fish market.

Outside the window, the scene seems too bizarre to be real. Did all these people really see the exhibition at the NGMA? Do they really think of me as some anarchist? On the news, several artists are varyingly astonished, appreciative and angry at the assault on the freedom of expression. The outbursts are embarrassingly emotional. And I have had my fill of half-joking references to how much an artist's worth appreciates after such a demonstration.

After eight phone calls, 32 emails and constant pings, I decide to recede to virtual underground, at least while this outrage lasts. I have already refused to comment on news channels and declined police protection. However, several police vans have parked themselves around the mob.

"Switch off the TV, Umi." My mother-in-law pushes herself up from the sofa and totters to the washbasin. "At least mute the sound and come away from the window. Come, we'll sit in my room," she instructs as she splashes water on her face again.

"Are the curtains drawn there? You're sure your headache is better?"

We spend the afternoon pretending to read, flipping through a stack of *Maayboli* and other Marathi periodicals. By mid-afternoon, I have grown accustomed to the drama. First, the synchronized shouts, then the high-pitched clanks of stone against the metal grill, followed by police announcements on the loudspeaker and the news anchor's pseudo-anxious proclamations.

"Bahar aao! Bahar aao!" the protesters scream.

"Should I?" I wink, attempting a weak joke. She sighs and shakes her head, a flicker of a smile erupting and dying at the ends of her lips.

I peek through the curtains. I am surprised by the

commitment to feel offended. Even as they are being pushed away by a ring of lathi-branding police officers, the protesters shout, "Jail mein band karo! Burn every painting! Insulting our gods! Our Sita Mata! Jail mein band karo! Bolo Sita Mata ki…"

"Jai!"

"Sita Mata Ki…"

"Jai!"

The painting is one of my more unremarkable ones, saved only by the acidity of the orange robes. The figures of two men and a woman lie in a forest, huddled against the cold, their clothes torn and sullied. They are in various versions of the foetal position, curled up amidst grass and flowers, while a bird and a snake hover in the branches above. The woman's shape and flowing sari produce a distinct 'S', her hair and garments following the breeze. A dark man faces her as he sleeps, their hands clasped together even in slumber. But the wilful loose end of her sari falls on the face of the other man who lies some distance behind her.

This second man's features are hidden by the fold of her cloth, and though his fingers don't really touch her, they ache to grasp something about her. Like he may be dreaming of catching her scent, gathering her laughter or seizing her warmth. The errant sari, in draping itself about his face, connects the man and the woman. An oblivious link, suppressed in waking hours, manifest only in twilight when day and night meet and dreams engage across sleeping eyes.

It is one of my quieter paintings, the kind that inspires a U certificate, and I am surprised at the stir it has created.

By late afternoon, my lawyer calls – though no case had been filed – to tell me that this would be a cakewalk. Apparently, we can simply use the boomerang technique by counter-accusing the plaintiffs of anti-religious sentiments since they have twisted the meaning of a naïve nature scene.

"Very clever." He means me and his tone is admiring.

"Yes, very clever." I mean him and my tone is anything but that.

Keeping my fingers crossed about the no-case-filed-yet status, I go about pretending to alternately work and relax, ignoring the commotion outside. My mother-in-law plays along and we amuse ourselves with cards for a while, but then I start losing too much money and she keeps demanding more shawls to keep out a chill that I don't feel.

"Khoop gaar zhala. I need something warm to sip on."

I nod and walk into the kitchen to make our third cup of tea, hoping some activity will break my losing streak. Outside the kitchen window – the only one not facing the mob – a lone figure sits across the street: a cobbler.

He faces the road, surrounded by cobbler paraphernalia. The throng has apparently forgotten the back of the building. He stitches away under a tiny shade held up by three sticks of wood. The daily stream of honks and people pass him by, and occasionally, he is blocked by a vehicle, engulfed in a cloud of fumes or hidden behind a loitering group. His hide-and-seek appearance brings a smile to my face. He seams and bangs while I hustle with the milk, both of us happy to use our hands, separated by 30 feet and a world.

As I stir sugar into the cups, he moves.

He gets up and stretches, a long, out-of-bed stretch. Then he turns and sits down again. Only this time, he faces the wall instead of the street.

He opens a box, unwraps some food and holds it to his face. Behind him, his tools lie spread out, held within a periphery of slippers. The world passes by as usual, beyond his circle of footwear, as do the fumes, the smells and the sounds.

I wonder at his need to face the other way, ostrich-like in its sad truth. He might have turned his back to the road to grab a few moments of privacy, but he is just as public as he was earlier. The smog probably churns with his vegetables, the honking bleats in his ears and the fragrance of the food is lost in the metallic odour of Mumbai's by-lanes. He is just as visible and invisible as he had been a minute earlier. The man plays a game of deception with himself. It is just a mirage he indulges in, a fleeting refuge from a constant world.

Do I seek a similar asylum too? It's not real, this sanctuary, but it's the only one I've got. When I paint, for a while a cool breeze swishes past my face, vaporizing my sweat and soothing my scars. For that stretch, my heartache abates and I can breathe again without the piercing stab I am accustomed to.

Once, when I was still fresh from exhibition reviews and fawning art students, a peppy journalist with two nose rings had probed, "Urmila Karmarkar, you were a bathroom artist – if I may – until you were discovered by a distant family member. Did you nurse dreams of such success?"

"Not really. I painted very infrequently."

"So when you got married, you had no idea that your husband's second uncle was the retired dean of Mumbai's most celebrated art school?"

"I knew very little about my husband, so knowing about his relatives was out of the question."

She had granted me a flicker of a smile. "And over lunch one Sunday, Prof Kothadiya saw some of your canvases and contacted a couple of art galleries and agents. Is that it?"

"Something like that."

"And then there was no looking back?"

"Well, I have had a couple of unflattering reviews…"

"Which have been vehemently opposed on a host of microblogging sites."

"The debate is quite evenly balanced actually. It's likely that *Seclusion* tries a little too hard."

"Yet, you have a great marketability ratio, Urmila. Usually, artists go through years of struggle, anonymity, heartache and even poverty. They yearn for all the things that seem to have fallen into your lap."

I had fumbled then, searching for an example that proved my suffering, almost apologizing for the ease with which I had slipped into the fraternity. Would anyone understand that my torment ran alongside each canvas? That I painted the story of another Urmila? That to truly know her grief, I had to live her life? That *Seclusion*, *Swallowed* and *Veil* were all me? And they were all her? Together, we formed a triangle with each canvas, feeding off one another.

Of course, with every successive discussion, I learned to attribute my fortune to the gods, destiny and ancestral blessings. Alternately I thanked a deity, a grandparent and a twist of fate, smiling wide enough to display happiness and small enough to express humility.

Soon, I was invited to conduct guest workshops at a couple of art institutions and the same journalist noticed my enthusiasm to help young artists. She was less resentful of my easy climb then, and over the next few chats, I found that I had graduated to 'Urmila ma'am'.

"Umi! Chaha zhaala ka?"

"Coming!"

I stop agitating the whirlpool inside the cups. The cobbler still faces the wall.

The rest of the evening passes under the aroma of ginger tea and the shadow of the cobbler's brown shirt. Occasionally, the flare of burning paper lights our window and dies behind the sheer curtains.

"Bahar aao! Bahar aao!" Do they actually expect me to comply? What if I really step outside?

I can hear a few neighbours shout down at them, "Go away. No one is at home. The house is locked."

"Umi! Stay away from the window!" Ma gasps when she walks into the kitchen and sees me peek at the cobbler again. "God knows who is watching this side of the building!"

"They're already dispersing, I think."

"What if they're back tomorrow? Umi, let's leave at night! We'll talk to that inspector and have the police escort us somewhere."

"For what, Ma? *They* are vandalising on the streets! Why should *we* hide like criminals?"

"No, the real criminal is hiding too far for us," she sighs and looks away.

"Ma!"

"Does he even know? Does he even care? Two women alone in this huge, mouldy house, with a mob at our throats!"

A sob shivers through her and I hold her close. I shut my eyes and try to picture his face. I struggle with the features. His eyes, when I find them, look through me. My art is my only ally in this search for love. The strokes tell my story and the canvas soaks away my rejection. The gust dies down at the end of each canvas, a haven of sorts. I wait to turn my back to the world as the cobbler did, and demand my own piece of wall.

Perhaps, in some manner, in absentia, my husband is fulfilling the first vow that the pundit had translated for us; he has brought me prosperity. A few years after the men left, we sold the family construction business since I was under no delusions of managing that strange, masculine domain. Although we still get rich dividends from its sale, the income from my art sustains me. Several paintings are picked up by neo-rich industrialists, many are silently auctioned, some have even changed owners for larger sums.

On TV, the camera zooms into a woman with deep kohl, a bandhini dupatta, and colourful plastic wristbands. There is something familiar about the tilt of her neck and the squeal in her reportage. Her eyes dart around the crowd even as the camera pans her inch by inch.

Isha Divani? Zara Imami? Ira Belani? Tina Chauthani? I've never been good at names. Faces yes (except his), faces always (except his), faces to the tiniest mole (except his), but names, never. I do remember her question though, posed under the fading lights of Samovar Café:

"Why do your paintings always leave something out? Something is always just outside the edge of the canvas…"

I'm sure I provided a long, meaningless reply – the only kind I know. How could I confess my rejection? Of course, my work is remarkable only because it seeks him, each canvas yearns to pull him into the frame so he may look at me once more.

Maybe if someone probed deeper, we would find the connection. After all, every curse has a reason, every demon a back story, every rishi a transformation, every poet a thief and every god a miraculous birth. Each piece of information is hyperlinked, connecting across space and time, to a yellow afternoon when I first sought love.

∞

I couldn't have been more than 10 years old. It was my parents wedding anniversary, and through the evening, Aai and Baba were predictably dull. In one corner of the living room, I held a pile of miniature steel utensils against my chest. I needed to set up my kitchen. The metallic toys rustled softly against the frills and bows of my dress. From the window above me, a draft of warm wind fluttered around my neck, cooling my sweat.

"Newspaper kutthe aahe?" My father put down his third cup of tea, switched off the television and walked towards the bathroom.

"Table!" My mother hollered from the kitchen.

Baba reached the dining table, tottering awkwardly, but no newspaper relieved the hunt in his eyes.

"Umi!"

I decided not to answer.

"UMI! Where is the newspaper?"

Baba had reached his threshold. He could wait for five minutes after his tea, no more. Everyone knew that as soon as he started his noisy slurping, they needed to keep the bathroom free.

Vanita, my distant cousin and my dearest friend, our damned, doomed, ill-starred Vanita, zipped from corner to corner and she discovered the cause of the agitation under a chair. Vani thrust the paper in Baba's hands just as his bowels were about to pour out their contents. I pinched my nose and started fanning the air around me. Vani, standing just outside the toilet, smiled as if she were in the Mughal Gardens.

The spluttering and sizzling from the kitchen attempted

to camouflage Baba's toilet routine but failed by a significant margin. By the time more tea and bhajjis were presented on the table, the flush had run for the third time and I had fizzed out yet another bottle of deodorant.

"Eeesh Umi! It'll stick to the food now!" Aai snatched the bottle from me and tucked it under her armpit.

Baba tossed a potato bhajji into his mouth.

"Garam!" He jumped from foot to foot, fanning his open mouth with one hand, while the other hand held his pyjama drawstring. Aai dunked a glass of water down his throat and dabbed his forehead with the end of her sari.

Their wedding anniversary and this was their great moment of love.

If asked by well-meaning relatives what the day's plans were, my father chuckled over the phone, "Kaay atta! After so many years of marriage, what party?" A couple of jokes followed, about aging couples or nagging wives or pouting mothers-in-law, with the listener guffawing awkwardly, as expected.

My mother, if she overheard these, joined in heartily. She sniggered at the caricatures, easing dollops of batter in the sizzling oil. Her responses perplexed me, and I couldn't figure out if they were a result of her maddening stupidity or her quiet wisdom.

Our house never saw roses or greeting cards, never knew the spark of a finger against a cheek or the whiff of musky cologne. My mother never wore chiffon saris and my father never seemed to notice the rustle of her clothes. In our tiny

1BHK, I slept between my parents every night. Sometimes, I wanted to stay up longer or just spread wider, and I suggested sleeping in the living room, but Baba wouldn't allow it. "Why waste electricity," he would mutter. Aai's smile never waned.

Baba, who hated euphemisms, referred to himself as eco-friendly. I believe in moderation when discussing one's parents, and I called him a miser. We were each allowed a single bucket of water a day, even in summers when the skin was parched. Only our perspiration cooled our faces as we sat on one bed under one fan. At mealtimes, the bulky pressure cooker and aluminium pan were plonked on the dining table since serving bowls were wasteful. Old saris were made into quilts and pillow covers, new ones were wrapped away for special occasions that never came. Empty milk sachets were washed and Baba took rotis and sandwiches in them to office; all the offers on the cling-wraps and aluminium foils of the world couldn't tempt Baba.

Yet, I could live with the rationed water and mismatched cushions, and use ketchup from complimentary takeaway sachets. What pierced me, like the geyser-less showers on November mornings, was their acceptance of a slipshod marriage. A large turmeric stain on Aai's nightgown welcomed Baba home every evening. He reciprocated by scratching his balls with such vigour that I had to look away.

Romantic melodies and item girls filled our living room of course, but their effect never resonated in their voices, not even in the sounds I caught accidentally. They were always talking about my marriage, but not once did they make marriage attractive. No compliments, no shared jokes, no secret eye contact, no shoulder rubs, not even a pet name.

Theirs was an arrangement of course, as I knew mine would also be, but did it have to be so loveless?

Through school and the first half of college, I searched for signs that I was mistaken, that behind my parents' unsightly conduct, lay hidden, secret passions marked 'confidential', delivered and received only in code, so clever that they camouflaged with ordinariness, and made every moment special and private. If they did, I never knew.

However, the next time I looked up from a Danielle Steel novel and found Baba discussing gold prices in the year I might get married, I decided – to fall in love. With my husband. In advance.

It's not as difficult as it sounds, perhaps easier than falling in love with a real husband in real time. In fact, every radio channel, every poster stuck in every first-class ladies' compartment and every Hindi movie had a catalogue of tips for me.

But still, an absent man is an absent man. I would have to go slowly. I needed very tiny steps.

I decided to start with the shoulders. They wouldn't be very broad, I knew. That's the stuff of fairy tales; no, his would be roomy when I wanted to snuggle up and yet slim enough to cut a lean figure. I pictured them, muscular and dark brown, like mounds of melting chocolate. They were marked by a set of prominent collarbones and housed a tiny well right in the middle. They had a birthmark as well, a large dot on the left, just where the neck ended. It was a mesmerizing mark, a black hole that I could disappear into.

Eventually, when I managed to clamber out of that hold, I

shifted my focus to his chin and mouth. His lips were as soft as his jaw was hard; they were as curved as his chin was angular. He had a long face, with a protruding muzzle and a stubble that stood on the verge of a beard.

If I looked very carefully, I would notice his lips twitching. The muscles around them trembled as if they were receiving tiny electric shocks at regular intervals. It was either the almost-invisible spasms of those muscles or the licking of his lips; very rarely would his face remain still.

Once I had sated myself – which took a considerable while – I found myself moving up the bridge of his nose and streak of his cheekbones. Only much later did I reach the oasis that I had been yearning for – his eyes. Clear but dark, an intense shade of brown leaning towards black, they looked back at me with softness. They blinked frequently, as if wondering at our premature romance. Even with that surprise, they couldn't restrict the laughter that tumbled out, the thrill of us gazing at one another.

Those were days tinged with the anticipation of desires that I wished would always evade me. As much as I yearned to see him in flesh, I was caught in the buzz he created every night behind my closed eyelids. He was always within reach and yet I dared not reach out, lest the stubble pricked my finger and I found that I wouldn't bleed.

For several years, I built a face and a marriage, never once stopping to think how much longer it would take to dissolve them.

The real trouble came much later. It came after the pimples, acne, fringe and chubby thighs had come and gone. It came with the first brush of pink over the cheekbones, the bend in the waist, the curve of the hips and the careless flick of the wrists.

Thin bangles tinkling at my wrists and the mogra in my hair announced my arrival as I brought in tea and pohe.

"Made by Urmila," Aai was quick to point out.

They rounded off a list of all my qualities, while I pretended I was not in the room.

"She is a fantastic cook. Next time you come, she'll make puranpolis. They're famous in the whole colony!"

"And variety dishes too. You'll never be bored. One day pasta, one day sev puri, then South Indian..."

"Our daughter is a little shy, don't mind. Nowadays, girls are so outspoken..."

"And sewing. Tell them about the sewing."

"Of course! See this framed embroidery here? Umi did it. And we don't go to tailors for simple things like sari falls and all."

"Very caring also. She bought that bird feeder there. She also insisted that our whole building separates all the wet garbage and dry garbage so the poor sweepers don't have to do it. Very modern in the right way, na?"

"Sings like a koel too! But only afterwards you'll hear – she's very shy, like I told."

Finally, after a stern glance from me, Aai whispered one truth, "She dabbles in art once in a while."

When I look back, I wonder why Aai, who never grudged me anything, was clearly uncomfortable with my colours. Like she knew that it was to strip me of myself, to transform me from a now-Urmila to a never-and-forever Urmila. From a one-and-only-you-are-unique-like-everybody-else Urmila to an Urmila who was a reflection of many echoes. An Urmila everyone knew but no one remembered. As if she knew that I'd walk down a lonely path, living a forgotten exile, surrounded only by the air of neglect.

Perhaps with the intuition that only mothers have, she had been anxiously dreading the husband whose face now evades me. The yugas are replete with the mighty who attempted to hinder destiny and failed. Aai, the Cassandra of my epic, could only look on as the clock ticked out my life.

I served the tea looking at their laps, too preoccupied with not spilling it. Carefully, the saved-for-special-occasions cups were passed into the palms of his mother, his father and his brother. This older brother, Purushottam, seemed eager to dispel my discomfort by relieving me of the shaking cups. He reached ahead and passed the sweets to his parents, offered to add sugar to the tea according to everyone's preferences and even ventured, "Please sit. Thank you for such a delicious spread."

"Thank you, also," he turned and looked at Vani, as if he knew that it was all a result of her kneading, chopping and frying.

Vani smiled but didn't look down at her feet, as was her habit. Instead, she ventured closer and took one laddoo from the plate that he held out.

I hadn't yet heard my husband-to-be's voice. Conversation was staccato, erupting from behind firm smiles. Every opinion expressed by every parent was vehemently agreed to by the remaining three parents.

All eyes settled on me every few seconds and I couldn't get a good look at him without seeming brazen. Only his lap sat within modesty-approved view. He wrung his fingers often and played with the single ring on his right hand. Eventually I managed to reach his chest and then even stolen a glance at his left shoulder, but his face evaded me. I wished Baba had insisted on a photograph before the meeting; he had only been concerned with the horoscope. Then, during an uncharacteristically animated and long burst of conversation, when I sensed that everyone would be too engrossed, I did it. I looked up.

He was facing my mother and I only got a profile. Sensing my gaze on his cheek, he slowly turned towards me. The eyes were large but distracted. They didn't dart fretfully like a caged pigeon. They didn't stare vacantly either, nor were they meditative. They were fixed on me like I was a curiosity, a novelty. And then, in an instant, the interest had waned. He watched with detachment, objectively, cerebrally, as one reads a newspaper – as if this wasn't his world or his reality; as if I was a new television programme that would be aired in his living room for an hour every day.

I was suddenly twitchy and restless. I shifted my position in my seat, rearranged the pallu over my shoulder and rotated the bangles around my wrists until the tinkling got too much and Aai glared the noise down. I was uneasy but didn't know why; what I did know was that he was completely oblivious to my anxiety, and this disquieted me further.

At the end of an hour, smiles abounded and sweets were stuffed into all our mouths. I touched his parents' feet and they held me in a tight embrace. He bent before Aai and Baba and was showered with hugs and blessings. Then the two mothers clasped each other, their eyes moist. Finally, the fathers graduated from firm handshakes to awkward squeezes of the shoulder and pats on the back.

Everyone embraced everyone else, except the two of us. We shook hands, like adversaries before a match.

That night as I lay down, I thought of the husband I had decided to fall in love with in advance. I thought of the knees, the fingers, the shoulder blades I had loved for so many years.

"Very nice boy," Vani offered, hovering around me. "Such a good family too. The brother was so courteous."

"Hmmm," I didn't want to get into this conversation.

"His brother was so respectful, na?" she continued.

I pretended to be asleep. Vani waited for a few seconds and then walked out towards the kitchen. I heard her opening the window just a little for the breeze to make its way in, and then adjusting her pillow.

"Goodnight," I offered finally, feeling guilty.

"Have a nice meeting in your dreams!" she teased in a hoarse whisper that carried across the darkness.

I didn't need a meeting; a glimpse would have sufficed. I replayed the evening repeatedly and looked at the scene from different angles. From the entrance, from the kitchen, through the eyes of Vani hovering in the kitchen, preparing the pohe that I had claimed. I saw his confident, lanky frame and the easy relationship he had with his teacup. But no matter how hard I looked, I couldn't remember his face. I knew the angle of his elbows and the straightness of his thighs. I knew the slight curve of his shoulder and his gentle stoop as he sat. I even knew his closely cut hair. But the rest was a blank. I had been so conscious of his neutral, curious gaze that I had failed to see him.

His cheeks, his forehead, his nose, his ears, his chin, his eyes – they were all smudges of brown, blots that I would spend the next several years studying but would never pin down. They evaded me each time, revelling in their abandon, certain they could never be reduced to the static constancy that I so craved.

Even now, sometimes I try to sketch his face on a paper napkin in a restaurant, on the writing pad beside the obsolete landline, on the soft bar of soap that I hold through long, thirsty showers. I usually manage the curve of his ears and the fluff of freshly washed hair, but within that frame, I face a mocking emptiness. His features remain a mystery; all I have is a brown rectangle. He has never let me grasp them. They flit away in reckless cruelty, caring not of the ruins that lie in their wake.

Four years and counting.

After fate unveiled my cards, my in-laws desired a pilgrimage to Rameshwaram. Being the undemanding kind, they scattered hints and sighs all about the house, so that I was always bumping into breaths heavy with longing. Ma brought brochures from travel agencies, took bhajan classes every evening, conferred with friends who had paid their respects and lamented with those who hadn't.

"At least we had the good fortune to visit Kashi a decade ago. But what use is Kashi without Rameshwaram?"

Papa believed that the spoons slipping away from his fingers and the medicine dribbling down his chin were clear signs; he clasped photographs of the abode of Vishnu with an urgency that worried us. Of course, he had a lot more heartbreak to endure, eventually slipping away in inches and years, scandalizing everyone with his last request. But there was no way to know that then.

In the absence of the sons, it fell on me to accompany them, a nurse in tow. We had no choice but to visit during Diwali, the tourist season; other times of the year were too hot, too cold or too wet for Ma and Papa.

On disembarking from the plane, swishing palms and hung, salty air greeted us. The warm, pickled landscape was dotted with lanterns and flowers of astonishing variety. A sticky car ride found us honking dangerously close to stalls frying fritters and doling out laddoos by the kilo.

Eventually, we slipped onto a smooth though narrow highway. The nurse, her chin hanging, and mouth open, slept, oblivious to everything that fell on her face. I tried to maintain an upbeat babble to keep awake, but since Ma had developed an aversion to air-conditioning, the wind hit my mouth each time I opened it. After swallowing a few fistfuls of air, I submitted to several rounds of miniscule siestas and a headache that would last the day.

Rameshwaram, one of the four dhams that promised liberation. We were in the hub of the devout.

The car wouldn't go through the final 100-metre stretch to the hotel since flower shops had taken over the road. We unloaded our bags, standing at a midpoint between the hotel, the main temple and the Agnitheertham. A stretch of the sea folded gently towards the temple, allowing for safe immersion of ashes, cleansing of sins and deference to the gods. Families paid homage in its waters alongside lone sadhus with matted hair and rudraksh garlands.

Papa's insistence that we stay in a stripped motel instead of a host of better options had reminded me a little too much of Baba. However, Papa's reasoning had nothing to do with thrift and everything to do with the view; The Tamil Nadu Lodge overlooked the waters that rose and ebbed to the chants of throngs of devotees. The rooms had tiny beds, lukewarm water, chipped tiles and paper-thin walls, but they had one thing right – large windows.

I leaned out, watching groups bathing and praying knee-deep in the Agnitheertham water inlet. The gentle throb of the waves interspersed with faint songs and chimes. The setting sun enveloped their distant bodies in a warm orange glow as they meditated in ink-blue puddles. I was at the epicentre of religious zeal, and there was little I could do but embrace it.

By the next morning, more of my elitist scepticism had washed away, too feeble in the face of unrelenting faith. We stood in line, inching towards the bath area. The temple held 22 wells, and each one offered different healing properties as well as a distinct taste. Papa would have liked to fetch water himself and bathe near every single well, but gave in to our collective pleas and agreed to the more practical route. Three helpers were hired to fetch water from each well and pour it over our heads while we prayed.

We stood in a common pond while a skinny boy with miraculously dry clothes ran buckets for me. On noticing that we didn't have a guide, he took it upon himself to supply a constant stream of nuggets along with the water.

"This one is especially good for arthritis. Taste it. Put your tongue out. I pour. Sweet, no?"

I attempted to answer but was prevented by the flow that ran into my mouth and nose. While I sat shivering, he ran off for the next bucket. Some feet away, Ma chanted loudly as the water washed over her. When her helper scurried off, she waded towards me and clasped my hand.

"Umi... Ask for Chhotu."

"Ma..."

"When the water is being poured, ask that he comes back. I am also asking. Trust me!"

It had been four years since I had seen my husband, long enough to despair and yet short enough to aspire. At what point does optimism end and hopelessness take over? How is it measured? In tears? In nightmares? In wrinkles? In paintings?

My runner boy returned with his bucket. As the coldness pricked me, I willed myself to picture my husband's face.

Come back to me.

Though the words echoed in my mouth, I was unable to see his features – an irregular long polygon, brown, gawky, nothing.

Another bucket. *Come back*! Again my words knocked about and again the featureless angular mound. I kept my eyes shut long after the last drop had run down my nose, intent on conjuring him up, if not in flesh, at least as a vision. Like a teenager all over again, I willed myself to shape his ears and outline his lips. I placed and removed a stream of possible eyes but rejected them all. Mixed brown and white and then a little yellow, a dash of deeper brown, but with every blend, his complexion dodged me.

A jolt of wetness shook me out of my desperate colours. I gasped and swallowed water, but the liquid kept my eyes glued. I steered myself away from my cold tingling skin and sought warmth in the elusive aura of my husband. I'd once dreamt him up in infinitesimal detail; now even the outline of a cheekbone defeated me.

Once more the sting and gush of water. "In this, you will taste salt. Can you imagine salt in a well? This is especially good water for ladies. Don't worry if it goes in your eyes."

By the ninth bucket, I had stopped feeling the bite of the water. I had to see him once. He may have slipped his hand out of mine, but surely, he couldn't destroy my memories so easily? Each icy cascade reminded me that in fact, he could. A veil had always characterized our meetings and even Rameshwaram was helpless in the face of Shree's stubborn distance.

There is no way to deal with the eventual other than submission. It took 16 buckets, but finally, for a few moments, I found that I could surrender to the moment – not to him or to my helplessness, but to the path below my feet. I could save myself from futile heartburn. As the water curtained around me, I cut myself off from the other groups, their squeals and mantras. A banter of cures washed over me, churning in the medley of splashes and squeals. First the water's cool slap, then its warm embrace – no desperate prayers for a reunion, no appeals against fate.

Even now, I am able to recall the bliss of that submission. The moments were as miniscule as dust and evaporated like dewdrops, but they were complete. For just that flash of an instant, I didn't want to be somewhere else or someone else; I embraced everything that had led up to this place, this time and this woman.

I lost count of how often my face was splattered with varied smells and stings, and soon, they stopped. When I opened my eyes, the world stood sharper.

"See madam? Everything will be all right. Whatever you want, especially children... sons, everything you can get."

After being hurried into a vast changing room and emerging

more wet than dry, we readied ourselves for the main temple darshan. I was subjected to kicks and elbowing by bent geriatrics as we jostled inch by inch towards the sanctum sanctorum. They stoically assumed that I would let them through first, although I stood ahead of them in the queue. The reasoning was irrefutable – in the line-up to Yama, they were closer.

Then Papa suggested, "We'll organize a special puja for Chhotu and Puru."

"What? Here?" I exclaimed foolishly. How could I have missed it? Attaining moksha remained a debatable prospect; their sons were just a wee bit more within reach.

"This is just the place," he added. "From here, Ram built the bridge to reach Sita."

"And after the war, Ram asked for forgiveness for his sins here."

"It's a sign, Umi. There's a reason why life brought you here."

How was I to tell them that *they* were the reason? Their aging hearts, persistent sighs and fleeing sons? Despite the years, every day we yearned for their footprints on the red 'Welcome' mat.

The next morning, Papa sent the nurse off to the Devasthanam office, which looked into the arrangement of special personal pujas. When we met the manager and a priest of the Devasthanam, we were in for a surprise.

"Such a special puja is only conducted on Fridays."

"But it's just Tuesday. Can't you make an ..."

"We can do everything, madam," I thought I noticed a tiny bow, just a momentary stoop, but then, he was significantly bent already. "But what's the use? It won't be effective unless it is performed on a Friday."

"How do we make the booking?" Papa asked. "It is so crowded now..."

"Can't it be performed on any other day?" I interrupted.

"I will make your booking for you." He shuffled towards me. "Madam, it must be a Friday. You are lucky; this Friday is the auspicious day of kartika shudha padyami, a very good day for prayers. They will be especially strong."

"Really? What is the significance of that?" This had to be Ma.

"Lord Vishnu, who took the Vamana avatar, as a dwarf and defeated the mighty king Bali with just three steps ... you might know the story... sister, on kartika shudha padyami Bali went to Patala – the underworld – and took over that kingdom. This day denotes his surrender to the mighty Vishnu and the end of pride and greed."

"So now we'll have to change our reservations," I picked up my phone. "I'll also have to talk to the hotel about extending our stay for another four days."

"You have waited so long, madam. You won't mind a few more days. It is often seen that the Lord decides when one may visit His abode and when one may leave."

"Then perhaps He would help me out with a room booking?"

"Umi! Don't… Punditji, sorry for…"

The man bent further. "Perhaps."

The hotel manager insisted that every room had been booked months in advance. He rattled off a list of other similar lodges: Hare Ram Hare Krishna Hotel, Blue Coral Cottage, Maharaja Deluxe Rooms – but none shared such proximity to the temple. Finally, after I exaggerated Papa's paralysis and agreed to pay for two rooms but use just one, he relented.

I had to move in with my in-laws and make do on the sofa, and find an alternate hotel for the nurse. It was well past lunchtime before all arrangements were finalized. My appetite had vanished with all the thinly veiled bribes that I found myself dishing out.

Ma and Papa hadn't bothered with lunch either; the looped conversation was enough.

"… just imagine if in a month, you see Chhotu walking home. Just imagine! Umi, come. Sit."

"No Ma. I'll lie down. I'm too scared to think of such things."

"Me too. But… just imagine!" Her voice began to shake. "Then what will it matter, all this hassle and all the…"

"But what if he doesn't?"

"But what if he *does*?"

"Hope is the worst," I whispered.

She took my hand. "It's just a little while longer. I know. A mother knows."

With two vacant days staring us in the face, we had little to do but make our way to the usual tourist spots. Considering the other option of remaining holed up in our unremarkable accommodation, even the bumpy ride to Dhanushkodi in a dilapidated jeep was welcome.

Our driver was more than enthusiastic. "From here, Hanuman took a huge leap and landed at Lanka. Jai Hanuman! And you'll see the starting of the bridge that the vanar sena built to cross the sea. Jai Sri Ram!"

We continued on the road along the shore for a while and I was glad to have the wind wailing in my ears. Ma, intent on catching every word of our guide, leaned in towards him, clutching her half-open windowpane for balance.

"Madam, see that?" The driver was adamant I show interest in the landscape. "Dhanushkodi was destroyed by a cyclone many years back. See the broken railway tracks there? And there is a road that side… Now no one lives here. It is called bhootgaav – ghost town. Last time the cyclone and tidal waves reached all the way to Rameshwaram! Imagine! They stopped just outside the temple at the feet of Lord Ram! Bolo Jai Sri Ram!"

He rattled away and I learnt to nod so I may ward off repetitions of his twang. Finally, he uttered the words that I had been waiting for. "See! Heaven, no?"

We scrambled out and trampled on the warm sand, eager

to reach the periphery of the brown grains. Two distinct seas embraced each other, like sisters who have loved and fought. The Bay of Bengal seemed older, her wave-less surface napping in the sun as old women are expected to. She was also deeper, our guide was quick to point out, and deceiving. Often, a benign stretch plunged several kilometres, tricking swimmers.

The Indian Ocean rippled and left froth and debris at our feet, sloshing and gurgling in the space between our toes. We washed our legs in her water, unmindful of the large surges and breakers that soared just a few feet away.

"See there? Those rocks? If you look from here, they form a line, no? Even though the bridge was broken, these pieces remain."

The boulders, though very far apart, largely fell in line, rising above the frolicking of the waves.

"So the water must be shallow here?" Ma asked.

"Oh no, madam! Do not make that mistake. Three foreign boys last year also said that and they went to swim. Only one came back. Only one! That's why all those policemen are here. See!"

We contented ourselves with ankle-high dips in the sea, Papa holding onto the nurse and me. After being tickled and teased for a while, the group gravitated towards a cluster of stalls selling coconut juice and roasted corn.

"You go, Ma." I couldn't take my eyes off the water. "I'll come in sometime."

I stood at the cusp, welcoming the current that twisted my

hair and stung my eyes. The floating stones hovered some distance away, tempting me with their nearness. The sun, though high, stood muted, mellowed by a fluff of clouds. It would be a couple of hours before it slipped away.

The spot where history, legend and mythology churned together, where one half of a couple embarked on a journey to find a beloved in a foreign land. Where a bridge once possibly stood, marking a union, however brief, a hope, however lost, and a love, however doomed.

I squinted but the land across remained out of reach. I had no messenger to fly to my beloved and report where he sat or how he lived. I didn't know what he thought of me, or if he thought of me at all.

I had no idea of the last meal he ate or the last time he was unwell or the colour of his bedsheet. We were not separated by a nourishing chasm of water but a desolate stretch of desert. No cool droplets hung on the dry dunes that stood between us. Instead, infinite grains of sand, unrelenting in their roundness, pricked my feet every moment of each day.

I bent and touched the water with my fingertips. A wordless prayer rippled behind my closed mouth. *Come home.* Return to the embrace of your wife, the commands of your duty and the words of the vows you once made.

The sun shook off its veils and darted a thick ribbon across the glinting water. The water gurgled and rested at my ankle. I took in the flowing blues for a few moments and turned to join the others. As the last of the ripples left my ankle, a hard object nudged my foot. I jumped. A coconut, unbroken.

On our way back to the hotel, it wobbled on my lap, staining my kurta with its wetness. The horizon turned dusky and dense, with the sun gravitating towards the sea. Above us, birds indulged in their last squawks of the day, screeching and flying across the treetops. I allowed myself the folly of a prayer, pleading to the sand, the waters, the birds, the breeze and the setting sun that would soon rise in the other half of the world. I prayed for them to carry my message across to the land that was his mistress.

PART II

Dhve Urjve - Vishnuthva - Anvethu

With this second vow of Saptapadi, as your husband, I promise you Urje: to grow strong together, physically, mentally and spiritually.

Although Vani's entry into our family could be vividly recalled, no one seemed to remember the days before she lived with us. Often Aai found herself reminiscing, "Remember when I taught you how to make chappatis, Vanita?" or "How excited you were to make papads in the microwave?" but even Aai could never recollect a day when the chappatis or papads were done by anyone else.

Vani was brought to our house under what were always described as 'tragic circumstances'. The tragedy was rarely discussed in her presence, but seldom left to rest once she turned her back. It so happened that my bond with Vani was preceded by a connection that our fathers shared. For one, they were related through a convoluted family tree – Baba's cousin's brother-in-law had married Vani's grandmother's cousin's niece. Vani's father had apparently done a disservice to himself by marrying a poorer, relatively plain girl with a leased, infertile field and a bedridden mother. "But those are the ways of the heart," my mother would sigh each time she recounted the story to me. "And these tragedies don't end with one generation," she'd indicate Vani with her chin.

This feeble link between Baba and Vani's father would have dissolved if it weren't for another, much stronger association. Both men had a common heritage in a village called Akola that specialized in scorching summers and the sweetest oranges. Although Baba had been to the place only a handful of times, he intuitively felt a strong affinity to anyone who reminded him of his grandfather's carefree, impoverished-but-unaware-of-it childhood. I remember some random childhood trips where we'd get into a hired car laden with books, electric coolers, calendars, even my old toys – all to be gifted to the school where Baba's father had studied. Aai's old saris also found their way there (the girls would learn how to make cushion covers from them) as well as an indiscriminate collection of marbles, battery-operated lanterns, jute bags, curtains and crockery sets. The single-storey, exposed-brick, Marathi-medium school seemed grateful for Baba's Santa Claus-like trips and reciprocated with baskets of oranges, tulsi saplings and glittery wall hangings made by the students.

A few times, some of the more promising boys were introduced to Baba with the hope that he would find them a way into Mumbai. Baba, not one to discourage, nevertheless managed to keep several of them at bay with casual, mid-assent comments on how much it cost to buy a kilo of cauliflower or a litre of petrol. Yet, he introduced one of them to an assistant film director who introduced him to a dresswalla who introduced him to a fashion designer, and now, the man is one of her many masterjis, working on brocade lehengas and embellished turbans. Another one found his way into a bakery. Baba got yet another man a job as a driver. Over the years, his informal placement agency had brought eight or nine men to Mumbai, and – the real mark of success – only three had returned.

However, his biggest favour had been for Vani's father, much before Vani was born.

Vani's parents' field had long demonstrated its moody, unreliable temperament. Aai often described to me how the land, which was more rock than mud, caused even the special, expensive seeds to wither before they could push above the earth. The family survived on the few buffaloes and chickens they had. Occasionally, Baba sent some medicines for Vani's grandmother. Once, on Diwali, Aai had sent the relatively recent bride a new sari.

Two years later, when I was just a toddler, we drove down the kachcha road to the school again. Once we had seen the newly constructed toilets, visited the temple and engaged in staccato formal conversation with Baba's grandfather's aging brother, we made our way towards Vani's parents' house.

Chandrashekhar and Savitri Phanse had prepared what must have been a lavish meal. "Including chicken," Aai always remembered to point out. "How they got everything ready, I don't know. They must have started as soon as they heard the car come towards the school. And soft ghee-rice for you because you were so little."

The house consisted of a large hexagonal room, surrounded by an expansive courtyard that had cracked under the heat. Two thin dogs sat with their tongues out, too hot to even bother looking in our direction. Once inside, we sat on cushions stuffed with straw but Aai said I soon ran into the cooking area. Various adults took turns keeping me away from the flame as Savitri Phanse pressed together fresh jowar bhakri for us.

They refused to eat with us. They took turns serving the food and spooning rice into my distracted mouth, threatening to give the rice to an imaginary sparrow if I refused it. Only after we were fed did Vani's parents approach the leftovers. While they hurriedly swallowed the meal, we were requested to make ourselves comfortable on their single divan and a tiny stool. Baba spread out and Aai fanned herself with her pallu after fixing her bangles high up on her hand, so they would not tinkle and draw attention to themselves. I lay on the cool floor with my dress hitched high, and Aai occasionally directed the waves of her pallu towards me.

A few minutes later, Vani's mother began clearing away the empty utensils. The noise shook Baba out of his intermittent nap. Chandrashekhar Phanse began some customary enquiries of people they both knew. When there were no more common connections left to discuss, Baba prepared himself for the request that hovered in the air.

"Joshi-sahib, would there be anything for me?" Chandrashekhar Phanse finally asked, his palms clasped together near his stomach.

"Mumbai takes more than it gives," Baba half-laughed and tried to dismiss the plea. "Just the distances, the commute, can kill a man!"

"I've got a 12 pass certificate also," Chandrashekhar Phanse said.

"Hmmm…"

"Anything is fine."

Baba nodded and frowned thoughtfully. "I'll have to see, Chandra."

"I know someone who can get me a BA certificate also. Will cost ₹800. But if I get something, then I can pay him after the salary."

"Oh," Baba's frown deepened.

Aai registered their desperation in silence, wishing again that she wasn't wearing gold bangles on her wrists. Recounting the story, she would tell me that she brought her pallu over her hands. "Our hired, dusty car, your frock with the satin bow, your Baba's leather shoes outside the door – it all felt obscene," she insisted.

"We cannot hold out much longer," Chandrashekhar Phanse's gaze fell to the floor. "We're already under too much debt."

"And then there's the other thing," Savitri Phanse spoke, looking first at her husband and then joining his contemplation of the floor.

When none of them ventured to elaborate, Aai asked, "What thing?"

The couple looked at each other.

"Tai, we are to have a child." Her hand touched her stomach lightly and she allowed herself a small smile.

"Arre waah!" My mother got up and held the other woman's hands. "That is wonderful."

"Not if it has to come into this world," she said, looking around the bare room.

"Don't you worry! Children come with their own fortune. Everything will change. You'll see!"

As it turned out, everything did change. First, Baba got Chandrashekhar Phanse a job as a peon in a friend's office. A little later, Chandrashekhar Phanse himself applied for another office-boy job at a different place, got the position and negotiated a better salary. Then, Vanita was born.

Considering the abundance that had preceded her birth, Vani's parents eagerly looked forward to the horoscope prepared soon after. The pundit listed the indecipherable first – Mesha was the rising sign. Its lord Mars was placed in the twelfth house in the watery sign of Meen rashi. The lord of Lagna occupied the twelfth house.

Then the juicy bits – a love marriage and foreign travel. Her parents looked at each other in disbelief. Health issues, which would escalate when in her thirties, but nothing that wouldn't be solved. She would have a kind and accommodating temperament and be loved by almost everyone. Not too bright, but she would stretch herself and aim high.

And finally, the blow – Mangal was in the fourth house. Discord in the family (never mind the kind and accommodating temperament mentioned earlier), bitterness, marital upheavals, death.

"A manglik!" her father cried in disbelief.

"But all the signs were so auspicious!" her grandmother insisted. "And the buffalo is pregnant again."

The pundit shook his head and dismissed her connections. "The signs begin from the time of birth, not before. If only she was born on a Tuesday!"

"Monday at 10:38 PM wouldn't be enough?" Savitri Phanse asked anxiously.

"Mangalvar would negate the position of Mangal in the horoscope," he sighed. "All is not lost though. You have to placate Mars, keep it shaant."

"Yes, yes, anything," Savitri Phanse rocked the infant in her arms.

"There is this puja, three days long, which would appease the ruler of her fourth house and dilute the effects. Not remove, just reduce. And she should immediately wear a ring with a red coral stone."

"Red is the colour of mangal," Vani's grandmother nodded, "and blood and death."

The pundit put on a serious face; all her melodrama was, ironically, diluting the gravity of the situation.

"Then you should donate red clothes to workers who use sharp iron objects," he added. "As soon as she is 10, she should fast every Tuesday starting with the first Tuesday of a new month in the rising moon."

He left Chandrashekhar Phanse with a long list of ingredients for the puja and a longer list of precautions and prophecies. The following Tuesday onwards, the entire family would begin chanting the Sundar Kand from the

Ramcharitamanas for 40 days at a stretch. This was followed by the Hanuman Chalisa. All on behalf of the little girl who could barely open her mouth to cry, let alone speak.

Chandrashekhar Phanse had to delay the puja by a few weeks as he accumulated loans for the arrangements. The puja needed large amounts of ghee, flowers, oil, rice and three pundits to preside over the proceedings. They also decided to buy red saris to give to the women who worked at construction sites.

After a year of prayers, chants, Tuesday-anxiety and visiting every Hanuman temple connected by bus, the family decided that they had probably done enough. Vani's parents resolved to play down the manglik aura. Everyone knew, of course, but they didn't want it hovering over the infant.

Vani grew up surrounded by the buffaloes, chickens and neglected fields. Her father visited them every few months and brought crates of oranges for Baba each summer.

Three years and two buffaloes later, her ailing grandmother died. They all agreed that it was a relief. The manglik connection resurfaced but such talk soon fizzled out. Another year and they managed to repair some of the crumbling walls and the roof of the house. Vani studied at the same Marathi medium school that had known Baba's benevolence, often using my abandoned notebooks, crayons and dresses.

When Vani was five, Savitri Phanse declared that she was pregnant again. Another crate of oranges found its way to our house. This time, Savitri Phanse decided to follow tradition and have the baby at her mother's house. She hadn't done so with Vani because of her old mother-in-law, but now she could afford a break. Five months pregnant, she took Vani to her maternal village, Kherdi near Chiplun, and tucked into the extra cream and special dry fruits rationed for her.

Chandrashekhar Phanse updated Baba during the monthly phone call that had now become customary. We learnt that Vani was excited about welcoming a baby; she was already behaving more like a grandmother than an older sister.

Another month, we were given details about the Kherdi arrangement. Savitri was enjoying the change. The place didn't have a hospital, but she got more rest and managed fewer responsibilities. Moreover, the previous delivery had been smooth – 17 minutes of labour, no complications, no stretch marks even – the goddess favoured Savitri.

His next phone call, however, came less than two weeks later.

"What happened, Chandra? Is everything all right?"

Baba heard the news in silence.

Savitri had gone into labour prematurely. At first, they thought they wouldn't be able to save the baby, but the mother would manage. Then they thought they wouldn't be able to save the mother, but the baby was strong. Eventually, they couldn't save either. Chandrashekhar Phanse had received the call at 4 AM, but he waited an agonizing three hours before waking us up.

"Yes, yes, go immediately," Baba spoke into the phone. "Do you need anything? You have a ticket? Money?"

They cremated Savitri Phanse and buried the child. Baba did not go to Kherdi for the funeral – instead, he began searching for a different accommodation for Chandrashekhar Phanse. The distraught man would have to bring his daughter to Mumbai with him, and his shared cot-basis room at Antop Hill wouldn't do. They needed something more suited to their distressed, fragmented family.

❧

My first memory of Vani was enveloped by the crowds of Chhatrapati Shivaji Terminus. I held Baba's hand as we waited on the platform. This was the first time she had stepped out of her village, and Baba explained to me that meeting another young girl would put her at ease.

Aai had arranged for me to miss school that day, and I was more excited about a free day than meeting some strange village girl. We were early. Baba and I strolled towards the local platforms just as a train crawled towards us. It stopped with a sigh. A cascade of colours and odours tumbled out from either side, making their way purposefully towards the front.

"Baba!"

His hand had slipped from mine for an instant.

"I'm here." He scooped me up and held me in his arms. His cream kurta was blotted at the armpits and the centre of his back. I ran my hand over his face to wipe away perspiration, and the bristles on his cheek stung my palm.

Around us, a sea of people hurried past, their faces as identical as they were distinct. Their limbs moved with routine briskness, their vigour picked up unconsciously, exercised in a mechanical fashion. Perched in Baba's arms, I looked above their bobbing heads. Dust hung in the arches, threatening to plummet on us.

I contemplated a massive, intricate cobweb. "Why did her mother die?"

He frowned.

"She was not well?"

No answer.

"Did she have a heart attack?" Recently, my friend's father had suffered a minor heart attack.

"No."

"What then?"

"I'll tell you when you grow up."

"Right now, I'm taller than you," I said, bringing my hand up to my head to show our difference in height.

"And heavier too!"

He shifted me from one arm to the other. The whiff of popcorn filled my nose and I pointed to the little stall. Baba put me down and we started walking towards the buttery aroma. He held my hand and I clutched his trousers with my other fist, hobbling awkwardly.

"When will they come?"

"A few more minutes."

"How old is she?"

"A little younger than you, two or three years."

"That's small! What will I play with her?"

Baba smiled. "Who said anything about playing?"

"Then what will I do?"

"Just talk."

"Talk what?"

Baba ignored me and ordered the popcorn. I crammed a few in my mouth. They left a yellow colour on my fingers and were already turning soft. But at least I had something to do. I offered the cone to Baba and he shook his head.

"Look, the train is coming into that platform. We have to go to the outstation platform."

From where I stood, I couldn't see any train but Baba pulled me along, holding me behind the neck as I marched beside him. Focusing on the dance of all our legs, I hopped, mock-skated and half-ran beside him.

Suddenly I was in front of her – pig-tailed, dirty-nosed Vani, clutching a packet of glucose biscuits and leaning all her weight on her father, half her face hidden behind his leg.

"Say hello," Baba nudged me ahead.

"Come here, Vanita. Vanu?" Her father tried to inch her away from the leg that she used as a pillar.

Neither of us complied.

"She is tired," Chandrashekhar Phanse said, apologizing for Vani.

"Won't you offer her some popcorn?" Baba asked.

I didn't move.

"No, no, she has anyway eaten too much in the train," Vani's father smiled.

Baba frowned at me.

"They will ease up on their own," Chandrashekhar Phanse said.

The men moved on to other talk. I vaguely remember something about selling a field and taking a room on hire in Thane. Then they lifted the bags that Vani's father had brought and began walking towards the exit.

Our fathers' hands were no longer free to hold either of us, and they kept darting anxious looks at us while we walked. I was worried too. The tracks were so close. I could easily slip through. Then the crowds, the pickpockets, the predators. I kept close to Baba. Since his hands were holding the bags, I reached for the strap of one bag. Maybe Vani would think I was strong and wanted to help him with the load.

By the time we reached the end of the platform, Vani had slipped beside me. Since I didn't offer my hand, she clutched the end of my t-shirt.

I looked at her confused face hungrily absorbing this new world. Her eyes darted all around, taking in the crowds, the sour smell of the train and the riot of noises. Somewhere on her person, I sensed the emptiness of her mother's death, and the goodbye she must not have said to her buffaloes, chickens, dogs and trees.

In a fleeting but wholehearted moment, I hurt for her. I let go of the bag. My hand reached for her fingers. They were stale and crumpled from the journey. A few more years and Vani would grow to become the sister I never had. And the sister-in-law I never wanted.

❧

After our first meeting, I didn't see Vanita for another three years. Baba sometimes met Chandrashekhar Phanse at the same station, unplanned, since they travelled the CST-Panvel route to their respective offices and back. I had all but forgotten the raggedy girl when she stormed back into our lives.

That evening, Baba's musical three-ring doorbell hadn't sounded even after all of Aai's soaps had aired and ended. Finally, just as Aai was about to start frantic phone calls, he called. From Narsee Monjee Hospital. Aai's anxious questions merited more than a broken phone line, and we rushed to the hospital.

We found Baba slumped on a bench in a waiting room. Vanita, muddy and tired, sat wailing beside him. The story unravelled between bouts of breathlessness and a fading blankness in Baba's eyes.

"Chandra and I were on the platform together, his daughter too. He had picked her up from some relative's house and was taking her home."

"Were you in the same compartment?"

Baba sighed. "He was in the second class."

"Then?"

"After Sewri, the train stopped."

"So?"

"There was no signal. It was not supposed to stop."

Aai put a hand on his shoulder.

"Come home now. We'll see…"

"Everyone started discussing some accident. But I didn't get up to see. Everyone else took turns peeping outside the door. I didn't move."

"So what? How were you supposed to know that…."

"I had a window seat."

It was out. He would never talk about it again, but it would cloud every moment that Baba stepped into. Twelve years in local trains had introduced a new caste system to Baba – second class standing, second class sitting, second class window seat in the wrong direction, second class window seat in the right direction, first class standing, first class sitting, first class window seat in the wrong direction and first class window seat in the right direction. Having made the climb to the highest rung, having tasted the wind of the creeks in his mouth, Baba had turned cold. While another man breathed through cracked ribs, he had only tapped his watch and pushed his head closer to the breeze, ignoring the envious looks the other classes darted in his direction.

"Shh… it's over." Aai massaged his shoulder.

"It was on the other side of the train. For 15 minutes, I didn't get up. Finally, I was so frustrated I went to the door just to stretch my legs. They were taking the stretcher past me when I looked out."

"Bas now!" Aai interrupted. "Enough. We'll talk when we go ho…"

"The compartment was overcrowded. He could barely get in at CST. He must have been standing at the edge. And that pole…"

Aai sighed. "First the mother, now the father. That girl has brought a heavy fate along."

Baba shot her a confused look.

Vani was initially sent to the relatives with whom she had been that evening, but they wouldn't have anything to do with her for more than a few days. She made them call Baba at work every day, imploring him to find an alternative. Baba, still shaken from the accident, brought her home.

Vani, however, wasn't content with this bland version. Her father's death wasn't so quick, simple or colourless. On moonless nights, she whispered to me that as soon as the train had stopped, she had jumped out. She had run back, parallel to the train tracks, followed by a handful of passengers until she found her father. He was lying in a gutter, smothered in dirt and blood.

"I could only recognize one eye, Umi-tai," she murmured. She said she had thrown her arms around his neck and refused to leave even when people started to pull them apart.

"I could feel his blood throbbing as it spilled out of his head."

I cringed.

"After sometime, your Baba reached the spot. He was the only person I recognized and trusted. I had met him at the station just before..."

Vani demonstrated how he had cajoled her, reassured her and eventually wheedled her into letting go of what had then become a corpse. In her father's dying moments, Vani claimed, Baba had promised to look after the orphan girl, educate her and eventually even get her married.

Although the scene was described in hushed tones, her intensity flamed through. Huddled in the narrow corridor that connected the living room with the bedroom, she brought to life the stench of the gutter.

"These two tiles are there no, Umi-tai? Like this plus one more. Such a fat ditch."

The reek clogged her nostrils and wet slush stuck around her ankles. The earth groped her, yanking her in, shooting its moss up to envelop her feet while she sat and sobbed, waiting for her father to respond.

"Your Baba picked me up from the gutter. He dusted my dress, cleaned my face with his handkerchief, held me close and said, 'Come, you shall stay with me. You shall be my second daughter.'"

Even in the moment of her heightened emotions, the scene had sounded suspiciously cinematic to me. But I knew better than to object. It was too important for her, and she needed her own story.

"Umi-tai, I have never removed this ring. See, the red stone is cutting into my skin! Why did this still happen?"

"There's no connection, Vani," I said for the hundredth time. "Don't you trust Aai and Baba? It's not true."

"What kind of person causes the death of the people who gave her life?" she continued melodramatically.

"Nonsense! Did you put that pole next to the railway tracks? Did you stuff 800 people into the compartment?"

"They say worship Hanuman, read the Hanuman Chalisa. Then they say girls can't go to the Hanuman temple. It's so confusing! Maybe that is why there is no proper effect."

I sighed. Anything I said was a waste of breath. Clearly, she was unaffected by all our repeated explanations. The fact that these connections were unclear did not deter Vani; it intensified the mystery and reinforced her struggle against what she believed was her fate. She wore prayer beads around her neck and a holy thread on her wrist. Her chanting increased, the prayers amplified, the temple visits stretched.

Until some random mornings when she'd get fed up and announce, "What's the point? They're both dead anyway! Who else do I have?" I would immediately exclaim, "But I am there na, and Aai and Baba. Don't we mean anything to you?"

To this, she would agree. "Yes, I should continue. I need to do it for you." Then we again insisted that it was unnecessary. It was most confusing.

Vani gnawed her way into our family, making herself indispensable to its stability. Perhaps it was her way of ensuring a place in a world that wanted to keep her at bay. No task was too big, no load too heavy, no food too complex, no shop too far, no night too late. She weaved through the household maniacally, packing my lunchbox, getting breakfast ready and filling the water tubs, all before the first of us had woken up. She learnt exactly how many teaspoons of dry coconut went into the aamti, how many drops of lemon juice Baba needed in his salad and in which direction the mirrors were supposed to be polished.

Increasingly she took over the kitchen – first the cleaning, then the shopping, then the chopping, then the rotis and eventually entire meals. Some evenings, Aai sat blankly in front of the TV, stealing glances at the kitchen and sighing. If Aai insisted on cooking, Vani offered to chop the onions and tomatoes; if she wanted to do the ironing, Vani was keen to fold.

After Vani became a fixture in the kitchen, the fridge abounded with chutneys and sherbets of all sorts. Large aluminium jars were perennially chock-a-block with karanji, chakli, laddoos, papads and farsan. She could dish out the most delectable raw mango kebabs, plonk brinjals in rich mustard gravies, conjure fritters out of jackfruit flowers and fashion chocolate cakes that could be steamed, so that even though she didn't know how to operate the oven, the house glowed with the sweet warmth of cocoa. Invariably, the abundance attracted tributes from our relatives and Vani dug her heels deeper into the household.

Baba did look into his promise of her education – if such a promise was made – and managed to send her to school until class 12. After that, Vani, who had never enjoyed dry cerebral gymnastics, put her foot down and sold her books to a second-hand bookstore.

Thereafter, her reign over the house solidified. Aai, after a few uncomfortable years, dealt with it as she had managed her husband's jokes and ball scratching. It was an odd experience to be laughed away. How, after all, is one supposed to complain that the girl does too much work?

Although I was too young to comprehend the complexities of household politics, I breathed in the air of suffering that settled over the house. My parents' concern over my closeness with Vani intensified. She had a hold over me that no one seemed able to shake off. I mimicked her brisk walk and animated chatter and wound a dupatta over my head even if the other girls in the building sniggered. At annual school functions, which Vani never attended, I searched for her in the sea of faces as prizes were handed out. Whether I was essaying the role of Antonio, debating over capital punishment or reciting Tagore, I yearned for Vani to cheer me on.

When we went shopping, Vani usually stayed back. But one day, I threw a tantrum at Dream Girl Collections and insisted that Vani see me parade in the latest fashions before I finalized any outfit. I refused to leave the changing room until Baba brought the bewildered girl on his scooter to approve my selection.

Later, Aai locked the bedroom door, sat me down and explained, "We cannot take her with us for every outing. It'll remind her of all the things she can't have."

"That's okay. I'll buy only half the clothes, chocolates and toys. We can give the other half to Vani."

However, while I was intent on weaving Vani into my world, Vani had other strategies. The first- and second-class compartments that had segregated our fathers were never too far from her thoughts, nor was the aura of misfortune that she carried around. She was so convinced about the exclusionary nature of our worlds that Vani focussed on capturing as much territory as she could on her side of the fence – the kitchen, the chores, the cleaning – instead of breaking down the fence altogether.

Of course, she loved me, her devotee, wholeheartedly, but she rained the affection with an intensity that kept drawing attention to itself. Her expressions were sincere, but always an oddity, a garish velvet cloak, heavy and weighing – a love that was always hot, never warm; always opaque, never transparent; always plonked on the centre table, never slipping into corners while I slept unaware.

Vani showed concern in a manner that disturbed instead of soothed. From Vani, I realized that even humming could be loud and a sleeping person could be jarring. I learnt from her, a manner that, like my husband once said to me, "makes your invitations repulsive." From her, I understood that caring was about taking over and not about surrendering.

Desirable or not, I loved Vani with the wholeheartedness of an infant and adulated her with an innocence that would make an onlooker weep. It didn't matter that I was only a guest in Vani's world of detergents and pots. I loved her because I couldn't otherwise. She was the sister I never had.

In any case, I knew that my day would come. It would be a day when I would part a curtain of mogras to place a garland around the man I had dreamed up. I would be radiant and beautiful, the centre of everyone's focus. On that day, it would only be Urmila.

Urmila this. Urmila that. Urmila here. Urmila there.

Except when that day came, it was never mine. Vani's story entwined with every recollection of the wedding. It was the day Vani shocked everyone, the day she did the unthinkable and became my sister-in-law.

On my wedding day, by the time I had parted the mogras, they had withered. The videographer had regaled me to a corner and I took my turn around the fire after Vani had taken her rounds with her new husband, by which time, the embers had died out.

On the back of a wedding photo, with Vani and me facing the camera, not touching, I had scribbled in a manner reminiscent of school-girl notes, "Et tu, Vani?"

Along with the transfers that are inevitable in any government employee's career, Baba shuttled between riding on two-wheelers and 64-wheelers. Wobbling on his bike and elbowing away in the train, he often dreamt of the comforts of air-conditioned sedans operating at just a flick of the wrist here and a click there. But for the longest time, we hadn't saved enough electricity, newspapers, cushion stuffing and empty milk sachets to afford an indulgence like that.

Yet, rickety school buses wouldn't do for me. Baba's bike seat might have been as tattered as the bus seat but he was adamant. "I don't want to look at your worried the-bus-is-here expression every morning!"

Instead, he'd kick-start the bike every morning, adding more kicks on cold mornings, and we'd make our way to school. From school, he went to work, and was invariably early. He could have spent that time with another cup of tea and an additional newspaper, but this was one calculation Baba never made.

Our combined morning routine began at 6:30 AM. While I would bathe, Baba packed my bag and polished my shoes. More often than not, I'd take too long in the bathroom and later the house resounded with his shrill gasps as he dunked cold water over his head, since the boiler needed time to heat up again – time that I hadn't accounted for him. On rainy days, he'd wrap me up and slip on my gumboots while I listed elaborate reasons to stay home with Vani. A few times every monsoon, the showers would greet us when we were halfway to school and Baba would park under a bus stand, only to realize that I had – again – forgotten my raincoat. Wordlessly zipping his large jacket over me, he'd brave through the patter while I made excuses to return home.

On those days, he sat in his air-conditioned office with his dripping shirt clinging to an old vest, dreading and welcoming the blasts of air that fell on his chest. If his boss frowned at his attire, Baba would mock-chuckle, "It'll dry off by the time the first customer arrives."

Until I skipped off to college – after which I was embarrassed by his lifts – Baba took a hot water bath only on weekends. He completed his morning tea quota on Sundays, guzzling cup after cup, scalding his tongue with the built-up urgency. He then tottered to the toilet with a newspaper in hand while I stifled my giggles and Vani brought out the air-freshener.

His biggest acts of love, however, were not on damp days with icy gusts, but on sweltering mornings on the bike. The heat in Mumbai was punctuated only by brief December weeks of coolness, with the rest of the year evaporating under the sun. Yet, I didn't even notice his affection through the decade that he played chauffeur. Until the day I sat pillion with another man.

Permission had been hard to get and even my husband-to-be was surprised at the suggestion.

"You can invite him home for tea," Aai had said. "We'll sit in the bedroom."

"Or for Tinku's birthday party next week," Baba suggested. "He'll get to meet the whole family. Plus there will already be arrangements for food and all…"

Eventually, Vani winked at me from across the kitchen and rustled together succulent kebabs, spicy, tangy chhole with a dry mango salad and caramel custard. Just as everyone had dug into dessert, she suggested gently, "It would be nice if Umi-tai gets to know him a little better. After two months, it'll all be so different and new for her. She needs to have a familiar face in the house na, a friend...."

So, three days later, I sat pillion awkwardly, holding onto the bar behind me, unsure if it was too soon to place my hand on my fiancé's shoulder. We joined the usual crawl towards the suburbs and he could rarely move beyond the second gear. Shree was a smooth rider if not particularly talkative, and I contented myself with looking at the Linking Road stalls of clothing and imitation jewellery. Around us, exhaust fumes rose and beggars squinted with outspread palms amidst a cacophony of honking.

Even all these together couldn't distract me from the intense heat. The afternoon sun glared at me while my arms blushed and perspired. With no wind to carry away the beads, they made their way down my temples and spine. I searched my handbag for a scarf, but Shree seemed perfectly accustomed to the sweltering air.

"Global warming must be more serious than I thought," I shouted so he could hear me through the helmet.

"What? Meaning?"

"It is so hot suddenly? Where did this come from?"

"Hmmm... you're not used to travelling at this time, I suppose."

"No, no! I would … you know, school and all."

"You want the helmet?"

I was just about to comment on the odds of a helmet doing any good, when it struck me. The heat hadn't been turned on; I had been pushed out of the shade.

For years, on traffic-jammed, sweltering mornings, Baba had ensured that the bike stopped in the shadow of a bus or we towed alongside a truck. At traffic signals, he had waited at the side under a tree instead of snaking ahead behind other bikes. Baba had never known the instinct to inch towards the signal.

Instead, he had always advanced at optimal speed in submission to weather conditions, moving from shade to shade, cover to cover. While cruising, the wind had blown away the heat and when stationary, my father had cooled my skin, silently.

Facing my husband-to-be's blue helmet on the shimmering Linking Road, I suddenly wished I were sitting on my father's bike instead. I itched to smell his shirt once more, to hold his waist and rest my head on his shoulders, to revel in the shadows he created.

That evening when I returned, I made special lemongrass tea for Baba. Aai grinned as I slipped off my bangles and earrings.

"So you had a good time, eh?" Vani chuckled. "Looks like someone is falling in love!"

I looked at Baba from across the room and nodded.

෴

We all had our secret attachments. Shree had Puru, Puru had virtue, Vani had her kitchen, Baba had his tightfistedness. Me? I had my name. After we were married, I fumed during every discussion that suggested the customary change of the bride's name. The ferocity of my retaliation and my forced courteous tone made my in-laws a little wary and more than a little guarded. As for me, I was secretly terrified of myself.

Growing up, I was accustomed to Aai being called Lata – her maiden first name – by one side of the family, and Sangeeta – her married first name – by the other half. Her passport, which hadn't been updated, certified that she was Lata Tembe, while her bank records identified her as Sangeeta Joshi. For her husband's colleagues, she was Mrs Bimal and the boys in the building knew her as Maggi aunty. Not for any culinary skill, but for her spiral, frizzy hair which she oiled every alternate day at the window. Meanwhile, every adolescent female of Chanakya Society knew her only as Umi-ki-mummy. For the vegetable seller, she was Joshi-madam and the fisherwoman bestowed upon her the name of our housing society – Chanakya. She would call out every Saturday, "Chanakya-tai, fresh rawas? Prawns?"

Despite this medley of terms and references, when the time came for me to take on a second name, I found that I couldn't comply. Perhaps it wouldn't have been brought up so vehemently if it weren't for the bent Meenabai's persistent questioning. "The chhoti soun, what have you named her? You haven't had the naming ceremony yet?"

Meenabai worked at the Karmarkar household only twice a week but her presence permeated each room each day. While her daughter-in-law, Geeta, toiled over the dishes and the sweeping, Meenabai looked after 'higher' work like tending to the house plants, helping the women rearrange their wardrobes, making lists of how much of oil and wheat flour were to be ordered and cleaning all the mandir idols. She had been with the family since my father-in-law's infancy, and commanded an uncomfortable authority. Over the years, her failing legs and curved spine excused her from displaying any accountability, but her tongue had lost none of its sharpness.

Once Vani and I came into the picture, we took over large portions of Meenabai's work, unwilling to allow dust to collect over the curios and idols. We secretly also hoped that it would make Meenabai a less frequent presence, but that wasn't to be. Work or not, she arrived precisely after breakfast on every scheduled day. For a couple of hours, she would gossip in the kitchen or express a gleeful, uneasy interest in Vani and me.

It was my lot to live in households with ambiguous relationships, and I never mastered the knack of negotiating them. Meenabai commanded the comforts of a matriarch while the dhobi, Hari-kaka, walked in and out of the kitchen as he pleased. Before taking the day's clothes, it was customary for him to settle down to a cup of extra-sweet mint tea. As per a routine established long before anyone cared to remember, Geeta put water to boil the moment Hari-kaka's bicycle sounded.

He'd hunch in the passage while she offered him Marie biscuits. Twice. "He only takes something if you offer twice. He's very humble that way," she explained to us, the new daughters-in-law. "After Mothe-sahib lost his parents, he made sure that the system they had set up never changed."

My father-in-law always had one foot in the past. I suspect that he experienced even the present in retrospect, once it had shifted and faded. Having lost his parents early, he was unable to let go of the things they had established – the large, heavy house, the old, dull construction business and the pompous servants. He hung on to each one with an anxious attachment, bestowing upon them an importance they should never have commanded.

While I came to accept Hari-kaka's treatment, I never could come to terms with Meenabai's presence, not least because she was a downright unpleasant sight. Over the decades, her back had started drooping and bending towards the floor, and her knees began spreading so that her body could balance itself. Her knees bent out so wide from waist to feet that her body resembled a kite, with her thin sari serving in place of paper. She once insisted that I help her sit on her special stool, adding, "I don't remember how it feels to have the knees touching each other."

Sure enough, her knees pointed in opposite directions even when she slept. With her mouth wide open, her nine-yard sari tucked up and behind, her pallu spread across her chest like a makeshift blanket, she looked like a wrecked, battered boat.

When my father-in-law was still a middle-aged man, Meenabai's body had started draining away all its fat and muscles. Following a strange bout of loose motions and vomiting, bit by bit, everything that filled Meenabai between the bones and the skin oozed away. Her skin lost its opaqueness and a translucency slithered over her. The pale colour merged with her bones, giving her a flowing cream complexion, the kind young girls vied for. However, with Meenabai's wrinkles, she resembled a melting plastic mannequin. First the grey of her hair, then the green of her veins, the dark brown scars of falls and burns, even the black of her eyes, all began to merge into folds of monochrome. Her pupils initially went brown, then olive green, then dull yellow until finally they lost all colour and were simply translucent darts of faint light.

Papa was extremely concerned and set aside special rations of whole buffalo cream for her each time she visited the house. He fooled her into drinking cod liver oil, telling the staunch vegetarian Meenabai that it had been extracted from pine nuts. Geeta was instructed to added dollops of ghee to Meenabai's dal and bhakri. But the weight refused to pile on. Daily rations of fresh butter, bowls of yogurt and sugar, even sweets saturated with jaggery and coconut did nothing to fill out the sagging skin over Meenabai's face and concave stomach.

By the time Vani and I kicked rice urns and stepped into the house, Meenabai did not know youth. If she had once been young, it was long forgotten, so that now, she only remembered herself first as an old woman, then as a very old woman, then as a woman so old it was embarrassing. A guest who had far outstayed her welcome.

The only place where she commanded the right to belong was the Karmarkar household. After all, she had been the nanny of the patriarch; no one else had taken him on the back and run around the house screaming, "Pashchim Express! PEEP PEEP! Move out of the way!" Only she had known the width of his little finger up her nose and the stench of his potty. She had seen him lose one tooth after another, getting four annas per molar, and 60 years later, he saw her mouth getting emptier by the month and presented her with a pair of dentures.

So, it seemed perfectly in place for her to ask what the new daughter-in-law's new name would be. However, I put up such a resistance that my parents were promptly invited over for tea.

"Urmila is beautiful," Ma explained. "It's just not… ours. We'll give you a lovely new name."

Aai twisted the end of her pallu, uncomfortable with the fuss I had created within weeks of being married. "You'll get used to it," she told me. "Even I did, even Kaivalya-tai, there's nothing to get worked up about."

"Shraddha is a very good name," my husband added. "Shraddha, devotion – it has a beautiful meaning."

I fingered my bangles and breathed heavily. "Yes I know. It's not about Shraddha or Savitri or Suneeta. I don't want to change my name. It doesn't…"

My husband gulped another sip of tea and interrupted. "But some people will anyway keep calling you Urmila. You'll just have more choice, that's all!"

"What if someone decides that from tomorrow you will have a different name?" I kept my voice low, but it was edged with annoyance. "What if you become a Mohan or a Lalit or something?"

"That doesn't make sense! Why should my…" my husband mumbled through crumbs.

"Chhotu, times have changed." This was Purushottam. "If Vahini doesn't want another name, then let it be. What does it matter, this word or that?"

My mother-in-law's face fell. "Puru! Of course it matters! It's tradition, culture. Don't those things matter to you? First the whole tamasha at the marriage and now…"

Aai cleared her throat. No one wanted reminders of that day.

"Throw the customs out of the window – all old people are foolish." Ma continued. "Every single generation before yours has been stupid. Only you have wisdom!"

"Kaivalya, it's not good for you to get worked up," my father-in-law said. "Puru, Urmila, it's not all mumbo-jumbo. It's scientific. Chhotu, as per your horoscopes, your marriage will be more compatible if your wife also has a name beginning with 'S'. It will bring in lots of prosperity, the pundit said. Harmony, peace, two children within a few years… And then also consider…"

"Maybe you should think of what happened to the Shindes." Only one voice would dare stop my father-in-law mid-sentence. He bent his head in her direction and offered a faint smile.

Everyone turned to face Meenabai. "What problems they had, eh? You tell them… tauba!" Meenabai held her earlobes and pulled them down while nodding from side to side.

"Of course, the Shindes! You must remember them?" Ma turned to Purushottam. "How many difficulties that couple had! Money would drain out instantly. Their investments fell, a house under construction stayed that way for eight years! No children after so many years of marriage!"

"Ma, they got the vaastu of the house changed," Purushottam pointed out.

"No! That was for the Kales! You're confusing our neighbours. They changed the girl's name from … I don't know, some Asha or Avni or something to Preeti. What a difference!" She snapped her fingers. "Like this!"

"Yes," joined my father-in-law. "The flat got constructed – it's fetching good rent now. Payal, their girl, must be five or six-years-old – Urmila you remember her, na? They were here last week along with Prashant. Small girl, very talkative…"

"And we are only particular about the letter!" added Ma. "Urmila can choose any name she wants from 'S.'"

"Yes, yes… Only remember you have to sign as per the new name. Okay?" Papa said.

I looked across the room at my husband, but his face had disappeared behind his teacup. He blended with the upholstery and said nothing more. Once Purushottam had expressed disapproval with the name-changing strategy, it seemed like his interest had simply vanished. He didn't seem as adamant as before; yet, he didn't offer any support.

Puru, who placed himself beside me, had run out of arguments. I knew that he sensed my discomfort, but he was outnumbered. Also, after the upheaval he had created at the wedding, he was cautious about contributing to yet another scene.

My mother's pallu now resembled a multi-coloured rope. The faint sound of a flush reminded me that Baba would soon be out of the bathroom and I straightened up to face yet another adversary.

With his entry, however, the discussion took a turn. When Aai apprised him of our conversation, he peered at my father-in-law.

"Karmarkar sahib, we weren't told about this name-changing business before the marriage."

"What! It's part of the tradition! It is understood, Joshi sahib!"

"But times are changing. Don't get me wrong – Sangeeta also changed her name. It's just that with youngsters, all this has to be specified nowadays. Tell me, Karmarkar sahib, we are doing all this to increase harmony in the house, right? Now look around you. Is it working? No, na?"

"It'll start working after…"

"These are signs, Karmarkar sahib. If the woman of the house is unhappy, the house is doomed. Now we know that already, na?" he chuckled a little. "After all these years of marriage, huh!" My father-in-law managed a tiny smile and I could sense some of the tension easing out.

"Let Urmila think about it, okay? Give her some time. Let her get the setting of your house first. Simultaneously, you check if there is any disharmony at all. How can we fix something that is not broken? And why break something just to fix it?"

His monologue marked the end of the debate for that day, and although the subject came up again, it was never tinged with the determination that had marked that evening.

Over the next few months, the queries dotted several social

occasions. At bhishis, parties, and Ganpati pujas, someone would casually ask, "What name have you given her?" and it was my mother-in-law's turn to twist her pallu.

"Not yet," she'd say to her friends hovering near the kitchen platform.

"Never," I would say to their daughters while we refilled sherbet glasses.

I suspected that sometimes my husband consciously brought up this subject when we were just about to go to bed. He knew that it put me off and probably did it so I'd leave him alone. After I'd disagree, he would shoot me a hurt expression and put on an elaborate show of drooping shoulders and frowns. Then he'd switch off the lights. However, within seconds of climbing into bed and adjusting himself a safe distance away, his snores rang through the room.

It didn't help that Vani was more than willing to change her name without anyone even suggesting it. On matching their horoscopes, we discovered that their names were already compatible; his 'P' and her 'V' were apparently an indication of progeny, foreign travel and a lifelong bond that would never get diluted. Yet, she insisted that tradition be maintained.

One morning we dished out uttapams and sambhar for breakfast, with Vani doing most of the work while I pretended to be knowledgeable. Vani had taken over handling the batter and all the accompaniments, leaving me to simply prepare coffee. I placed the milk on the gas to boil and started spooning coffee and sugar into six cups – extra strong for Puru, no sugar for the parents-in-law, very sweet for Vani and black for myself.

My husband seemed to have no preference; he ate whatever was placed before him and neither approved of nor censured the food.

I mentioned to Vani that Shree had begun sulking again over the name business when Vani started to coax me, "Come on, Umi. We'll both do it!"

"I'll take another name from 'V' and you take one from 'S'."

"It's not as simple as that!"

"It is! The complication is in your head. See when we were born, we didn't have a choice, right? Our parents chose. So think of this as a way of exerting our choice over our identities. It's actually a wonderful thing! It is not all old-fashioned, it's actually very modern if you think of it this way…"

"But I like Urmila!"

"That's because you're used to it! Have you ever known another name? Then how can you say? I am already feeling very good about Veena… so musical, or even Vandana… Which do you like?"

"Please Vani, don't! If you start doing this, it will reflect so poorly on me!"

"So what can I do, Umi-tai? How will they accept me? You tell me!"

"They won't! You can make hazaar fancy dishes for them and give them foot massages every day, but it won't make a difference! Do you really think a name will change things? Even if you change it to Sita, it won't make a difference!"

Her face fell. One batch of uttapams was charred, the other turned sour.

"But that's why I want to do this," Vani whispered. "Maybe they'll feel that in some way, I have changed my fate. Our destiny is tied with our names. Don't you want to shake that off, Umi?"

"You are too desperate! You'll latch on to any nonsense," I sighed.

"Come on," she insisted. "It'll be fun! Just think you are choosing a name for your daughter."

"It's not like that…" I turned to pour the hot water for coffee.

We were not alone. My mother-in-law stood glaring at Vani's back. "This is not some game or amusement, Vanita," she began through clenched teeth. "There is a reason behind everything. It is not to be taken lightly."

Vani blushed. "I didn't mean it that way. I just thought that…"

"A name is not a piece of clothing. You can't drop and change whenever it fancies you! Please don't put such things into Urmila's head."

At that instant, the milk boiled over and Vani rushed to the stove. "It's all gone!"

"It's okay," I reached over to clean up.

Ma shook her head and let out a heavy sigh. "As far as destiny goes, you have affected this family enough. No need for any more interference."

The fermented odour of strained harmony hung over the family long after that morning. When Purushottam and Vani left for Dubai, exiled from the house, followed by my husband, the name-changing business was forgotten. They all had bigger problems to worry about and it suddenly didn't matter how I was addressed. Even Meenabai gave up on reminders.

Ironically, however, I know that I would have easily given in once he left. The night he chose to leave me behind and follow his brother instead, I turned superstitious. Vulnerable and heartbroken, I only needed the carrot of his return to follow any suggestions. Was there some truth in the horoscope reading? After all, the evidence couldn't be any less apparent. Had the astrologer foreseen this? Would I have lived a different marriage if I was a Sunanda or Savitri?

Would my husband have upheld the second vow he took, to help each other grow stronger, physically, mentally, spiritually? It was a farce, this promise. I have not grown; I remain static, frozen in the time that he was with me, living in the past, holding on to desires that have turned bitter. He is still under the shadow of his brother, stunted, like a frail bush in the shade of a large tree. His branches do not spread, certainly not to me; his roots just entangle further with the thick base that is silently, unknowingly, strangling him.

Maybe I should have turned into Suman or Suhasini or Supriya. Perhaps I'd have a different story to tell. Perhaps I'd have lived that ideal life, which in its beautiful ordinariness can never have anything remarkable to say. Maybe I'd never have felt the need to pick up a paintbrush and search for the man who left me behind. Maybe he would be right here, caressing my fingertips, looking into my eyes, reassuring me that I'd never have to face a lonely night, that the pillow beside me would always rise and fall to the rhythm of his breath.

∽⌒⌐

The moment a desire dies is a sharp one. As pointed as the splutter of a mustard seed, as shrill as a whine, as heavy as a star on a clear night. I had delayed that moment for as long as I could, looking away when it threatened to burst. Its fear lurked around my dupattas and beneath my slippers, covered but heady.

Most nights, I massaged eucalyptus oil on Shree's knees; he was uncomfortable with the ritual but his mother insisted. The weak knees were a chronic condition, persistent since his childhood; his knees would buckle under trees, stiffen during races and cramp on cold evenings.

For my father, this was a clear character sketch – fear of responsibility. One evening, Baba ventured, "Umi, your husband needs to take charge. Maybe it's time you and he moved out of that house..."

"Baba! They would be aghast if I suggested it."

"See his constant knee-ache? Men who cannot stand up for their duties, the dharma charted out for them... this is a symptom."

"Baba, please!"

"Trust your father, Umi. He needs to take more responsibility, not more massages."

For the first several months, I defended my husband with a zeal that would have put off Shree had he known about it. He was mine, with all his flaws; I was more than aware of them and the world need not be any wiser. There is something noble in the act of secretly shielding a lover, even an undeserving one.

I evaded Baba's responsibility theory, but when teamed with Aai's anxieties, the trap closed in tighter. "Such constant pain signifies inflexibility. The man is as obstinate as an oil stain."

"Please Aai, it's not like he restricts me or anything."

"But he restricts himself. He won't let go. See this knee joint? It can only bend forward. And for especially rigid people, the knee joint clamps even more, always in pain, can't move."

"Aai, even the elbow can bend only forward."

"The elbow doesn't take the weight of the head and heart, Umi. It doesn't bear the consequences of our decisions or our inaction."

"So? What is the connection?"

"Umi, uff! You must get your eyes checked. All sceptics have poor vision."

At such a point, the discussion would whirlwind out of hand and my parents would only be left with remnants of philosophy that were too random to piece together. He never admitted it, but I know that Baba blamed himself. I had married the first man my father had suggested and the now casual front I put up jabbed him. His guilt oozed into everything he held dear. The consecutive cups of tea in the morning reduced and dried up, the extended naps were restless visions, his trips to the bathroom turned painful and shorter, and some mornings, they weren't necessary at all.

My father worked on all fronts. He first tried to gauge how far along I had emotionally attached myself to the man, then reasoned with Shree and argued with his parents about the benefits of nuclear families. It took many months of hopeful reconciliations, twitchy naps and persistent constipation, but he eventually resigned to having failed.

Though I was oblivious of Baba's sacrifices in my childhood, I couldn't remain insensible to the way my father gnawed at himself in my youth. Baba wasn't the sort one could understand easily and carried the curse of being appreciated only in retrospect. He made a partner of his failures, accompanied at all times by the downward eyes and the dragging gait that is characteristic of those who live in blame.

I tried to mask the initial differences and later distance with my husband. But Aai and Baba were selective about what they believed even in the first few weeks. They suspected that only half my statements were true and the other half those I wished to be true. Not wanting to jinx the first or puncture the second, they usually played along. But I know their smiles faltered as soon as I turned away.

Of course, the marriage considerably increased my fortunes – even before my art attracted fame – as I became assimilated into a prominent business family. Added, the thrift and foresight of ancestors had allowed the Karmarkars a large property, a larger inheritance of gold, bonds and shares, and some political pull as well.

A couple of times, Mamta, Shree's sister, suggested that I open a boutique – the acceptable thing for ambitious daughters-in-law of the family to engage in. When I confessed that I had little understanding of clothes, she pondered for a while and said, "Maybe I could talk to Dad about an art boutique. It'll be nice to have someone from the family dabble in something fresh!"

So, over dinner, the topic of the day was art. "I remember once being mesmerized by this painting of a marketplace in the rain," Mamta began. "It was so realistic, it looked like a photograph! Everything from the water droplets to the puddles and shadows...."

My mother-in-law joined in, chewing noisily. "It is a real skill to paint like that. Urmila, do you make such paintings?"

I shifted. Shree looked at me, his roti held in the air. I shook my head and looked down.

"Well, you must try to."

"I'm sure Urmila's art has its own strength and beauty." This was Purushottam, my ally at the dining table. Though we met only at mealtimes, in subtle ways he forwarded my cause, whether it was suggesting a holiday with Shree – that didn't materialize – or getting another servant to attend to his father. Often, I was grateful just for his presence. He recognized my loneliness and didn't foolishly try to abate it with polite enquiries.

"In all these years, I have only seen a handful of her paintings," Vani said. "Umi can be quite secretive."

Normally, a statement like that would invite a deluge of probes and pleadings of tell-us and show-us, but not when Vani spoke. Not for the past few weeks.

"Can you do some flower vases?" Papa asked. "We could do with some pretty pictures around the house." I smiled and nodded.

More discussion continued about the blossoms on trees, snow-covered mountaintops and the realism of a flowing river while I resolved not to contradict anyone.

"I'd like one of children," Ma suddenly said, looking at me. "Little smiling infants. Shree, you should keep a couple in your room too."

Mamta giggled and nudged Shree. His face registered panic and shame, the dismay of a child painfully aware of the dirty way in which it had been born.

Across the table, Purushottam and Vani looked at each other, noting that it was not required of them.

PART III

Threeni Vruthaya - Vishnuthva - Anvethu

With this third vow of Saptapadi, as your husband, I promise you Rayasposha: to acquire wealth by righteous means and spend it wisely.

It's 6 AM, a Tuesday, and I have already downed half a cup of coffee. The other half waits amidst tubs of paints. This is the way I recognize the passing of yet another night. In an hour, the milkman will arrive, and 15 minutes later, Geeta will walk through the door. I usually look forward to this little window when my canvas screams and the house listens. But today, there is only silence, inside and out.

After the protests last week, a lull seems to have settled over the world. There is no sign of agitation. Everything has been swept away. There is a newness to the compound, as if it has been whitewashed. Perhaps it is just the shifty light of dawn playing games with me.

I decide to switch on the television to check if the media retain any memory of the outrage. I keep the volume low so that the sounds don't reach my sleeping mother-in-law.

"The Delhi-Gorakhpur express derailed at around 2 AM and although we cannot confirm the casualties at this stage, initial numbers suggest that the figure is upwards of eight."

Click.

"... rain clouds continue to loom. However, the showers will be moderate over the next 48 hours."

Click.

"Whirlpool, whirlpool. New Whirlpool White Magic. Now with advanced hand agitator. Give your clothes a new whitest white!"

Click.

"The cabinet minister is engulfed in yet another controversy but Mr Chattan insists that he has been framed and that he was, in fact, visiting his sister at the time that the video allegedly captures him accepting the suitcase ..."

I cannot take the barrage any longer and switch off the TV. Now, the silence is grave-like in its stillness. Being absent from the news is a relief. In the few days since the protests, worse things have happened and the sacrilege of my paints has been forgotten. Perhaps that's all the protesters needed – to get it out of their systems and inspire some anxiety.

My paraphernalia lies scattered in the room I once shared with my husband. Now, only the bed gives it a semblance of domesticity. Paintings sprawl on the floor, hang unfinished from awkward angles on every wall, block the bathroom door and pile up over the desk. Brushes, rags and half-empty tins punctuate the room. Just the sight of all the colours is enough to give anyone a headache, but this has been my refuge for more years than I wish to count.

I know that I should be grateful. My unguided hand and untutored eye have found admirers. They sell for large sums, each one of these canvases that depict absence. In a restricted universe, my name is familiar, even sought after. He, of course, continues to ignore me. Occasionally, a supplement might carry a review of an exhibition or a summary of an auction. But it's always the same news wrapped in different words:

The oil-on-canvas titled *Nothing* attracted the highest number of bidders. The use of deep reds and stark whites, positioned seemingly haphazardly but leading to a blob of vacuum, saw steep rises with each successive offer...

Privation – a woman whose head is covered by a sari but the sindoor lies outside her face at the edge of the painting – was picked up for an undisclosed amount...

No, I don't attempt to depict emptiness. In fact, I pile on the colours, layering them, stretching them beyond the canvas. Yet, these do not fill me. And here I am, downing coffee, inhaling paint, etching out both a living and a reason to continue living. My husband's third vow to me is too ridiculous to even be a joke.

I start dabbing paint on the canvas directly with my fingers. The strokes are shaky, but I persevere. I touch the canvas with quick, light tips, feeling tiny currents teasing me. It is always different and special when brushes are kept out of the equation, so much so that I don't allow myself the indulgence too often. Special moments should be spaced out, I've learnt, or I'll run out of reasons to continue.

I don't realize when my strokes become bigger and faster.

My fingertips dab urgently, shaking the canvas so I have to hold it with the other hand. A pair of ears has taken shape, then a hand with long, rough fingers, a forehead full of creases. I play with the brown. It needs to be lighter, darker, deeper, fresher. Cheekbones, jaw, hairline. Does he part it on the right or the left? I cannot remember. My fingers think left. They jump. From the neck to the ears to the eyebrows. I need the exact shape. I shall see it soon, I tell myself. Yes, soon, I shall see the face. And perhaps, it will see me too.

∽✍

My childhood daydreams of marriage were always tinged with the sadness of separation from Vani. I loved her dearly and worshipped her with a secretive, silent fury checked only by pride. I remember envying Vani's tasks – scrubbing clothes in the bathroom surrounded by suds and slipperiness, standing on a stool to clean the fans, kneading the warm, gooey chapatti dough. Most of all, I envied that she was asked to chop vegetables – not just rinse them under the tap as I was instructed – but actually peel and cut.

Vani could chop like a dream. She would hold an animated conversation with me, debating the intricacies of my relationship with my friends, or fix her gaze on a bird outside the window or stare at Shah Rukh Khan romancing on jagged mountaintops, and all while her hands worked away. She transformed cucumbers into little light emeralds, carrots into six-petal orange flowers, and onions into a heap of translucent cubes before the first tear dared to sting the eye. While she made merry carving vegetables, splashing in water and fussing over the plants, I was forced to focus on the revolution of the earth and the minutiae of prime numbers.

I sulked. I fought. I reasoned. I bribed. But Vani wouldn't hear of exchanging roles. "If you don't study, Umi-tai, you'll become like me!"

That didn't seem such a bad proposition, except when I considered that Vani slept on a cot in the kitchen and all her possessions could fit in the two cabinets beside the gas cylinder. Sometimes, while I studied, Vani ironed and folded clothes, but she couldn't keep her eyes off the diagrams and photographs in my textbooks. She disliked reading but gravitated towards the self-important aura of scholarship. Sometimes, she'd ask timidly if I could study aloud. On the days that I did give in, I read slowly, gesticulating, using my eyes, my tone, my whole body to fill in the gaps that language could not.

Some afternoons, when I was particularly frustrated at not being allowed to temper the dal or trim the plants, I brought on my own revenge. I agreed to read to Vani, but chose a complex Civics or Geography chapter that was filled with jargon and then rattled away in a self-important accent. I would watch Vani's eyebrows crinkle and crease, and she couldn't keep up with folding clothes. She didn't follow the explanations and spent the rest of the day looking vacantly through all of us. Those evenings, our eyes ran when she chopped onions for salad, but I was adamant. If she kept me out of her world, I would keep her out of mine.

Despite these cruelties I inflicted, I could neither imagine nor bear a childhood without Vani in the frame. That is how she was – all-absorbing, sucking away the vacuum until she was ever-present.

One day, I did some research of my own. From the moment Aai's alarm sounded in the morning until the sigh of Vani lying on her cot in the kitchen, I counted how many times our names were called out. On my graph paper, I made tally marks while sitting in the centre of the living room all day, pretending to study.

Every other sentence was punctuated by 'Vani', 'Vanita' or 'Vanu'.

"Vani! Stir the aamti!"

"Did you iron those shirts, Vanita?"

"Vani! Answer the door!"

"Uff! What heat! Vanita, make some taak, will you?"

"Umi? Done with your homework ka? It's been over two hours now!"

Finally, a tally mark for me.

"I have a test tomorrow, Aai. Difficult aahes."

When Baba opened the door, I gained some more points but not for long. Vani always dominated over dinner.

That night, the accounts showed 44 Vanitas and 8 Urmilas. I applied it to all the mathematics I was studying that year:

A ratio of 11:2, an improper fraction of 5½; in the world of division, there was a remainder of 1. In the bar diagram, Vani's bar was long and sleek, mine was short and plump.

In a pie diagram, she was a huge hungry mouth, ready to swallow me whole. Vani expanded for over 304.7^0 out of 360^0, while I cowered and shrank.

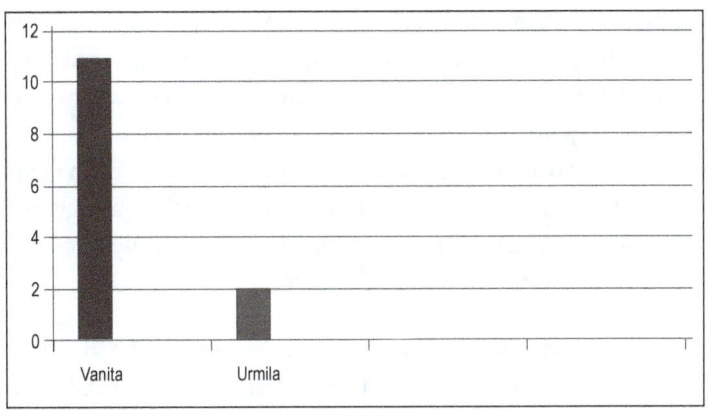

Yet, I couldn't help but love her. If I hadn't been sulking and keeping score that day, her bar and pie would have stretched out of the sheet, for I would have called for her the most.

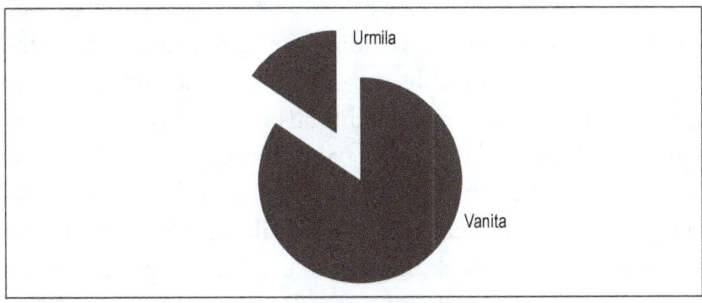

Perhaps I was destined to find disappointment in those I loved. For all my love for Vani, on the most anticipated day of my life, she left me grasping a garland of dead flowers. She didn't mean to steal the show on my wedding day; yet, she did. Just as my husband probably didn't mean to reject me on our wedding night; yet, he did.

They had a lot in common, the two loves of my life – a fixation for decorum, the ability to complicate relationships, a naivety that breaks hearts and is oblivious to the fact, and the curious, useful knack of merging into shadows at will. However, what linked Vani and Shree the most was the one person they both adored. And it was not me. When the time came to choose, they knew which path to follow; it didn't lead to me. I paled before that man; in fact, I vanished altogether. When he entered the room, the rest of us were simply artefacts; when he left it, the room didn't matter.

But I must give my husband the benefit of the doubt – perhaps what then seemed disinterest was actually his awkwardness. The only sensation that remains vivid is my pain. It is as fresh as on the day it was inflicted, and still stabs like a blunt knife.

We had been married a week and Shree hadn't approached me in bed. Sure, on the wedding night, embarrassed by the giggling relatives outside our door, we had attempted to grope each other in orange light. His face had already started sprouting bristles. He had probably shaved very early, owing to the rituals at dawn, and by the time I knew his touch, it was deep into the night; technically, it was already the next day. His stubble tickled my neck. A burst of laughter erupted from me before I could check it and echoed around the room. A few girls outside imitated the sound. I turned red. Shree stiffened and withdrew.

I pulled him closer and resumed the search for his lips. He played along for a while. I wanted him slow and hungry, yearning but restrained. He was too hesitant. When his nervousness settled, his eyes started drooping. Sometimes, I believe that only his discomfort kept him awake for those minutes. Soon, he sat up straight, placed some distance between us and said, "You must be very tired."

"No. Yes, I mean I am ... who wouldn't be? But it's okay."

I looked directly into his eyes. My chin was turned up, my pallu already fallen on the bed. I had undone 17 safety pins before climbing into bed, not wanting him to haggle with them.

"Do you want to get into something more comfortable? All those things must be poking you."

I wasn't ready for that question. In every film I could recall, the bridegroom relieved the bride of the heavy silks.

"Uh ... no, I mean ... it's okay."

The giggles outside intensified.

"I'll drive them off." He attempted to get up from the bed, but I held his hand.

"They won't listen. Let them be."

My hand was still on his when he wrestled it gently and freed himself.

"Listen," He pulled a stool close to the bed and sat on it. "All this has happened so fast. Maybe we should wait... It's... strange."

I wished then that I was covered with 17,000 safety pins, that my pallu was three inches thick and my skin devoid of sensation. I took a deep breath. "We could talk," I offered.

"I'm tired. Tomorrow?" his casual voice pierced my ears.

I lay unsure while he fidgeted with pillows and blankets. Already, the bed reeked of dead and squashed flowers. In the soft glow, I could see only silhouettes, and sound had already been my undoing. I smelt my way through that hour. First the overpowering fragrance of his perfume, mixed with perspiration and the sandalwood of rituals. Then the jasmine and marigolds, decaying by the minute, pulped by our tossing bodies and the cold surfaces of my bangles. We fell asleep with the corpses of marigolds separating us.

The delicacy of the moment lost that night never surfaced again. With each new night, I entered our room with desperate hope, but his hands danced clumsily, and worse, obligingly. In the blackness, tears stung my eyes and I gave up whatever little pretence of pleasure I had put on. Relieved, Shree pulled the blanket around him. It took him the tiniest flicker of disinterest to turn his back to me, and a series of encouragements to approach me.

One night, after deciding finally to consummate our marriage, I started to undress in front of him. Only the glow of the diya kept beside the garlanded photograph of the gods cast light on my skin. They stood resplendent, the trio – Ram, Sita and Hanuman – all glowing in the wake of virtue. The couple's hands were raised in perpetual blessing, while Hanuman stood on bent knee, looking up at a point in the space between their arms. As was customary, Shree bowed before the threesome, ate a piece of the sugar that had rested at their feet all day and then climbed into bed.

Casually, I made a big show of slipping off my bangles and

necklaces. Then, the sari was made to slide off and pile on the floor. Sitting in a small blouse and a low petticoat, I massaged lotion on my arms and legs, humming a tune to myself, seemingly unaware of his gaze. In the dim light, my skin was honey, my hair a tasselled curtain. I had applied thick kohl to my eyes for added depth and mystery. For several years, I had imagined this scene – the day my husband, whom I had fallen in love with in advance, would make love to me. When I stole glances at the mirror, it echoed my confidence; I was as tempting in the flesh as in my reveries.

I slowly unhooked all the buttons of my blouse and slid it off. I had a black lace bra on. Still humming, I pretended to struggle with the hook and casually walked up to him, gesturing for help.

Shree struggled with the hook and his battle was real. It was too tiny and delicate for his large, thick fingers. He tugged me backwards with the bra strap until he was seated on the bed and eye-level with the hook. Then he fumbled and found his reading glasses. He walked across the room and switched on the tube-light.

The white light awoke the reposing room. The bed, the chair, the table jumped at us from their slumber. The curtains were bright and jarring again. The photographs of his grandparents mocked us from the wall, the ceiling fan churned in dizzy mirth. Only the garlanded images of Ram, Sita and Hanuman stared through us, refusing to acknowledge my helplessness.

He strolled back to his seat on the bed without looking at me. As he peered at the hook, I crossed my arms about my chest. I was naked in the white light. Naked because his gaze did not cover my body. In the omniscient glare, I was muscle, tissue and skin, as if I lay on a surgeon's table. My curves were lost, the fluttering in my heart dismissed, the goosebumps on my skin ignored.

"Why do they make these kinds of hooks?" Shree muttered from behind his glasses. "As it is, they are at the back... how did you manage this before?"

I was still fumbling with the answer when I felt the tightness give way.

"Ah! Here, it's out. Breathe freely now."

I turned around to face him, but he was already fidgeting with the pillows.

The next morning at breakfast, his sister commented about how quiet I was. I just smiled and continued serving upma. Shree approved.

I realized soon that my banter put him off. He liked me receded and ebbed. He liked me as backdrop, beautiful and unobtrusive. My sight was too loud, my clothes too bright, my hair too untamed, my laughter too quick. I had to learn restraint.

Sometimes, I wondered whether our marriage had taken place with his approval, but then I learnt the truth. The question was whether his marriage had taken place with his approval; I wasn't the variable that mattered.

With Purushottam brushing away all suggestions of marriage for several years, my in-laws had given up on him and focused their attention on the younger son. Shree first excused himself because his older brother was still a bachelor. Then when it became clear that Purushottam might always remain a bachelor, Shree started arguing against the requirement of the institution. When those concerns were resolved, he found fault with every girl they mentioned. Finally, when his father suffered a paralytic stroke and his mother was clearly too old and weak to care for both of them, Shree relented. I was the first girl they met after Shree gave in.

It is another thing that I had poured my heart out to him several years before I saw him in my parents' living room.

Marriage is an act of balance. On the one hand, you feel right about something and you make a decision. On the other hand, once you decide, you make it right. I figured that since I had fallen in love with my husband, I now had to do everything in my power to make him feel the same way about me. So, attentively, I gauged his reactions to everything I said, ate, wore and did.

He was happiest with me when:

I cooked sabudana khichdi (Puru's favourite, not his),

I massaged his father's legs,

I took over supervising the maid,

I relieved his sister of all her chores,

I chatted over tea with his mother,

I wore cotton saris,

I didn't wear bangles,

I spoke less in company and at the dining table and

I fell asleep immediately after he entered our room.

Between caring for a paralytic man and figuring out my husband, I barely had time to pick up my brushes. The few afternoons when I sought the palette, even I was shocked by the brazenness of the colours. No pastels appeared, no neat lines or smooth curves. Instead, a woman with a blurred face dominated the canvas, restless and fierce, as if she would walk away any second and slam a door that stood just outside the frame. She could never be relegated to the background and was usually upset. I tried several times, but I couldn't bring her to lie down or stare at a lily or knit a shawl.

The only canvases that didn't have women were those with clocks. These were much more disturbing than any female form, and with each batch, I wished it was the last.

I still cannot bear to sell my first clock painting. Every colour of the palette has thrown itself on that scene. The lowest layer depicts a commonplace round clock, the most ordinary kind. Above that lie pairs of hands, more than a dozen of them stacked one on top of the other, each illustrating a different time. The blue pair shows 3:50; the amber, 7:25; the green, 6:05; the purple, 1:45. On top of these are piled ochre, maroon, ink, grey, lime, fuchsia and khaki. Each colour ticks a different time and the clock rotates untamed and giddy.

∽❧

The day I learnt to mistrust time was slippery with cunning. I was plumper than I was tall, a tot in oily pigtails with a handkerchief pinned to the pinafore. The air drooped wet and taut about me, sticking to my scalp. Beads of sweat collected under my double chin and in the folds of baby fat behind my knees.

It had rained all afternoon and the muck from my gumboots was stubborn. As always, Aai nagged me about cleaning my shoes, putting away my schoolbag and placing the uniform in the washing machine before I was even granted the luxury of a long sigh. Vani was yet to feature in our lives; once she arrived, my paraphernalia always found its place without drawing attention to itself.

The academic year had begun only a couple of weeks earlier and homework was some way off. But what was the point of a free afternoon if a wall of rain curtained it? The compound was already an ankle-deep brown pool, and sheets of water rattled away on the tin awning of our window. It was an afternoon that invited toasted sandwiches, hot chocolate and board games.

After an hour of numb channel-surfing, I insisted that Aai play a game of Ludo with me. She was sprinting between a pile of unwashed dishes, the ironing board and dinner preparations. Naturally, the first few mild requests had no effect on her. After a lot of whining, she agreed, "Okay! We'll play. Just give me 10 minutes."

"How much is 10 minutes?"

"Count till 600."

"600! That's too much, Aai!"

"Who will cook dinner? And iron your Baba's shirt for tomorrow?"

"Onetwothreefourfivesixseveneightnineteneleventwelve thirteen…" I gulped a mouthful of air. "Fourteenfifteen sixteenseventeeneighteennineteen…:

"Arre not like this, Umi. Take a breath after each count. One. Two. Three."

"Four. Five. Six. Hurry up. Seven. Eight. It's too much. Nine. Ten."

"You watch TV for 10 minutes. Then I'll come."

"If I watch TV, how will you know when 10 minutes are over?"

Aai let go of the clothes and stood over me. "See that clock?"

"Ya."

"Where is the big hand?"

"On four."

"When it reaches six, it means that 10 minutes are over."

"Really? I don't have to count?"

She was back in the kitchen. "Really."

It sounded too simple to be true. I was certain she was trying to trick me and squeeze out enough time to finish all the vessels and clothes. Maybe the hand would move every two days – how could I be sure? Certainly, she preferred her detergents to Ludo with me.

So, I hurried to tear a piece of paper from my notebook and find a pencil. I stood opposite the clock and counted, slowly, with breaths. I had never counted to 600 without stopping, not even at school. Intermittently, so that I didn't lose track, I wrote down the numbers I was counting. After each number, I ensured that there was a sharp intake of breath, similar to the kind of yoga Aai did every morning.

Four hundred and sixty three. Slurp. Four hundred and sixty four. Slurp. Four hundred and sixty five. Slurp.

Finally, when my mouth was dry, I reached 600.

"Done!"

"Good. I'm also done. Get the Ludo from the drawer."

I rolled the dice and rejoiced. Six! In the first try! What were the chances of that! Plonk-plonk-plonk-plonk-plonk-plonk. There, six.

"Your turn."

As Aai played, my eyes fell on the clock. I had become so engrossed in counting, that I had forgotten the purpose of the exercise. I should have kept track of the time. The big hand was still on four.

I was right; she had tricked me. Tears stung my eyes. What if I hadn't taken the effort to count? I might have had to wait for days!

I didn't want to play with Aai anymore, but I had already nagged her so much that I couldn't just refuse. With each round, I palmed the dice reluctantly and marched my piece ahead with angry deliberation. It no longer mattered that I was in the lead. The charms of Ludo were lost to me and Aai sensed it.

"Call Sonal and Neeta home if you want. I'll make soup. Your turn."

"Sonal is at her cousin's house today. Five."

"And Neeta? Your turn."

"Three. I think I'll open those new colours Ramesh-kaka bought me."

"Or you could watch that new cartoon Sheela-moushi gave – Princess and the Pea."

"I don't like princesses."

"Oh! Why? Your turn."

"Everyone keeps telling them what to do." I glanced at the big hand on the clock. It was still on four.

"And my princess? Does everyone keep telling her also what to do? Your turn."

"I want to paint."

"So paint, na."

"All the art sheets are over! I've told you five times and still…" I just wanted to finish the game.

"Okay. Once the rain stops we'll buy more. Your turn."

"Can we buy 50?"

"50!"

"So we don't have to keep going!"

I didn't paint the clock until several years later, but I learnt to mistrust it. I eventually surmised that its stillness was a result of Baba trying to save on batteries, but by then, the damage was done. Every time I looked at it, it was with suspicion. The more I thought about it, the more proof I found of its illogical nature. Some mornings when Aai woke me up, I could have sworn that the night had never passed. I had slept for just a moment. Why, I couldn't even count to five in that much time. But sure enough, the sun was staring through the window and Baba was in the toilet with the newspaper. Then I'd rap urgently on the door and Baba would shout, "One minute!" Dutifully, I'd stare at the clock and start counting. I'd press my thighs together and push in, leaning on the wall, afraid to even breathe too hard. Before I'd reach 50, Baba's flush would sound. Yet, I was certain that it couldn't be just 50 seconds; it must have been four minutes at least.

Time played games with me – and not just the seconds and minutes. Whole hours, days and weeks would trick and tease me, until I learnt that it was capricious by nature.

Which is probably why I was perplexed by the Math sums that I faced later; I could never map time along the X-axis at equidistant points.

If you are travelling from Kanpur to Delhi, which is a

distance of 408 km, and your train moves at 65 km/hour, how long will you take to reach Delhi?

It depends. On whether I am munching on Lays and Pepsi while reading a book. Or whether I fall asleep at the start of the journey and only wake up halfway. Will it then amount to half the time for me?

Or

Three men can chop a tree in 7 hours. How long will 5 men take to chop the same tree?

It depends. If they are chopping it for building a fire to cook dinner, they'll certainly finish by dinnertime. If they are not whistling while working, it'll take longer.

Perhaps the two most distrustful inventions were the clock and the calendar. Both were a sham, giving an illusion of order and uniformity, but actually dividing us from ourselves. We don't live evenly and neatly. Each moment is distinct. One moment may stretch on, another just gallop by; one may be a distant memory and another may expand until it spreads across every experience. Why, there are entire periods of time that I have not lived at all, and then spans that are saturated with meaning.

Who can calculate the length of time between my husband sprinkling sindoor into the parting of my hair and him tying the mangalsutra around my neck? It couldn't have been more than a few seconds. Yet, all these years, I have lived within those moments.

Or, the duration between me slipping off my clothes and

Shree turning away, pulling the bedspread over his shoulders. The tick of the seconds hand stretches wider than the blanket, looming over my dry lips, engulfing within itself the entire night, the following day, the week, the month and every shred of breath that escapes my lungs.

Some canvases held a single pulse of the clock while others spanned several ages. Some instances spread wide, embracing the sun, while others dug deep, freezing the tick to its core.

Six years and counting.

A friend once asked me, "Why did you stay all these years? Why didn't you do anything for so long?"

But it couldn't have been so many years. How long is a trance, how slow an itch?

Time, however, wasn't the only element that played with me. Mirrors found their way into my paintings. Startling images stared back from each canvas. In one, a woman in a bright red sari stood between two parallel mirrors. On both sides, the redness multiplied infinitely until I thought I would turn blind with the reverberation. Her bindi resembled spots of blood, freshly smudged. Her wrists flicked delicately and her arms were soft and rounded. Wisps of hair ran down her ears, neck and breasts. A half-smile appeared on her face, and yet, whenever I looked at the canvas, I could only think of a crime scene. Perhaps it was the redness, perhaps the imposing duplicates which refused to stop reproducing. Later, the press dubbed it *Narcissus' Sister at the Shrink*.

I was given my share of titles too.

"She has specialized in Epic Art, focusing on the women of several famous stories."

"Urmila Karmarkar's work is distinctly feminist and can be identified by…"

"She draws her themes from Indian myths and reminds us to ask…"

The first few times, I launched into explanations, split the nuances of feminism and debated over scenes from several epics, but these were exhausting and futile exercises.

When I was invited to conduct art workshops, I sensibly devoted more energy to the eager participants than the compartments that these speeches slotted me into. I was aptly rewarded. When we worked together, we were complete in ourselves.

Sometimes, I looked at the canvases of other artists, and saw what they had found. Some had found style, some colours; some had found vent, others technique; many had found themselves, but none had found joy. It's the nature of art, I suppose. It plays with your soul, wringing it, elevating it, storming it, overwhelming it. Art is complex. It asks to be hung on walls and for red ribbons that say, "Do not step beyond this line".

Joy on the other hand, is a simple emotion, ready to evaporate at the smallest trick of the mind. It surprised me, that emotion, gurgling up to my lips at the start of each workshop. It flitted around me with ease, as plain and transparent as air. I wished those afternoons to never end.

The light air would persist, escorting me home. Through fuming streets and over broken footpaths, I would forget to be complicated. I would forget that I had a husband and yet didn't have one. It didn't matter whether Vani was damned or cursed. Those moments belonged to simple uncoloured things like the aroma of paanipuri, meows of kittens and the smoothness of the chiffon dupatta around my neck.

It lasted until I reached the threshold of the house. The sight of the door burst through the ease that had shielded me up to that instant. Then, sighs took over; the ebb and flow of tears rang in my ears despite the loud commercials and sitcoms that we waded through each evening. Empty spaces haunted every corner I turned to.

Maybe we should have shifted into an easier home – one that was fresh and crisp and small, that didn't have a history etched in each room or a secret breathed into every wall. Instead, we sat at the oversized dining table, watched TV on a sofa that was too wide and retired to beds that remained half-empty.

As I look back, I am struck by the sham that we played out. Every morning I picked one of the many bindis that adorned the right corner of the dressing-table mirror and stuck it between my eyebrows. The tiny gold cups of the mangalsutra hung between my breasts while I went about making breakfast. I didn't really know a husband, but wore all the symbols of a married woman – green bangles, silver toe-rings, vermillion and a shelf-load of other colours and metals.

When Aai had meticulously arranged for the various rings, bangles and necklaces, neither of us suspected that that they would just be empty badges.

The morning had buzzed with anticipation. There were just a few days to go before the wedding, and Aai resolutely cancelled my spa treatment for an afternoon of tradition-lessons. We were off to Jhaveri Bazaar, a lane astonishingly dirty and cramped for the kind of business it performed. Already, a few days earlier, my ears had been pricked along the 'C' curve and studded with diamonds. Next we were off to a different jeweller, this time to pierce the nose.

"These are not just silly rituals!" Aai had argued all the way. "It is for scientific reasons. All these points are acupressure points."

"So?"

"So if you have earrings or a nose-ring pushing in at that spot, it is good for health."

"Then why don't men do it?"

She slapped her forehead. "For your information, earlier even men used to wear all this. Don't you remember the serials on TV? *Ramayana*? How radiant all the princes would look with their long earrings and necklaces? Even cummerbunds and bangles…"

"It doesn't look good now. Not even on girls."

"The boys have already abandoned all these customs. Now it's up to us to keep our culture alive."

"There's a reason why the men stopped, Aai! My ears are

already hurting; I can't bear the nose ring now. Can't we do it next week?"

"But by then you'll be married!"

"So? We'll do it after marriage."

I remember Aai chuckling. She chortled into the end of her pallu and shook her head.

"What?"

"Nothing… nose ring after marriage…" A fresh gush of snickering erupted and her dimples deepened. But within a few seconds, she had turned thoughtful.

"Come, let's first have some sugarcane juice," she suggested. "That new 'Cane and Syrup' outlet has opened here." She pointed to the end of the road. "Very hygienic."

I was happy to defer the nose piercing, however brief the interval. We debated over the sugarcane juice – with lemon, mint, orange, ginger, pineapple, honey or jaljeera – and eventually armed ourselves with two frothy glasses. Aai chose a relatively secluded corner and settled down on a plastic chair, flopping her purse on the table between us. It had been a sultry morning, with the recent drizzle steaming up at us from the roads. Her hair had frizzled so it reached several inches above her head and mine fell limp and sticky on my neck. We downed the juice too soon to feel satiated and I went off to order another round. It was only when we had slushed through half of the second round that she cleared her throat.

She put on her expression of purpose and began most casually, "Umi, about the nose ring…"

"Hmm?"

"We'll choose a nice big one, not the stud kind, the round ring... like Madhuri Dixit's in what's that movie?"

"I don't know."

"Arre, it's at the tip of my tongue!"

"*Beta*? *Tezaab*?"

"No, no..."

"Accha forget it. Doesn't matter."

"No it matters... the point is that the nose ring will be round – probably with pearls like your set – and a gold chain will link the nose ring to your earrings."

"That'll be so heavy!"

"No, no. These are special chains – thin like a thread – especially for brides."

"Whatever!"

"Beta, look at me. Forget that juice for a minute!"

Aai was squirming and I raised an eyebrow. "What?"

"See, the nose ring is very big. And it is linked to the earring with a thread."

"Aai, you already told me that."

"Yes. So the point is that on the wedding night... The husband, to do anything... I mean he first has to remove the nose ring."

"What?"

Impatient, she spoke rapidly. "Arre, he has to remove the nosering! First find his name in your mehndi. That you know na? So first he has to find his name in your mehndi, then he must remove the nosering. Otherwise how will you... kiss?"

"Oh!"

"Yes... oh!"

"He'll put his finger in my nose!"

"No, no... it's an easy clasp. Don't worry!"

I imagined him struggling with a fat finger in my nostril and burped a large blob of sour juice. Aai had regained her composure and joined in with a chuckle. Seeing her sudden shift from twitchy to relaxed, I laughed and shook my head. Within a second, Aai joined in, holding her stomach and chortling. One hand on her belly and the other on her mouth, she turned even pinker.

"Why... why do you think they refer to the suhaag raat as nath utharna?"

"They call it that? I've never heard it!" I exclaimed. "We don't have to use such code words!"

That had been the extent of the sex education I received from my mother but the nose ring persisted. It was never removed – not by Shree on our wedding night, not ever. Over the years, the shape and size changed. On the wedding day, it was a Brahmani nath, with bosra pearls and rubies. Later I stuck to a thin gold band. Then I chose a diamond stud instead of the dangling metal. And now, a plain gold dot rests on my left nostril.

The last stage of hope is the abandonment of symbols. The symbols adorn me, simultaneously providing a mockery of my marriage and the collage of a dream. Perhaps one day, Shree will embody everything the symbols stand for. For now, the rings, bindis, necklaces and sindoor act as substitutes. They touch my fingertips and the gaps of my toes, the cleft of my breasts and the tip of my forehead. They caress me where I thirst for his touch.

☙

They say that I am imagining it. For the past several weeks, my colours have been staging a rebellion. They merge as they wish and I can never be sure if red and blue would make magenta. They stray out of the lines I assign to them and run into corners. They openly refuse my strokes, insisting on patterns I never intended.

They insist that like my colours, my mind has congealed, clotted like curd. But even they should be able to see that my stomach has swollen. Where it once curved in, it has begun to arch out. A smooth mound like an infant's, with a large, sore belly button.

Yet it is hollow, there is no denying it. Every month, I am reminded of the hollow redness of the sindoor. It trickles out like the paint, refusing to form the outlines I ache for.

As I wash the angry, hurting redness away, I imagine the

spaces inside. Spaces that wait, growing increasingly impatient. My body has been softening and curving, moulding itself into a cradle. My breasts have grown heavier, my fingers lighter, as if they are learning to touch a new cheek or hold a tiny finger. My voice has developed a song-like quality, the kind I would once find annoying in kindergarten teachers.

The signs are there for all to see, and yet, I have missed them for years. I was so engrossed in seeking an absent husband that I have overlooked the absence of a child. Did the emptiness in my paintings, the suspended limbs and vacant faces echo not the absence of a man, but the void in my womb? The minute I think about it, lightness settles over me, like a face waiting to be recognized. I know I must stop fighting the signs. That evening, I look up at the fertility clinic that has lined our road all these years. Maybe I will walk into it. At just the thought, the roads seem to widen, the trees droop lower and the traffic honks in rhythm.

Within a few months of our marriage, on sniffing some discord, my mother had made the suggestion – have a baby.

"All marriages can work," I remember her contemplating while dunking whole tomatoes in boiling water. "We just have to wait long enough. And a child will be the glue to hold you together until then."

"What's with this glue talk?" I laughed and waved her off.

I had forgotten how perceptive she could be. With Vani out of the house, my mother had reclaimed her old self. She cooked a single dish every morning, which took them through all the meals of the day. Baba looked after the many pots of tea, Aai trimmed the plants, he made the bed, she looked into the clothes. The bookshelf remained undusted for days and she couldn't hide her relief ("There are more important things in life than clean surfaces"). Some dinners consisted only of instant noodles and a walk down to the new frozen-yogurt parlour. They lived more like roommates now, finally able to abandon the veneer of marriage. After Baba's retirement, the frantic office routine was replaced by Dev Anand songs on TV, a constant stream of assorted beverages and midmorning siestas. Aai went off for music recitals with her friends, while Baba called his gang over for cards and misal bought from Sai Anand Family Restaurant.

The days when I visited saw an unnatural bustle in the kitchen. On this afternoon, Aai had already made pakodas and was now fussing over a salad. "A child doesn't just make a man a father. You'll see – he will become a husband."

"I don't know, Aai. It's a little strange."

"You've always wanted children! Do you really want to wait? Has he indicated that he doesn't want them?"

"No. We haven't discussed children." I rescued some tomatoes from the boiling water and carefully arranged them on a large plate to cool.

"Discussions are not always good."

"Aai, let it be."

"Listen," she turned to face me. "Just tell him that you want a little version of himself."

"That's corny!"

"Arre, it works. Say that he's too much for you to handle – you want smaller hands, tiny feet, little giggles. Keep it light."

"Is that what you said to Baba?"

She nudged me and smiled. "It's what your Baba said to me!"

"And you were okay with that?"

"If I was a little apprehensive, one look at you changed everything." She pinched my cheek and walked towards the fridge. "Where are the curry leaves? Did you see any?"

I handed over the box and began peeling garlic. "Still, I don't think he's ready for a child, Aai."

"No one is. What's the problem with just checking? See where he stands? Just remember – nothing too heavy."

So, I did. On a carefully selected evening, I casually perched on the stool in front of our dressing table. A few photo albums lay scattered on the table, placed strategically by Vani. I pretended to notice them when struggling with a bracelet.

"Is that you or Puru?"

He took a cursory look. "Guess."

"The smile looks like his," I said.

"I suppose I have his smile then."

"Babies are so adorable!" I flipped through some more pictures.

"Hmmm. Makes you wonder what happens to them later."

I wasn't sure whether I should continue. Perhaps I wasn't the best person to prod, and certainly, I could do without another rebuke.

"The other day, Roopali-kaku was talking about how it's been a year or so..." It was true. She had mentioned the upcoming double-wedding-anniversary. "Something about the right time for children and all." I kept it casual, even managing a small chuckle.

"Please don't start taking her seriously. Ma does that enough as it is."

"No, no. No hurry, of course." I pretended to flip through the photographs, looking for another opening.

"What are both of you doing here?" I pointed to a photograph.

He put on his glasses and peered. "Fancy dress."

"But you're in a sari!" I giggled. "What are you guys supposed to be?"

"Krishna and Radha. See the flute that Dada is trying to hide behind his back? Ma insisted that we couldn't go as Ram and Laxman for the fourth time in a row. Stop laughing!"

But he was smiling too. "We won a consolation prize or something. And the costume guy let us keep the peacock feather."

"It must be so special to share everything with a sibling. I kept pestering Aai and Baba!"

"But Vanita-vahini is…"

"Of course! She's like a sister. But you know, it's different. She's not… not…"

"What? Not good? Not lucky?"

"No! She's…"

"Not good enough? Say it, Urmila."

His jaw tightened. He pushed away the album and turned towards me.

"That's not what I was about to… you know that!"

"Everyone has to stop treating her like this." His voice was low.

"I have never treated her badly! Even my parents…"

"How much should she go through? It's self-fulfilling, all this bad luck nonsense. People themselves create misery in the house because they expect it!"

"She herself believes it. First she needs to…"

He put his hand up and sighed. "You don't seem thrilled to have her here, Urmila."

I looked away. "Two days ago, you spoke to me about everything happening so fast, things have to settle down. It's just a very big change. And sudden!"

"Oh please! All your 'we are sisters' talk is nonsense! You love her in a condescending way, because of the manglik stigma. Ask me how siblings are."

"Everyone doesn't have the same kind..."

"They're trying for a child, you know!"

I didn't. "What?"

"Dada told me. He said it would help the situation. They really want a child." My husband got up and started putting away the photographs.

Why hadn't Vani said anything? Here she was helping me with my plans and I was clueless about her decision.

He began fidgeting with the albums. "It's been a few months since they decided."

"Why didn't you tell me earlier?"

"All this pressure isn't helping, Urmila. This expectation – it's the most unfair of them all! Do you notice that they only want it from us? No one is asking Dada about children."

"Why are we talking like this to each other? Why do we always end up like this, Shree?" I got up and started walking away.

"Earlier he was supposed to lead everything. The house, the business," my husband continued. "Now suddenly they don't want his example, don't want his wife, don't want his children!"

I couldn't bear to continue the conversation. Not knowing where to escape, I abruptly walked into the bathroom. I started splashing water on my face. For several minutes, I let it run from my cheeks, down my neck, spotting my kameez. Finally, I walked out, still dripping.

My husband was lying on his side of the bed, staring at the fan. As I walked closer, he shut his eyes.

"You need to give everyone time, Shree." I lay down beside him and switched off the light. I placed my hand on his chest and patted it gently. Bringing my pillow closer, I shifted towards him.

"No one is giving me time," he muttered and turned away. His blanket found its way up to his ears.

So, they were trying to conceive. Maybe they are trying now, I thought. I looked at the curved, covered, scoffing form of my husband and shook away the thought. Comparisons would do no good.

In the darkness, I listened to the soft churning of the fan, and for the softer breath of my husband. These would have to do for now, since I wasn't to hear the words I wanted. His loving pleas wouldn't fill my ears and my repressed moans wouldn't fill my throat. The pillow needed to go back to the left; I needed to go back to the left. Slowly, I shuffled to my side.

I found my way to the unsteady beats of my heart, and silently, sincerely, lulled it to a calm that would afford me a semblance of sleep.

The next morning, the air seemed alight with promise. Instead of burying himself in the newspaper, my husband whistled and helped me fold the blanket. Then, like hesitant guests, we tried to tuck the bed sheet tight, one on each side of the bed. When we tried to place the pillows – each working with one – they didn't align in a straight line. At the next attempt, they were too close, then too far, then too flat. I couldn't suppress a giggle. Shree finally took the pillow from me and dumped both resolutely on the bed.

Before it could get more awkward, I made my way to the kitchen and watched Geeta stir up an aromatic upma. As Vani and I set about the breakfast routine, I saw my husband walk into Puru's room. They emerged a few minutes later and continued what seemed to be an engaging conversation, out on the balcony. Puru was nodding a lot, patting my husband's arm, smiling broadly.

A soft cordiality surrounded us, and my husband and I were united in a mutually polite series of smiles. Although we were still distant, at least he wasn't agitated. Certainly, something had shifted.

Late in the evening, Aai called. I stepped into our bedroom to talk at leisure. Shree followed me and locked the door behind him. He fidgeted with the cupboards and folded some clothes, while I provided Aai with long hmmms and short replies. Aai must have sensed my hesitation and soon hung up. Once I disconnected, Shree sat me on the bed and took both my hands in his.

"Urmila, I've been thinking."

I waited. This was already unusual.

He cleared his throat. "You're right. We should have a child. Why wait?"

I hadn't expected this. If only I could speak to Aai right away, again. But my husband was holding my hands. I managed a soft, unnecessary, "Really?"

"Yes, I gave it a lot of thought. A child will be good for us. There is no need to delay it."

As if to prove his point, my husband ran his hands up my arms, touching me lightly with his fingertips. When he reached my shoulder, he slid off the dupatta.

"What made you change your mind?"

He slid closer and held his mouth against my neck, breathing lightly. "Just," he whispered in my ear.

I arched my back in anticipation and then checked myself. This was not how I had imagined it to be. I hadn't washed my hair, my underarms were unshaved, a trickle of sweat ran down my spine, I wore a dull, old kameez. And I had told Geeta I would supervise the chhole that was planned for dinner.

I kissed his mouth, his eyes, his neck. When I reached his ear, I whispered, "Wait, let me freshen up."

Instead, he turned me around suddenly and I lay sprawled on the bed. My husband towered over me and smiled. He bent, and reaching over me, switched off the light. Only the glow of some streetlights filtered through the window.

"I have to tell Geeta…"

"Shhh!" he put a finger on my mouth, but I could see that he was pleased with the resistance.

I decided to play it his way. "But what if she knocks?"

As if to demonstrate how little he cared about distractions, he slid a hand into my kameez and squeezed my waist. Then, he reached for the knot of my salwar and pulled it free. He lifted my hips. I was wearing floral cotton panties and I cringed at the memory of putting them on that morning. But I needn't have worried; Shree wasn't even looking. His eyes were staring straight ahead of him, focused, resolute.

"This is quite sudden," I said, just so he would look at me.

"They say a child completes the equation, balances everything."

The mathematical analogy was odd, but I didn't comment. I sat myself up and tugged at the kameez. He lifted it above my head and took in the sight of my breasts. Despite the white cotton bra, I could see that he was tempted. For the first time perhaps, my husband perceived me as a sexual being. Just this thought quickened my pulse and I could feel the slight heaving of my breasts.

I turned around. It worked. My husband inched closer and took off the pin that held my hair in a limp bun at the nape of my neck. The strands fell all over my back. Parting them slowly, he reached for the clasp of my bra. One tiny pinch and my breasts swayed loose. I shut my eyes and allowed myself a soft sigh. Kissing my back, Shree eased the straps off my shoulders. He resumed caressing my back with hesitant fingertips and inched his way across my ribs.

He cupped my breasts from below, taking their weight in his hands. I ached to turn and press myself against his body, but his hold was too firm. He leaned over and kissed my neck.

Then, almost as suddenly as he had begun, he let go of me and began undressing. Within moments, he had both of us naked, facing each other. My husband took my hand and sat me on the bed. A slight push and once again, I was supine. He parted my legs and stood between them.

Although I had longed for this moment, I needed it to stretch. "Why such a hurry?" I stroked his face with my fingertips.

"Maybe I can't wait to make you a mummy." He smiled.

"You better not change your mind later!" I joked. "There's no return policy."

"Why would I ever want to return something so adorable? And you would play with it, run after it, fuss over it…"

"And you? What about us…"

"Oh, I'll fuss over the baby too! And once that little bundle appears, you'll have no time for me or anyone else!"

He laughed, but I was uneasy.

"But that's not…" I began.

"Shh!"

He spread my legs further and slowly guided himself inside me. Just a couple of inches in and he stopped. A warmth flooded over me and I allowed a soft moan to escape. I dug my heels into the mattress and raised my hips. He entered deeper, waited for a couple of seconds and then thrust all the way in.

I cried out. Immediately his palm clasped my mouth.

Shree continued moving, awkwardly, pushing and pausing, an irregular tempo. We needed to work out a rhythm. My eyes shut, I traced his back with my fingers. I tugged at his hair and followed his spine. When I reached my husband's buttocks, I pressed them down and pushed my hips up, trying to establish a pace.

A few seconds later, he flicked my hand away. Now, I was burning and sore, and the screams I swallowed were more of pain than ecstasy. Yet, I couldn't bear for him to stop.

"Shree?" I said just to distract him for a moment.

"Hmmm..." His palms were now grasping my shoulders tight and his thrusts were getting harder.

I had to make up a conversation. "So this baby we're making..."

He grunted.

"... are you thinking of a boy or a girl?"

He ignored my question and his pace remained unchanged. I opened my eyes and looked at him. My husband was still staring straight ahead, his expression intent, serious.

"What if it's a messy girl like me?"

Again, he ignored me. His stomach slapped against mine. A film of perspiration coated our bodies. It was a strange sensation, this awkward, raw coupling and the intermittent waves of pleasure that tingled through me, as if my body couldn't decide whether to like it or not.

"I like this side of my husband," I murmured. "And maybe the kid will ask for a sibling."

For the first time, he spoke. "Even better, you'll be twice as busy."

It took a moment to register. There was a determined edge to that statement.

"What do you mean?" My voice was no longer low and husky.

"Nothing."

"No, why did you say that?"

He stopped moving, propped himself on his elbows and said, "Are we going to just keep chatting like this?"

I tried to shift, but his weight came down too heavily on me. A part of me wanted to brush aside his statement and continue our conflicted pleasure. I wanted his hands on my back, wanted his toes pressing against my ankles, wanted his mouth on my breast. I wanted him towering, groaning, entering, thrusting, losing himself in me. More than anything else, I wanted him to want this again and again, before breakfast and after dinner and all the hours in between. But I couldn't let that tone go.

"Why did you say it'll be good if I'm busy?"

"A child will take up your time and you'll become busy. That's all."

"So you're trying to distract me with a live doll? That's why you changed your mind?"

My legs were still spread in anticipation. My husband knew my yearning, sensed my hips rising to meet him.

He reached lower and put his mouth on my ear. His tongue found my earlobe. "Urmila, shhh! Just lie back and enjoy."

He pushed deeper into me and his pace started to quicken. Our hips slapped against each other hungrily.

But I couldn't forget. He was trying to replace himself. I knew it in my gut. It was probably what the brothers had discussed all morning.

My husband started thrusting harder and for the first time, he shut his eyes. As his thrusts reached a crescendo, he reached for my breasts and squeezed them hard. I stifled a cry. I lay conflicted, eager but anxious, thrilled and terrified – desired and yet, simultaneously, completely, unwanted.

Before I could stop myself, I took a deep breath and pushed. Shree slid out of me and slipped to my right. His semen spurted all over my thigh and our hastily discarded clothes. Shocked, white, it seemed to glare at me angrily. Shree cupped his penis, trying to prevent stains on the bed sheet.

"Why did… what is wrong with…" He was breathing heavily and his voice was cold.

I looked away.

He tottered to the bathroom, fuming but silent.

"Not like this, Shree," I said to his retreating figure. "A baby cannot replace you."

"What is that supposed to mean?" he shouted. "Why do you have to suffocate me so much?"

"So you tell me – what should I do?" I hastily began covering myself again. My old, faded clothes were suddenly comforting.

"Let go of me!" He returned from the bathroom, scowling.

"How can I let go of what is not mine? Maybe if you really…"

"Really what? Rip out my fucking soul?"

I had never heard him swear before. Shree slammed the bathroom door behind him.

He wasn't too off the mark; I did want his soul. Isn't that was love is about – soul mates? Belonging to the other person for eternity? Except he made me sound like the devil incarnate.

Even now, every time I recall the scene, my husband's statement reminds me of some of the women I paint. They never smile, but some of them look like they have just laughed – a cunning sound, high-pitched, mirthless, shrieking and sudden – the devil's laughter. When I look at their faces, I remember that evening when I hugged my knees as my husband stormed into the bathroom, his soul intact, his semen spilling over the floor.

PART IV

Chathvaari Maayo - Vishnuthva - Anvethu

With this fourth vow of Saptapadi, as your husband, I promise you Mayobhav: to develop harmonious relationships and bestow prosperity.

Since the day Vani stepped into our lives, she maintained an air of being wounded. She was a victim in a world so cruel that it wouldn't even afford her a culprit. It was in her stars, she demonstrated with each shrug and each sigh. She was supposed to be the one in a thousand who would carry the misfortunes of humanity on her shoulders.

When she gave Aai hour-long head massages, it emphasized not the intensity of Aai's headache, but the depth of Vani's altruism. When I followed her around, imitating her gait and her speech, she stressed her tolerance of my intrusion, not the extent of my devotion. When she enthusiastically offered four different kinds of parathas for breakfast, it was the reflection of a wonderful person in a demanding setup.

Puru had a thing for victims. He was privileged and didn't know how to handle it in a world full of sufferers. Any other man born into a wealthy, indulgent, respected family would probably feel entitled, powerful. But Puru lived in the shadow of guilt, his eyes downcast. Guilt at reaping rewards whose seeds he did not sow, at enjoying fortunes he did not earn. His health was robust, his mind sharp, his genes beneficially selective, he worked hard because it came to him easily, his family doted on him, women dared second peeks at his enviable frame, the servants anticipated his desires before he could express them; even the eunuchs at traffic signals could conjure up no further blessings. He was miserable.

Added, Puru's mind played with numbers. We were given statistics at every turn of a conversation. Did we know that 80 per cent of Indians lived on less than 80 rupees a day? That only 16 out of 1000 people in the country had access to the Internet? That this meant 98 per cent of the population didn't have the basic facility which drove our lives and our businesses? He emphasized that we did not even want to know the percentage of people who lived in houses made of mud, wood and leaves. Could we imagine that 63 per cent of the country didn't have toilets?

Once, while a team of cardiologists, orthodontists and neurosurgeons stood by my father-in-law, Puru murmured that for others, there was less than one doctor for every 1000 Indians. In an unjust, random world, he fell on the right side of the fence, and was haunted by the faceless masses that didn't share his luck.

He was always petting stray dogs, packing extra vegetable rolls for beggars, installing more bird feeders around the housing society, coaxing the milkman's son to appear for various entrance tests or asking his many office peons about the rains and harvests in their native villages.

Yet, no one imagined his quiet, tentative romance with Vani. I wonder when Vani found the time. I conjured up an image of them meeting in the vegetable market, strolling with radishes, haggling over mint leaves and squeezing in a quick drink at the juice stall. I wouldn't be surprised; it was entirely harmonious with her idea of romance – small, simple bursts during routine chores that didn't interfere with one's work. Leisurely gazes or long-drawn chats over coffee and croissants wouldn't work for her. They were too unproductive and fattening. And they weren't in her stars.

Of course, Vani and Puru didn't need excuses to meet; there were legitimate reasons because of the upcoming wedding. Since the groom was shy and the bride busy with beauty treatments, they took on many proxy responsibilities. Also, unlike convention, my family was not required to host the entire function. When Shree's parents insisted on splitting all costs and efforts, Baba had been pleased, but Puru and Vani had their own reasons to celebrate.

Vani had to pick up my blouse from the tailor, and Puru was heading the same way; perhaps he could give her a lift. The blouse needed to be tightened and Puru was again taking the same route; perhaps he could take her there and drop her back. Maybe they would take a detour to the printer's office and finalize the text for the invitation cards. I learnt these details much later, and Vani insisted that they never articulated their feelings, that just being in each other's company was enough.

"I couldn't believe that he might like me, Umi. I kept thinking I was imagining it," she once confessed. "After all, you were to marry his younger brother and me? I'm a manglik."

"Vani! Stop using their words."

She grinned. "I know. It just sounds so dramatic."

"So you never once told him?"

"No, in fact I would call him 'Dada'! Older brother!"

"But he must have indicated it?"

"Puru is so attentive to everyone. How could I have guessed?"

"So what would you talk about?" I asked.

"About the bride and groom, what else! How happy Umi is, how Chhotu needs a haircut, whether your outfits match properly, how you will adjust to a joint family, how Chhotu couldn't bear the idea of marriage till he set eyes on you!"

"So Shree and I were unwitting allies to your hide-and-seek games!"

She smiled and left it at that, but I could imagine how it must have panned out. After all, Shree was Puru's devotee as much as I had once been Vani's shadow. Vani and Puru had this power in common. Their biggest fans were going to tie the knot, and it provided the perfect platform for their faltering feelings to blossom. In the light of this bond, it must have been possible to dream away the chasm that separated them.

Vani, who never let me forget the first- and second-class compartments of our fathers, discarded her caution for Puru. Despite having woven herself into several labels, she did manage to come up for air. She must have hoped, must have indulged in an unprecedented optimism because I knew that she spurned all other suitors. Perhaps she believed that her stars owed her this shift.

Marriage proposals for Vani had begun much before they did for me. The mangal dosha wasn't as much as a deterrent as I had feared, because there were several manglik men awaiting a bride. Vani was alone, orphaned, and hence, available earlier and coveted more. The first proposal came from the owner of a car repair shop. The next was from a supervisor at a security arrangement firm. The third suitor ran a small hotel at the end of the lane. She hated them all, and opposed each one with surprising intensity.

This one was a womanizer, that one still lived at the edge of his mother's pallu, yet another was overstocked with testosterone and thought a wife was just a combination of a maid, punching bag and whore.

A few times, Baba tried to reason with her, but it would only end with Vani in tears, clutching my mother's feet. "Please, Tai, don't give me away to that spineless man. If you are tired of me, just say so and I will walk away!"

It was always a variation of the same theme – proposal and protests, suggestions and sobs, worrying and weeping.

Once, Baba joked, "Maybe we'll send you off with Umi as her dowry!" He was closer to the mark than we could have imagined.

Her fuss, which would have put off other men, made Ravi Kaluskar even more resolute. Manglik or not, I agreed with Vani wholeheartedly on her rejection of the arrogant man with reeking breath and a leering gaze. He was a partner in his brother-in-law's thriving rentals business (33 per cent partner, as he proudly declared when his parents sat in our living room, discussing a possible alliance with Vani). Rumours suggested that it was an arrangement that his sister orchestrated because Ravi was throwing his life away. He had barely managed to push through a correspondence degree, and then flitted from one aimless job to another. The mother vehemently blamed the horoscope charts and the mangal dosha, but I suspect it had more to do with his fondness for the bottle. In fact, if it wasn't for the manglik denominator, he wouldn't have had any basis to even dream of a match with Vani.

After he was made a partner in the rentals business, Ravi Kaluskar went about proclaiming his newfound status and income. He did so by offering cars to neighbours at discounted rates for weddings, holidays and out-of-town guests. Sometimes, he drove the cars himself, ostensibly out of affection, but more likely to get a rear-view insight into the lives of others.

Once, we had rented a sedan for a two-day trip to Shirdi, and he kept increasing the air conditioning, forcing Vani to squeeze her arms together while Ravi adjusted the mirror to focus on her cleavage. Perversion aside, it was very risky too, and more than once, I instructed him to turn down the air conditioning. He carried with him the musky stench of alcohol and the futile whiff of the mints he used to camouflage it. It was a miracle we made it back whole.

Later, Ravi would follow her to the market, relentlessly offer lifts and often ring our doorbell, asking to speak to Vani. She spurned all his advances, ignored him on the streets, stopped drying clothes at the window if he stood in the compound, shut the door on his face and took me along on days when the market couldn't be avoided.

138

I believe something within him snapped at this public rejection, so complete and unambiguous in its refusal. Ravi vowed to avenge the insult.

He stopped loitering; his stroll now had a purpose, his gaze a mission as it followed Vani. Despite the haze of alcohol, he managed to do it cleverly, stealthily, with the ease of a professional. This resolve struck me much later, after all the damage had been done, the tears shed, the reputations soiled, after our destiny had unveiled itself.

∽◌

The weeks that led to my wedding were replete with warnings. The tulsi that had stood on our balcony since I was a toddler, withered and couldn't be coaxed back to life. Our tailor was suddenly summoned to his village to attend to an emergency and my trousseau remained incomplete. My father was diagnosed with diabetes and could only take the smallest bites of the ceremonial sweets. On the morning of the engagement, I was to bathe in rose-scented milk, except when I took the first mugful, I realized that it had curdled. Gradually, the omens led me to the epicentre whose ripples send tremors even after all these years.

On the day we came to know about Ravi Kaluskar's plans, they had already been in action for several months. I was placing the last hairpin in my elaborate hair-do. The shehnai players had taken their seats, the diyas on the stage were lit, the caterers had heated the oil for cocktail samosas.

And Ravi had already downed his gives-me-a-boost drink

at 11 AM. Vani stood fussing over my sari when he swayed forcefully into the room, reeking.

"Here you are, in the bride's room! Considering your closeness with the bridegroom's brother, I thought you'd be on that side of the family."

Vani looked up at him, her face pale.

"You know what I mean ... shouldn't you be checking on his sherwani, maybe tying, untying the pyjama?"

The eight fretting women in the room fell silent. My heart sank. Yet, it felt light, like a feathery fist tumbling down a pipe, like I could finally stop wondering what could go wrong.

"What are you doing?" I managed a high-pitched shriek.

"Celebrating your marriage, what else? Two girls from this family frolicking with two boys from that family. It's all so convenient. Come, let's all celebrate!"

He fished out a small bottle from his pocket and took a glug.

"He's drunk and talking nonsense, Umi-tai." Vani said. "Someone take him away." Her face was red and on the verge of crying.

"Of course, throw me out! After all, you're too good for me! That rich chikna is a better catch. So how did you tempt him? Have you even told him the truth about yourself?"

"What is he talking about?" I dreaded the answer even as I asked. But he ignored me.

"Of course you would reject all of us. Your sights were set higher, higher than that one even," he said, pointing to me. "The older brother! Waah, I salute your cunning!"

By now, he was back at the door and a group had gathered outside – a few distant uncles, a couple of cousins, and Purushottam. My eyes fell on Baba at the periphery of the circle. His dilemma was visible on his face; he didn't know whether it would be wiser to intervene or ignore the man. Aai hissed at Baba and pushed him ahead.

"Kaay challa aahes? Stop this drama!" But his voice shook.

"Aye Kaka, don't interfere…"

"What don't interfere? Eh? On our family function, you come and do this drama? What do you want?"

How I wished for both of them to shush and vanish, for everyone to be most concerned about whether the laddoos would have enough dry fruits in them or the puris would be adequately fluffy. Or for their attention to stay fixed on the traditional belpan vajratik necklace I wore and the perfect mehndi on my hands. But Ravi's audience, including Shree's parents, breathed in every word that Ravi uttered.

Outside, as if to echo the scene, June clouds started to gather. In a few seconds, it became distinctly darker and the tube-lights emphasized the dim sky. The heat had reached its summit; it would release itself in teardrops soon.

"For how much do you lease her out? To your cousins and brothers, you pimp!" he screamed at Baba.

Another louder, collective gasp ran around the room. My father lunged at him but Ravi's tirade went on. "I've always wondered why you took in this orphan girl. But it looks like she earns her keep!"

Vani was now sobbing, her kajal running down her face. I ached to enfold her, smother her and yet strangle her for what I knew was to befall. I took a step ahead and stopped. I couldn't; I was hurting too much.

"I've seen her with him a dozen times! All coy and teasing. And the man – he couldn't hide the tent in his pants!"

"How dare you make baseless allegations?" Baba shook Ravi violently.

"You don't believe me? Ask him yourself. There he is!"

Ravi pointed at Purushottam. Purushottam had been walking towards Vani but stopped.

I saw Baba turn red with this new suggestion. "You have no right to walk in here and talk nonsense!" he pushed Ravi's shoulders. Ravi, in turn, leaned his considerable weight on Baba, sending him shuffling backwards.

I knew I had to do something; this wasn't the time for inert spectatorship. I clinked all over as I ran to the two of them while they wrestled with each other.

"It's my wedding!" I shrieked.

First Ravi let go. Then my father released his hold. I saw my future in-laws and husband staring at me with crinkled faces. The crowd looked at me expectantly, as if awaiting an explanation. I continued in a softer tone, "All this is ridiculous. With the ceremonies, there were so many errands. So Vani would go for…"

"Ah! Perfect excuse, isn't it? I had warned her, hadn't I? She cannot shake me off just like that – after all, where would she get another match? No, I had to learn the real reason. It was him."

Again, he pointed dramatically at Purushottam, and everyone turned towards him.

"Just stop him!" My mother-in-law cried as a splash of red covered her aging, translucent cheeks.

Vani turned to her and sobbed, "We were running errands for the wedding."

"What a sham! What an actress! Superb. The next Miss India – Vanita Phanse!"

Ravi clapped his hands as he walked intently around the periphery of his audience. He contorted his face, cringed and squeaked, as if to imitate Vani. "Ravi, stop pestering me, don't you know that I am actually not like you. I'll get one of the big ones. So what if I'm manglik?"

My mother-in-law inhaled sharply. Of course, she didn't know of Vani's horoscope; there had been no reason for her to be informed.

Vani let out a hoarse whisper. "Stop it, Ravi." And then turning to me, "He's talking nonsense!" Vani fell at Aai's feet. "I'm very sorry! I have ruined your family's happiness. I don't know how this happened."

Aai looked away but Ravi held her shoulder and lifted her from the ground. "No, no, this grovelling doesn't suit you, madamji. Wait till I tell everyone about your favourite positions!"

"Stop!" Vani barely managed to squeak.

His gaze now circled his disgusted audience, whose curiosity was thinly masked. "They would meet in the car, always in the one with tinted windows."

"Don't listen to him!"

"So many times I followed them behind Sarthak College, after dark. The place is always deserted then, only couples in cars."

He licked his lips. He might have been beamed from one of those prime time soaps; his hold over everyone was hypnotic. Even Baba stood rapt.

Ravi walked towards my mother and joined his palms together. "Aunty, she wasn't late because the shops were too crowded or there was too much traffic. No. Oh no, no! She was sitting in the car, with that brother, her dupatta discarded. Aahaha!"

The mahurat had passed. The pundit had taken position at the doorway like everyone else. The fire had been abandoned.

Outside, the rain drummed away; I hadn't noticed when it had started, but now it was unmistakable. It rose to the crescendos of Ravi's revelations and throbbed when he grimaced. A wet, sticky air hung about us, blotching my yellow silk blouse and frizzing my hair until it spread gawkily about my head.

"Don't ask what would happen next!" Ravi shook his head, stuck out his tongue and touched his index finger alternately to each ear. "The car would shake so much I was afraid it would roll off!"

Vani had huddled up in a corner of the floor, her hands covering her ears, sobbing copiously. I wished I could do the same, but I was rooted by spasms of helplessness.

Vani kept shaking her head, murmuring, "It's not like… that."

My gaze fell on the full-length mirror mandatorily present in the vadhu room of every marriage hall. I was distorted. One eye had a deep kajal outline; the other one was bare. One earring was firmly fixed; the other one still lay on the dresser. My gold-and-Swarovski shoes stood beside the make-up bag and the pins on my pleats were showing. My eyes were angry, my cheeks pitiful, my lips trembling with rage and misery.

"We will not be insulted like this!" I had never heard my prospective father-in-law shout, and was startled.

"Really? You have a lot of respect, eh? Teach some to that son of yours! Raising the hopes of that poor, unfortunate girl. God knows what false promises he must have made!"

Then for the first time, the ring of spectators was broken. Purushottam stepped in. I saw him reach Ravi and place a firm hand around his shoulder. He steadied him and led him to a corner. He spoke through his teeth, a low hissing, meant just for Ravi. We only heard the calming whistle of his whisper, and an occasional snarl as his lips curled. They stood huddled for several minutes and not once did Purushottam's grip loosen, not once did his rustling voice falter.

Purushottam's intent gaze did not leave the man for a second, while he towered over Ravi. When finally, we had begun to breathe regularly and the pundit had glanced thrice at the forsaken pyre, the tide changed again.

With a sudden jerk, Ravi shook himself off Purushottam's hold, ran past a group of shocked teenaged girls with elaborate hairdos, and zigzagged out of the hall. As he ran, he screamed, "Apologize! Never! She treated me like shit. Thinks she's too good. Now let everyone know that truth about her and about you!"

His holler was first met by a loaded silence and then the murmuring started. An animated high-pitched buzz met my ears, speculating, deliberating, adding embellishments to my embarrassment.

My in-laws-to-be caught hold of my husband-to-be and conferred as they led him out of my sight. My parent's panicked and trailed after them. A group of aunts shadowed Aai and a bunch of friends monitored their progress with live commentary.

"They're leaving the mandap!"

"Girish-kaka is holding the car keys!"

"Bimal-kaka is touching Girish-kaka's feet!"

"Purushottam is talking to Bimal-kaka."

"Kaivalya-kaku has sat in the car and rolled up her window."

"Oh no! All their pagdis are out..."

"Sangeeta-tai is sobbing!"

"Vani has reached them... she's talking! Sangeeta-tai pushed her away!"

"Purushottam is talking to Vani! Vani is looking quite shocked... more shocked even than..."

"They're making big gestures. What does that mean?"

Finally, when I was quite sick of hearing the nails hammer down, someone screamed, "They're walking back! They're coming!"

My beautician sprang into action and started stabbing eyeliner on my eye. Someone slipped shoes on my feet; my pallu was straightened. Three additional pins were tucked into my bun and an old aunt dabbed a handkerchief over my perspiring face.

"Keep your fingers crossed!" she whispered.

"Here, hold this piece of salt and lime in your hand," another woman offered, warding off evil.

Once the vibrations had been cleansed and my face touched up, the circle of women opened up. The entourage looked sober and confused. After their entry, the circle regrouped and was shut.

My parents reached me first and placed a hand on each shoulder. Then my husband-to-be-or-not-to-be stood, shifting his weight. I kept staring at him, but he would give me no clue. His parents' expression was unreadable too. Only Purushottam and Vani were composed – a little too composed, like actors in a play who worked guiltlessly, aware that the murders they committed were not theirs to pay for, for their characters were to blame.

They unsettled me more than Ravi, and I almost wished him back with his drama, just so this moment could disappear.

Baba cleared his throat. Aai sniffed. My prospective in-laws stood pale. Vani made brief eye contact and whispered to no one in particular, "I cannot say it." She then stared at her feet.

It was left to Purushottam again. When he opened his mouth, I realized why he had had no success with Ravi. The man was blunt. "I have decided to marry Vanita."

He was stating something monumental then, but all I could think of was the stink of my rotting gajra. The strings of flowers on my forehead, hanging beside my ear, had been purchased the previous evening and refrigerated. Nothing had prepared them for the perspiration-saturated drama that marked the day. The edges of the white flowers had turned brown and started crinkling. Each time I shook my head or stood at a certain angle from the fan, the stench burst through my nostrils.

I suppose I should have broken the silence. When I didn't, Purushottam continued, "It is best for everyone and Vanita has agreed. It is the only way the insult to your family and mine can be reversed."

My mother-in-law cleared her throat – a supposedly harmless sound, a shallow rumbling of the throat made before saying something important, or before not saying something important.

I broke the silence. "So… this is true?"

"It's not like what he said. We never…" Purushottam looked away before continuing. "People will talk for a while, but at least the family honour will be maintained."

"So Vani and you … ?" I probed again. Vani's gaze now fell to her feet and I got my answer.

"She is a very good woman," Purushottam said, cryptically.

"How could you do this?" my mother-in-law gasped.

"It wasn't like that, Ma. But I like her."

My mother-in-law hissed from behind her frown. "The girl is a manglik!"

"Ma, all these things…"

"You cannot risk your life!"

"It is all superstition!"

"You cannot take a chance with your life, Puru. She's an orphan – did you ever wonder why?"

On noticing Puru's inclination, for the first time, my husband-to-be expressed an opinion. "Ma, we just discussed it. Please! We will do all the pujas," my husband continued. "I'm sure there is a way to stop the effects."

"If you don't believe in it, what is the point of the pujas?" my mother-in-law asked. "And if you do believe, then you'll know that they are useless."

"This is the only girl that Dada has liked, after so many years, Ma! Are we going to let him remain alone because of some superstition?"

"With all this embarrassment, you're pressuring me! Puru, of all the girls in the world, you had to find a manglik!" She was breathing heavily, her voice strained.

Vani stood right there, but clearly, my mother-in-law was not concerned.

"Ma," my husband said, "This is not in anyone's hands. If Dada has chosen her, if he likes her, we must accept his choice."

Purushottam seemed uncomfortable with this suggestion of a romance. "We must go ahead with the ceremony. There have been enough delays," he said, effectively scattering everyone towards preparations.

A flurry of arms and voices rippled all around me, running and rescheduling. There were new guests to be apprised of, older ones to be confer with, confused children to shush, additional puja material to buy, the photographer to negotiate with, doors to rush out of, calls to answer and adolescents to stop from smirking.

I have a hazy memory of my father discussing fate and my mother examining more mundane arrangements while Vanita sniffled. I vaguely remember the pundit's frantic phone conversation as he was obliged to cancel his afternoon appointments to accommodate two weddings, pocketing a weighty fee rise.

There was probably some amount of confusion and a significant amount of debate. Certainly, aunts were hustling and uncles grunting while children were revelling in their luck with all the free entertainment. Somewhere in that fog, I recollect a scamper for an appropriate outfit for Vani.

But my one sharp memory is not of action, but of inaction. I remember the stillness that settled over me while the world revolved around its own issues. Like ripples, the paralysis washed from the toes to my head, until I could neither move nor think.

Once again, the mocking tinkle of bangles pierced my ears and Vani's face punctured my sight. I knew that no matter when they called me out to the mandap, it would be a few minutes too soon, or perhaps, it was several minutes too late. The more time moves ahead, the more it is moving back, completing yet another circle, returning once again to that familiar starting point.

Purushottam, being the older brother, went first. My father did the kanyadaan, my mother gave a ring off her finger for Purushottam to place on Vani's finger. The garlands meant for us were used by them; we later got makeshift ones that had far too many leaves and just six flowers of a mismatched nature. Only the essentials were incorporated. The cousins did not dare hide any shoes; my brothers did not pinch my husband's ear, symbolically warning him to take care of me or else… No one threw rings into scented milk to ascertain who would find them first and thereby dominate in the relationship. I did not place a new one-rupee coin in my husband's purse to welcome Laxmi into the house.

And no one noticed when immediately after the rituals, the first face I looked at was not my husband's. As a young girl, I had often heard from my aunts, "Make sure you look at your husband's face immediately after the wedding is solemnized and the white curtain is dropped. Then, his face will be imprinted in your eyes and when Yama's time comes, he will look into your eyes and grant you the same husband in your next birth. It's a bad omen if you look elsewhere, so don't get distracted."

Yet, my first vision was of Vanita and Purushottam sitting by the stage, radiant in the glow of their baffling union.

I know that symbols have no value except those assigned to them. Even Baba once said that mythology was the amusement of a particular breed of aunts. I also understand that wedding rituals are just that – rituals. Why then does his face elude me? Why, after so many years, is it as obscure as a foreign tongue? Why do his features mix and merge like a surreal cubist painting?

Maybe if I had disciplined myself to look at his face, then I would not have been the person I am now. Maybe I wouldn't seek his face every morning as I confront yet another canvas and yet another hope. If only I could clearly remember what my husband looks like, I would position him in a certain moment of the past, and that clarity would free me of the looming, cloudy ghost that I follow.

Roopali-kaku's gaze was as black as the kohl she applied on my temple to ward off evil. Her breath fogged with misgivings. Her eyes danced on the mehndi of my hand, curdling its fragrance. But it was not always so, I heard. At one time, the sight of her struck red, puncturing the hearts of many Deshmukhs and Deshashths alike. A local beauty (winner of the Bombay Queen Pageant) with a very non-local aura (the daughter of an Air Force officer), she once enchanted the streets she walked on.

Of course, all this reached me through the maid's fervent whispers, while kneading dough, when boiling the Ayurvedic medicine for Papa, during the wait for the puris to fluff in the oil. It was a broken story, and Geeta provided fragments that sometimes overlapped and at other times were lost. The tale seemed to absorb the environment of its telling and I couldn't help but notice its delicious garnish. It picked up from Geeta's fingers the bitterness of turmeric, the crackle of mustard seeds and the softness of ghee.

Roopali-kaku's parents were friends with my father-in-law's parents, Geeta explained. They had the same chartered accountant. Tax reports led to tea sessions, which led to table tennis, which led to tours to Devgarh – the common village of their separate ancestry. "Always stuck together like this!" Geeta pinched together two bits of dough and frowned.

She hit the dough repeatedly with her fists and continued, "The thick-as-hung-curd-fathers were afraid of only one thing.

And that one thing came true." For despite the camaraderie between the men, when Roopali-kaku shunned all the overt and covert offers that came her way and eyed Papa, both sets of parents scowled at the suggestion.

My in-laws are Brahmins. Roopali-kaku's family is Gowli. It was one thing to break bread together and share a sense of humour, and an entirely different matter to mix blood. But Roopali-kaku was adamant. She fasted, she prayed, she wept, she bribed. When her own parents didn't budge, she shifted her charms to her prospective in-laws. Her subtleties caused them to shuffle away in embarrassed excuses and she shifted her target to the man in question.

Apparently, my father-in-law was aghast; apparently he hadn't shown any interest in her at all to warrant such a response. Geeta claimed that his indifference towards her was exactly what had warmed her heart.

"Not that all that chamcha-giri made any difference to Babuji!" Geeta was convinced. "No, he was not affected by her angrezi and her dhumak-dhumak!"

"But Geeta, what does it matter – all this Brahmin or not? We're all made by the same…"

"Hai Ram! Umi-tai! Tauba!" She stuck out her tongue and touched her index finger to both earlobes.

Just then, Vani entered the kitchen. Immediately Geeta straightened up. "Now it is different. At that time, even speaking of such things was tauba. In our family, we marry only in our caste and only from our village… never outside."

Vani threw a look at me, picked up a plate and walked out. I wanted to follow her; she must have thought I was prompting Geeta, but the puris would have burnt.

"Geeta! Hold your tongue when Vani is around."

She muttered something under her breath and turned away. The coldness between the two women often made me hesitate to enter the kitchen. Until a few months ago, Vani and Geeta would have fallen into the same category – second-class citizens in an upper-class household. Now, by a cruel twist of fate, Vani had been elevated to the status of the older daughter-in-law, complete with ornaments and locker keys, while Geeta remained between heaps of washing and piles of peeled potatoes. The intrigues of the household ran deeper with every passing day, and I had to struggle to remain afloat lest they entwined me in their snaps and clasps. Often, I struggled for air that was unsaturated with conspiracies.

Of course, in her mind, Vani probably wasn't a bundle of contradictions. It didn't confound her that she was the older daughter-in-law of a staunchly conservative joint family, a former semi-maid with a damning prophecy, and simultaneously rich and destitute. It didn't really confuse me either; for me, she was simply the sister I never had.

"So then what happened with Roopali-kaku and Babuji?" I continued.

"What was to happen? Babuji is not one to disregard the rules of dharma. He flatly refused."

"Then?" I could see that already her mood had deflated and all the spice from her narration had washed away.

"Then what? After a year or so his marriage was fixed with memsahib."

"Oh"

"Mind you," she leaned towards me. "Roopali-kaku married only after Babuji was married and Purushottam sahib was born."

"Accha."

"Three years younger than him, she was, and still she waited – waited for some calamity to fall and her fate to change. "But it was one good thing after another. First Babuji got married. Then, after 10 months, memsahib gave birth to a rose-like son. Puru sahib… and after one year… Chhotu sahib came."

"Anyway, all this is so long back," I offered, putting the saga in perspective. "Who would remember?"

"A widow always lives in the past," Geeta offered cryptically.

"What?"

"So young she lost her husband – after five, six years only. Heart attack. And Babuji is always helping around. So, he must be friendly with her. But she should not be all friend-friend always!"

"So does Ma know about Roopali-kaku?"

The knife clanked from her hands. She swung around to face me, distress clouding her eyes. "Please Umi-tai… memsahib must never know!"

I couldn't see what she was so worked up about.

She shook her head vehemently. "All these years, no one has told her. What's the use? It won't do good, no? They have become so close now, no? Plus Umi-tai, you only said – who remembers these things? Even Babuji must have forgotten, no? The children have never known. It's just that my mother-in-law was working in this house then … so she said…"

"Yes. Meenabai has been here very long."

She beamed. "And after some years, I also hope to take leave and send my soun… we will start looking for a girl for my Ramesh."

As much as Geeta played down Roopali-kaku's presence, it had etched itself irrevocably into the pillars and walls of our house. At bhishis and at casual tea sessions, I saw the way she worked on Ma, and was amazed at how deep and long vengeance could run in the woman's veins. I saw that when she couldn't win over the man, she had decided to operate his house by proxy, through his wife.

As the women chronicled their friendship to me over unsuspecting shopping sessions, I connected the dots. In the first year that my mother-in-law had entered the house as a fresh, anxious bride, Roopali-kaku had led her by the elbow and eased away her apprehensions. She offered to shop together, so the bride may learn the food preferences of her household. Together, they arranged the garden so the plants were not at risk of withering under the novice's touch. The duo even refurnished sections of the house – "they love wood in this family… yes, teak, not sheesham… they prefer the light variety."

Naturally, by the end of the year, Roopali-kaku was indispensable and bosom pals with Ma. I suspect that she was glad about the past being kept under wraps from her new friend; the fact that Ma didn't know must have been a heady thrill for Roopali-kaku, a sign that the new bride was not yet privy to the family secrets or her husband's love-interests.

"Your Roopali-kaku saved me when I first entered this house! I didn't know how to make chappatis!" Ma slapped her knee and doubled up.

"We used to pretend that we were chatting in the kitchen, but I was secretly kneading the dough myself!" Roopali-kaku added.

"Then she took me to her house on some pretext and I practised there! Imagine! My in-laws never realized!"

"But under the excuse of teaching you cooking, I found a friend! The benefit was all mine!"

"I don't know what I would have done otherwise…"

"The terror of being a new bride! Of course I couldn't leave Kaivalya without a hand!"

"When Puru and Chhotu were small, they used to call Roopali Chhoti-Ma… half the time she attended to their nappies and cries for mashed potatoes…"

This breakthrough surprised me. "Now they don't call you Chhoti-Ma?"

"No, these boys! Once they grew up, the habit stopped."

I smiled. They knew. At least they knew something. I noticed that both Puru and Shree were courteous to her, but the familiarity ended there. When she stayed back for dinner or accompanied us during family birthday celebrations, they weren't the ones who pushed for her inclusion.

Roopali-kaku looked at me and her expression changed. At some moments, I suspected, she saw me as her new adversary; I wasn't being won over by her guise. She pasted a huge smile on her face and exclaimed, "Why, Urmila, until a few years ago, I knew the size of your husband's underwear! Kaivalya and I shopped together for it!"

I checked the shock in my eyes, but she saw. Round one was hers.

Sometimes I think back and chide myself for my ego. Perhaps if I had played along and stroked her vanity, if I had concealed my aversion to her underhand methods, then she might not have felt compelled to axe Puru and Vani out of our existence.

When Roopali-kaku saw that I wouldn't join her informal camp that aimed to alienate Vani, her anger took on stormier proportions. They were tiny, at first, the taunts. The kind that could be passed away as an unfamiliar sense of humour or strange witticisms. Once these were woven into our speech and became the new norm of conversation, she increased the level. With each successive month, Ma learnt new references for Vani and subjected her to newer derisions.

They concluded that though she had lived with us since childhood, she had the accent of a villager.

Vanita either got too pally with the servants or was too uptight around them, as Roopali-kaku surmised. "The woman cannot really identify her role in the household. She's always oscillating. What else can be expected?"

Most times, when I tried to speak for her, it backfired. For some reason, my justifications always led to conclusions I had never intended and only further weakened Vani's case. Like the time I explained that Vani couldn't have been responsible for the open kitchen cabinets, which had led to the rat eating all the dry fruits.

"How could Vani have left the cabinets open? She hasn't stepped into the kitchen all day!" Ma had smiled smugly.

"Of course, she wouldn't," Roopali-kaku sniggered. "Vanita is not the maid here, after all."

Another time, in the privacy of her bedroom, I had tried to soften Ma. I could do nothing about Vani's circumstances but I offered a new perspective to our relationship. After a long explanation of how Vani was brought up like a sister to me and how she was an asset to our family, I concluded with, "My parents considered her to be their daughter and always treated her that way."

Ma had smiled. "Yes beta, she is a daughter to us as well. But you know what daughters are, don't you? Paraya dhun. Wealth of another. A temporary resident."

The hostility escalated with a measure so gradual that it could never be observed in any present moment; only a comparison over months would reveal the difference. And Ma, too quick to chide Vani, didn't see how it made Puru wince.

She didn't see that it brought the two together, united because they were fighting a common enemy – an ill-fated existence in an unforgiving world. Puru, whose ideals had been scattered and unfocused, now had someone to fight for. He found a purpose in Vani. Everyone spoke of rationality, equality, kindness – but they couldn't really live it. Puru, through his example, upheld righteousness. Vani was wronged and unfortunate, but she was also uncomplaining, and this made her struggle nobler. The subtler the taunts, and the harder she tried to be cheerful, the harsher they fell on Puru's ears. Their affection, which might have been guarded earlier, found its full measure in the air of these domestic intrigues. While the rest of us became more estranged and conflicted, Puru and Vani gravitated towards each other, huddling together in the wake of the frosty reception to their wedding.

PART V

Pasubhyaha - Vishnuthva - Anvethu

With this fifth vow of Saptapadi, as your wife, I promise you Praja: to raise strong and virtuous children with you.

A few months into the dramatic, impulsive, twin marriages of her sons, Ma summoned up the courage to resume interactions with friends. Disappearing from the social scene would only invite more gossip, and Papa suggested re-establishing their routine with as little awkwardness as possible.

It would be better to start with a home advantage, even better to garner the sympathetic votes of women, she decided, and hence the announcement of the bhishi. Bhishis sprung from generations where women stayed within the confines of their kind and organized innovative ways of commerce. Every month, Ma's coterie of 12 would meet, contributing ₹10,000 each to the kitty. A tiny fraction of this would be handed over to the host to meet the expenses of refreshments; the rest went into the investment of the month.

For a regular business of close to ₹120,000 a month – in cash – small-time jewellers were willing to drop a tax component of gold. Maybe add a tiny silver idol of Hanuman if each woman bought Ram and Sita. During the wedding season, the first floor of Kala Niketan or Sari Bhandaar was booked and the shopkeeper took over the arrangement of refreshments.

"Saris are also an investment," Ma explained. "My wedding sari was woven in pure gold thread… should be worth more than ₹60,000-65,000 now."

That particular month, however, was not about saris, stocks or gold. Vani and I were duly informed that the bhishi of the month would involve providing informal cash loans at higher interest rates.

The night before, our husbands sat us down and explained the importance of these gatherings in Ma's life. These were not only her friends; they were the mirrors through which she gathered reflections of self-image and pride. They were the ones for whom she formulated elaborate recipes and scouted rare spices. When she went shopping for clothes, she imagined their expressions in the dressing room.

Shree then expounded the three rules of bhishis that were never to be challenged:

[1] The most important person of each bhishi was its host. The woman who held the bhishi at her place took on the role of supreme matriarch, regardless of whether older women were present.

[2] At the start of the meal and the end of the meal, the food on each guest's plate would be of the same quantity. The host would necessarily pile on second and third helpings of everything. If the jalebi was eaten, another one would be added; if the tikki was over, another one would be provided. When a guest couldn't take a bite more, she would simply stop

eating, irrespective of how much food remained on the plate.

[3] The host took her role very seriously. A host never requested a guest to help with anything and if a guest did offer to help, it meant that the host was inefficient. "You, Ma and Vahini are joint hosts," Shree emphasized. "So make sure that everything goes smoothly."

I nodded. Vani looked about her and nervously asked me to go through the whole thing again the next morning.

Looking at our anxious expressions, Shree offered, "I know, it's quite ridiculous."

"Completely over the top," Puru agreed, sighing.

Vani ventured hesitantly. "What happened? Anything in particular?"

"Nothing," Shree looked away.

Purushottam sighed. "Roopali-kaku commented that Chhotu does not seem as proactive in the business as I am... thinks he just dabbles away in the background while I am taking the lead."

"Arre! Who is she to say that we must break up the commercial and residential constructions? Just because there are two brothers, it's not compulsory that the business has to be divided!"

"I know," Puru placed a hand on Shree's shoulder. "That's just the way *her* sons are."

"Why doesn't Ma understand this? For months, she went

on about expanding and diversifying. Puru will handle this; you handle that!"

"She takes her friends' suggestions too seriously. You don't bother your head about it. And you shouldn't either." Puru looked at Vani and me, and we nodded.

I look my husband's hand in mine. "They must be close friends for so long... it's natural. We mustn't offend them." After a few seconds, he stole his hand away from mine.

Yet, as the morning of the bhishi crept over us, he asked me what sari I planned to wear and how I would tie my hair. "Use those heavy earrings," he added. "Ma will like everyone to compliment you."

I approached the bhishi with a frightened eagerness, while Vani managed to play out a fraction of the same zeal. We mentally rehearsed possible conversations and expressions, aware of the thorough scrutiny we would receive. Any daughter-in-law would have been subject to inspection, but we were objects of greater study due to the circumstances under which we had been married.

At sharp 5 PM, the bell rang. "Come, come!" Ma ushered them into the living room, which was already saturated with the fragrance of chhole and saffron jalebis.

"Ah Urmila! Come, let me look at you properly. On the wedding day, the bride is buried under so much jewellery and make-up and flowers. I hardly got a chance..."

"Urmila, you remember Sangeeta-kaku?"

I smiled while the older woman took my face in both her hands.

"Ah! A pari."

Vani nudged me. I bent down and was appropriately blessed. Next, Vani bent to touch her feet.

"Oh you are already blessed, my dear! What more could I possibly add, Vanita?" she said, indicating the large living room and all its artefacts of wealth.

Vani's smile faltered. "Kaku, your blessings will…"

"She speaks!" Sangeeta-kaku grinned at the other women. "That day, we didn't get to hear much of her voice, did we?"

Fortunately, she was interrupted. Unfortunately, it was by her daughter-in-law, Sakshi.

"Mummy! Don't embarrass the girl. Times are changing. Which woman isn't ambitious? You wouldn't let me settle for just anyone, na?"

I huddled closer to Vani. She moved two steps away.

A trio of women arrived at the door just then and Ma took the opportunity to move out of earshot. Her cheeks were flushed, her voice shaking.

As Shree had predicted, the women fawned over my lattice-drop earrings and admired the interplay of gold and platinum. Three women surrounded me, one examining each ear, the third busy with her notebook and pen, taking down the address of the jeweller.

Vani stood outside the circle. With each passing second, her smile shrank. Soon I shuffled out of the circle and walked towards Vani, but she muttered something about arranging water and escaped into the kitchen.

Even when all of them had been served water and had declined tea until the business of the day was taken care of, Vani remained in the kitchen. As the chatter progressed, I unlearnt the gossip that I had expected from these gatherings. These kitty-parties-of-sorts were nowhere close to superficial chinwag-and-tattle sessions. Instead, they presented a microcosm of the world of business. Tips on stocks were exchanged in earnest. Larsen and Toubro was up. It was the right time to buy HDFC. Get rid of any Cicso holdings. Always hold on to the Tata Motors portfolio.

After the warm-up, we moved to the main business of the month. Keerti-kaku, who gave informal cash loans to businessmen, sourced her liquidity from this meeting. Every lakh of rupees entrusted to her was multiplied to a lakh and twenty within a year. No one asked who her clients were. Keerti-kaku, the least tech-savvy of the lot, wrote amounts in a diary and placed the money in an Amarsons' plastic bag. That was it – no receipt, no proof.

"I've been giving her three lakh a year for two years now," Sangeeta-kaku whispered at my perplexed face.

The ₹10,000 contribution was the mandatory lower limit, but everyone gave significantly more and I had to force myself to stop gaping; I had never seen so much cash handled so casually. The only rule was that all amounts be multiples of ₹10,000. "Otherwise, it's too much khitpit," Keerti-kaku explained. "Each unit of ₹10,000 will be returned in exactly a year, with an interest of ₹2,000."

The lower agenda of the day was matchmaking. Two horoscopes, three photographs and three bio-data were passed along, each eliciting insider comments about the proposed girl or boy. The files of each prospect were passed around clockwise to everyone except Vani. She sat on a stool at an awkward angle; she could technically be inside the living room and also inside the kitchen. The women were confused about whether she was sitting with them or not, and Vani too couldn't arrive at a conclusion.

"To think that a few months ago, we looked at Urmila's horoscope like this. And now she sits among us," Sakshi said.

"Yes," added Roopali-kaku. "It's too bad we didn't have the same pleasure of choosing Puru's wife."

For a long moment, the living room was silent. Finally, Sakshi chose to intervene. "We did check out so many girls for him, remember? Mrs Rane's niece? And that architect from Pune?"

Roopali-kaku nodded. "But what to do? He just wasn't interested in marriage."

"Didn't like a single girl. He didn't meet anyone, did he?"

Everyone looked at Ma. She squirmed and pretended to adjust her dupatta. "One or two."

"I started thinking – my God, our Puru is so particular!" Roopali-kaku said. "Actually it is quite the opposite! Very large-hearted of him. It's one thing to take a risk with Keerti's investment scheme," she winked at Keerti-kaku who was adjusting the Amarsons bag. "But this chance... a true romantic!" Roopali-kaku smiled and adjusted her sari pleats.

Vani turned red. She pressed closer into the wall against which she was leaning. Ma busied herself with everyone's water glasses. I cleared my throat and called on my most non-confrontational tone.

"Kaku, sometimes we can't see it right away, but the best plans have already been made for us."

"Such a young mouth and such wise words! Your horoscope didn't tell us about this trait!" Half the group started giggling and some of the tension dissipated.

The conversation changed track for a while. Sometimes, separated by large spans, a smile appeared even on Vani's face. Someone would unwittingly provide an insight on her husband or use a double entendre.

Too soon, however, everyone launched into the next sub-agenda. Gayatri-kaku was running for mayor. Everyone was to pool in resources to forward her campaign. Roopali-kaku offered the services of her cook since a daily entourage of guests and supporters would inevitably need to be entertained. Three women pressed envelopes into her lap while she protested and held on to them.

"Anything you need, just let us know."

"There are so many places to visit and you know how the press is – always clicking photos."

"Hmmm… Now you've become a celebrity."

"That's the problem! I have already repeated all my saris once. I need some more. You know – modest but classy. I bought five last month, but how long will they last?"

I decided to speak up. "Kaku, you can take some of mine."

Ma beamed for the first time that evening.

"I got so many recently because of the wedding."

"No, no! I can't take away a new bride's clothes! What will people say? And your husband…"

"Gayatri," Veena-kaku elbowed her. "Don't worry. He will be happy! What do newlyweds have to do with clothes anyway?"

Immediately the group snorted and tittered, while I shuffled into the bedroom. In the interim, I heard them discuss men's problems, huddling significantly closer.

"Viagra and all is fine. But who is to tell them they need it?"

"Exactly. Just telling them will counter the effect of the pill…"

"That is why I just crush it and put it in his milk at night!"

"Really?"

"Just give flavoured milk. So the taste and texture are hidden. Masala milk, Bournvita… anything. The best part is that you can choose the nights!"

Veena-kaku dug into her purse and fished out three round bottles.

"This is for the opposite effect. You know… if they are away on a business trip or something."

"Ah!"

"A few days before, start giving one tablespoon daily."

I had to remind myself to clamp my jaw and control my disbelief. How precious to witness this scene with Vani and laugh over it later! I looked in Vani's direction, but she had disappeared into the kitchen, her little stool jarring in its emptiness.

Lately, laughter had evaded us. Heaviness hung about our conversations. As a child, if I had known that Vani and I would marry brothers and live in the same house, I would have been delighted. Now, I see how false such dreams are. The two daughters-in-law of the house spoke in measured tones, walked without tinkles and strictly stayed within the realm of practical discussions.

When I returned, Veena-kaku was holding up a bottle. "This is even more useful– reduces snoring."

"I've tried everything. Snores are here to stay and sleep is meant to fly."

"Pallavi, don't give up so easily. See, this opens up the nasal passage, allowing free movement of air. So the sound is automatically reduced."

"Fine. I'll take one. But if it doesn't work …"

"Then we'll take sleeping pills ourselves! Theek?"

Only once finance, politics and men were taken care of, did

they give in to their hunger pangs and the aroma of chhole-bhature.

"Kaay re Kaivalya, you are still sticking to vegetarian food, na?" Veena-kaku said. "Or have you started allowing non-vegetarian too? They must be eating it…" she nodded towards Vani.

"We have to change with the times." Gayatri-kaku interjected before Ma could respond. "These are modern times and look how open-minded Kaivalya is… The Karmarkars have always been into social work but see – they walk the talk."

Vani entered the living room, holding a tray laden with aloo tikkis and sherbet.

"Old habits die hard, don't they, Roopali?"

"Don't be so cruel!" exclaimed Roopali-kaku, smiling. "Differences are good. You know… everyone contributes something. Vani will know all about shrewdly running the kitchen. Kaivalya can cut her groceries budget by half!"

"I think from the next bhishi onwards, we should give you only ₹300 for the food expenses!" Veena-kaku added, smirking. "So much more will be left for our investments…"

The same nervous laughter that had accompanied earlier jibes rang across the room. It died down in an instant, as insincere mirth is inclined to. For several minutes, only the clang of spoons could be heard. Vani, visibly nervous about her role, had been imploring the group to take larger helpings, but decided it was not her place and hastily stopped. Ma excused herself, went off to her bedroom and stayed there for over 10 minutes.

I decided to pick up a plate and piled it with food, if only to give my hands something to do. Vani remained unsure. I gestured to her to help herself, but she shook her head. Roopali-kaku noticed our exchange and immediately started cajoling Vani to eat with us.

"Arre Vanita, why aren't you eating?"

"Kaku… I'll…"

"No, no! Come on, take a plate. The days of eating after the family are over for you, eh?"

A plate was thrust into her hand and a ladleful of chhole dunked in the centre.

"It's not that… Actually I never used to…"

"Yes I know, dear. You're not used to it, but the ways for you are different now. We don't want to embarrass the family now, do we?"

When my mother-in-law walked out of her bedroom, the first thing she saw was her guest serving her older daughter-in-law. Roopali-kaku had lifted the salad bowl and was piling some on Vani's plate, while I stood flushed and ruffled. Otherwise, the world had gone quiet. Everyone's spoons seemed to stand suspended in the air.

Ma's bhishi had turned itself over on its head. The look on her face was unmistakable; she was determined to undo this insult and its cause, never mind that to do so, she would be playing into the hands of the woman who had once coveted her husband.

Roopali-kaku was so subtle and complete in winning over Ma that the woman's closeness with Papa seemed logical. In fact, Ma saw it as an extension, a consequence of the women's friendship, never realizing that in fact, Roopali-kaku tolerated her presence in order to gain access to the man, his house and all he held dear.

It was not uncommon to wake up any morning and find Roopali-kaku serving aloo parathas to my father-in-law ("Sunita made a special ragi-infused dough for his strength");taking mango milkshake to his room ("These mangoes are from Ratnagiri – Ashok sent them from his farm"); or rubbing oil on the soles of his feet ("They taught us this special acupressure technique for the nervous system") she offset these intimacies by devilishly teasing Ma, insisting that Ma sit at the dining table or his dinner would be tasteless, that she wear the green sari because it was his favourite colour, that she leave her hair loose because it took 10 years off her face. It probably thrilled Roopali-kaku, this game, the power she wielded on both sides. And when Ma realized that her presence at the table didn't really alter the taste of her husband's dinner, that the green sari didn't even register with the man, that the loose hair looked dull, scanty and grey, it must have given Roopali-kaku an even bigger kick.

Some evenings, when she knew that Ma was out, Roopali-kaku would come over earlier than usual and huddle with my father-in-law, presumably discussing the children, the weather, the changing skyline of the city or any of the long list of ailments that haunted the man. However, each time, she'd call

Ma first, explain that she was in the neighbourhood or that she finished early from the parlour or the book club was cancelled. She'd make a show about returning home or visiting another day, prompting Ma to exclaim that she'd be home in another 40 minutes, why not just wait?

Roopali-kaku ensured that these suggestions always came from Ma. She perfected an elaborate pretence of not overstepping, and then walked all over the unsuspecting woman.

So, it shouldn't have surprised me to wake up from a nap and see Roopali-kaku heading into my father-in-law's room. However, something about the visit struck me as uncommon. For one, the entire family was out, picnicking at Water Kingdom. For another, this retreat from the heat and our domestic strains had been suggested by Roopali-kaku herself. She even insisted that Geeta go along to help Ma. When Ma extended the invitation to her best friend, she refused, insisting that it was a family trip and everyone needed to connect with each other in a low-pressure, fun environment. Of course, it was understood that my father-in-law wouldn't join in; Papa, though well enough to engage in unavoidable excursions, was certainly not in any position to frolic in an artificial wave pool or even handle the long drive.

We spent two days in anticipation, then another day packing and planning. However, by the morning of the trip, the heat wave got the better of me and I came down with a sudden fever and throbbing headache.

Everyone insisted on cancelling or postponing the trip, particularly Vani, who was easily unnerved in my absence.

However, we had already invested too much attention, emotion, and perhaps, ambition in that little picnic. They had to go, I insisted. I'd stay home with Papa. Perhaps it was a blessing in disguise, and they would get undiluted time with Vani, and possibly shed their mental limitations of her.

I spent the morning nursing my headache with steam inhalations and mugs of green tea. Papa sat in the living room, providing the occasional advice or admonishment, witnessing my helpless submission to the pounding in my head. Finally, after a quick lunch of curd and rice, I found that I could lie down, and soon drifted into a long, sweet sleep.

It must have been around 5 PM when I awoke to the jingle of my cell phone. They were leaving from Water Kingdom. They had a great time. The rides were fewer than they expected. Was I feeling better? After our reciprocal asking and answering, I decided to get a bite to eat, when I noticed Roopali-kaku saunter into Papa's room.

Perhaps she didn't know I was at home. Perhaps for once, I would shake her plans and watch her stoic face falter in embarrassment. I decided to play it casual, simply walk into the room and ask Papa if he would like tea. I even looked forward to the excuse she would be forced to conjure up. Resolute, I walked towards the room, trying to keep my step light but not sneaky. I was just about to knock and enter when her raised, shrill voice reached me.

"Suddenly these things are acceptable to you? After hurting me so much?"

My father-in-law coughed but met the tone of her

accusation. "Times have changed! And it's not like he took my permission – just went ahead! What is done is done."

"Yes, it's very simple for you, isn't it? Only during our time you were being so difficult!"

"Why these complaints after all these years? Hasn't everything worked out well? Your children, my children…"

"What a thing to say to a widow!"

There was no way I could enter now. I remained at the door, unsure but curious, ready to flee at the slightest hint of being discovered.

"You know what I mean," my father-in-law sighed.

"And yet I coped with everything, until you reopened my scars." Roopali-kaku's voice was high-pitched and heavy with emotion. "You watched calmly while your son married a manglik!"

"I did not watch calm…"

"You allowed it! All this means nothing to you now! She lives in this house, she pays the servants, she greets me like I am a guest!"

The haze that had surrounded me finally lifted. My father-in-law's past had come to catch up with him. Of course, Roopali-kaku couldn't stand Vani. Just a generation ago, the woman's overtures had been scoffed and her heart broken, all because of a diminutive caste variation. And now, a stranger, an orphan, an ill-fated nobody had perched herself as the older daughter-in-law and prospective matriarch. With Roopali-kaku, no allowances had been made for the keen friendship the fathers shared, for her legendary beauty or for the tears she shed in the bathroom. Why the sudden acceptance of this adharma now?

There was no question of Roopali-kaku's intentions; I only wondered how far my father-in-law would allow them to play out. Quite far, as it turned out.

"Those days..." she was saying. "I kept telling myself that it wasn't in our hands; it wasn't in your hands. Or was that just an excuse? Were you just playing me?"

"From where has all this suddenly come up?" My father-in-law raised his voice. Shrill, quivering but loud, it hammered past the door. I took a step back.

Roopali-kaku ignored his question. "How do you tolerate it? Your son is shirking everything that you were so particular about. He blatantly defies his upbringing, the values of the family. Tell me – did he really think of you once? How you would take it?"

"This new generation..." my father-in-law began.

"The problem isn't the new generation – it's the old generation. Actually, you don't have a problem with him marrying that cursed village girl! If you really wanted, we could have also... been together. But no, never. The truth is that you played with my feelings and then made up these excuses."

"What is the point of all this?" he finally asked.

"The point is that this has to stop!" she hollered. "You wouldn't allow it then, you can't allow it now!"

"But they're already married!"

"End it. How can she stay in this house, cursed, like the messenger of death? How can she, after everything I have been through?"

My father-in-law must have been aghast for his next statement was barely a whisper. "End it? Do you know what you are suggesting?"

"Do *you* know what I am suggesting, Vishwas?" she answered. "Do you know that I have kept your letters, your cards?"

"You want me to separate them?"

"Save your son, and for that matter, your wife. Those letters are well preserved. Just ask the damned girl to leave!"

"Puru will never allow it."

"If he feels so much for the unfortunate villager, he is welcome to walk out with her."

"Roopali! This time you have crossed…"

"I haven't," she retorted before he could finish. "All these years and you don't really know me. You didn't care for me then; you can't be bothered to understand me now."

"Not when you're talking of breaking my son's marriage!" He began coughing and I was tempted to barge into the room. Instead, I remained frozen while he drank back his coughs and gruffly refused the assistance that Roopali-kaku was probably offering.

"I should have known," he finally managed. "I was a fool."

"No," she said. Her tone was no longer pleading and angry. This time she spoke softly, saturated with sweetness, menacing in the sudden shift. "No, Vishwas. I have been a fool too long. You will be stupid only if you brush me aside like you once did, only if those letters were to find their way into Kaivalya's hands. Now, that would be a foolish thing to do, wouldn't it?"

"How dare you…" another coughing fit took over and Papa couldn't finish. I waited several seconds for his broken breath to turn steady, but it rose and fell hoarsely, haltingly.

"Here," Roopali-kaku must have offered him water in the steel tumbler that is always at his bedside. However, the next second, it clanged to the floor, either because Papa was too feeble to hold it or, more likely, because he had flung it away.

I had heard enough. I decided that this would be a good time to make my presence felt. "Papa…?" I opened the door and put on a surprised face for Roopali-kaku.

His fit prevented him from speaking, but Roopali-kaku also seemed to have lost her voice.

Leaving the door ajar, I sprinted to the kitchen, found another glass and quickly helped my father-in-law sip some water. By then, both seemed to have recovered, and Roopali-kaku mumbled some story about having left behind a sari when she had gone shopping with Ma the previous week.

I did not probe, but my silence revealed the holes in her excuse more than any questions could. She looked around, declared that she couldn't find the elusive garment and would probably ask Kaivalya about it, and then hurried away, unable to meet my mute rebuff.

That evening, I hovered around my father-in-law, taking longer than usual with his medicines and his tea, just in case he decided to open up. Instead, he wrapped himself tighter, declining the second cup, escaping into the bathroom and feigning a nap beneath his restless eyelids.

Soon, the picnickers returned, their arms tanned, their toes still wrinkled and pale from the water. When they had left in the morning, my flushed face had seen them off; now, Papa's stooped, pained frame greeted them in the living room. Whatever bonding the picnic might have generated, I knew that it was too delicate to withstand the storm that was to follow.

Puru and Shree immediately helped him to his room and changed him out of the kurta that was now stained with sweat. Soon however, Shree appeared in our bedroom, explaining that Papa had wanted to talk to Puru privately.

"His health is slipping," my husband explained. "Papa must be anxious about the business again."

I nodded and went about my routine of preparing for the night. I needed to be alone, needed to hold together the fragments that were breaking before me. Perhaps my father-in-law would explain the whole thing to Puru, maybe brainstorm a way out. Maybe they would pacify Roopali-kaku, keep her at bay. Maybe in a few weeks, this would be forgotten and I would be able to ignore my discovery.

Of course, nothing of the sort happened as I soon learnt. Papa said he couldn't see his son falling into a life of misfortune and ill luck. At the slightest mention of Vani's inappropriateness, Puru turned defensive. He became excessively polite and compliant, making Papa even more agitated and angry. Papa stormed, Puru feigned patience; Papa declared phoney ultimatums, Puru received them earnestly; Papa played the card of his failing health, Puru emphasized the importance of a non-fractured family in the face of an illness.

No one could say for sure when the discussion – if it can be called that – started. And no one could ascertain when – if ever – it ended. At some point, we just resigned ourselves to our waiting beds and the illusion of sleep, tossing over the wreckage that we had already become.

∽∽

On the following Sunday, a distant politician friend who was acquainted with Roopali-kaku was invited to lunch. He was the personal assistant of the personal assistant of the leader of the opposition party, and his intervention had been requested to approve the sale of a large plot under litigation. He knew Roopali-kaku through some favour she had done for him when he was just a faceless party worker. Now, he was happy to be able to repay her, and Puru and Shree were quite particular about him leaving pleased and satiated with our hospitality.

I am certain Roopali-kaku must have apprised him of Vani's background; nothing else can justify the man's aversion to her. When Vani welcomed him at the door with a namaskar, he looked away and instructed, "Malkana saang Gokhale sahib ale." Inform your employer that Mr Gokhale is here.

Vani began fumbling with a reply, but I gathered my wits and turned to Geeta who was standing behind Vani. "Didn't you hear? Go tell Papa."

My intervention ensured that everyone could pretend that he had addressed Geeta, but he refused to play along. He ignored Vani with determined singularity. Although she sat at the table with us, passing him pickle and stuffed brinjal curry, he barely glanced at her. He refused the papad when Vani offered it to him, but happily helped himself to the plate a few seconds later. My mother-in-law registered these hints with frowns; my father-in-law recorded them expressionless. Both Shree and Puru were unable to eat beyond a few bites and exchanged disturbed glances. Roopali-kaku must have been quite thorough in her instructions, and the man played his part perfectly.

That evening, in three separate bedrooms, three separate arguments ensued about one single issue.

Shree and I fought over how each one was not doing enough to ensure harmony.

My parents-in-law fought over how the reputation they had built through sacrifices was dissolving before their eyes.

Purushottam and Vani fought about separating. Not from each other. From us. He insisted it was the only way out. She pleaded to give it one more chance. He reasoned, she sobbed; he argued, she cajoled; he disputed, she sighed.

"Umi," she confided in me later, "I can tolerate all the labels that the world throws at me – luckless, illiterate, maid, orphan.

But I won't be able to bear being called a home-breaker! How can I let him leave his parents, his family?"

However, the politician's aversion was just the first part of Roopali-kaku's plan. She instigated every acquaintance and his grandmother against Vani. To one, Roopali-kaku emphasized the village background; to another, Vani's lack of education; to a third, the cheeky courtship; and of course, the trump card was Vani's mangal dosha. This was used to explain away the most routine of misfortunes and the most disconnected disasters.

Papa and Ma tolerated all the barbs with a stoic façade. They pretended that the taunts hadn't registered and learnt to ignore entire chunks of conversation. However, the condescending remarks of politicians, neighbours and geriatric relatives did not break our home. They created fissures and blew sourness through our windows, but their clever subtleties just hastened the departure. Instead, our home was fractured by the direct disgust of a mere dhobi.

It was an unremarkable evening, the deceiving sky giving no hint that it was about to fall right on us and tear open the ground we stood on. A cloak of normalcy enveloped us all– the salty, hung air, the fragrance of basmati rice flavoured with ghee, the creaking of the cane that Papa used to limp around, Geeta's halting gossip and Vani's silence.

The only exception that evening was the fuss over the aamti. Puru liked it a certain way, thickened with tender pumpkin pulp, spotted with bits of lotus stem and garnished with shredded coconut. Vani had chanced upon all the ingredients in the market, which led to an unprecedented hustle in the kitchen. The tricky lotus stem had to be washed delicately and the pumpkin steamed for just the right number of seconds before it was run through the juicer with exactly four tablespoons of water and half a lemon. The complex procedure was not without its reward though, as the most delectable aroma I had ever inhaled filled the kitchen.

All that was left was for our husbands to return, the salad to be sliced and the table to be set. The usual trickle of small politicians and businessmen had come and gone – since Papa's health had been acting up, most of his 'maintaining relations' activity had shifted from the office sphere into the living room. Ma had shopped for curtains with Roopali-kaku and come home looking pleased. Her sons were expected any moment now, and she checked with Geeta on the status of the aamti. Tiny bubbles had started erupting; once they evolved into larger ones, she needed to turn off the gas and hold the steam down with a heavy lid.

It was a Tuesday. As was usual on Tuesdays, Thursdays and Saturdays, Hari-kaka's cycle entered the compound at precisely 7:30 PM. I walked into our bedroom to bring out the clothes that needed ironing. His entrance was usually announced by a medley of sounds – cycle-bell, slippers, the plonk of his other bundles, his voluble namaskars to Papa, whom he believed to be turning deaf, ruminations on the weather, slurps of mint tea and praise of whatever seemed to be sizzling in the kitchen. This evening, he ushered in silence.

I had been blind to the signs. This wasn't the first time he declined his customary tea before unfolding the bundles of clothes. Lately, he had begun to avoid this ritual, sometimes providing feeble excuses like how late it was or how it looked like rain. A few times, he just shook his head decisively, offering no explanation. This spell continued for so long that even Geeta refused to keep offering the cup. "He's not some king or something," she fumed, "If he wants it, he'll ask."

A few months earlier, Vani and I had decided how to divide the responsibilities of the household. Naturally, she took on more than I did, and handling Hari-kaka was among her tasks. Vani counted the clothes, checked the earlier lot and paid him at the end of the month. She even began a system of providing hangers for saris and trousers, so they may have as few folds as possible. When Hari-kaka protested that he wouldn't be able to carry these on his cycle, she went out and demonstrated how they may be balanced on the handlebar. To compensate for the extra effort, she added, "Don't worry, Hari-kaka, you were taking ₹10 for saris, right? We'll make it ₹15. That should cover it."

However, within a month, he increased the rates of all garments. A few months later, yet another price hike was imposed "for all saris and trousers only". His work seemed to turn sloppy and Vani resorted to checking the clothes when they arrived. He'd receive her suggestions with a frown. When she looked at him for a more detailed response, he forced a small nod. Vani and I, new to the household, assumed this was his default demeanour.

I realized later that Hari-kaka was one of the many who craved balance and stability, even if he fell on the wrong side of the equation. Now, there was a shift. Vani's entry, her migration to the other side, her privileges and power over him, turned him sour and bitter. He had defined his relationship with the Karmarkars on strict parameters. It was his place to work, their place to reward, his place to request, their place to grant, his place to please and their place to receive. Never mind that he had the short end of the stick; Hari-kaka was more interested in the stability that this structure provided than the specific benefits or losses he experienced.

What made it worse was a mere coincidence. The first evening that Vani tallied his services for the month and handed him his pay, Hari-kaka's mother suffered a stroke. He had cycled home, the money tucked away in his shirt pocket, only to be welcomed by a frantic wife and a semi-paralyzed mother. Although they rushed her to the hospital, she lost movement in one leg. Later, Papa offered to show her to some specialists but Hari-kaka declined. The damage was done.

At our place, Roopali-kaku only displayed elaborate sympathy for the man's mother. But when the dhobi came to her house, she let forth a different lament. She implored Hari-kaka to see the signs. Whatever that woman touched was bound to be cursed. Did he want that woman's money to feed his family? Would his sons gain prosperity from such hands? Wasn't all this just the beginning of the end? Compelled by Puru, manipulated by Vani, the Karmarkars had drifted. Did Hari-kaka also want to tie his fate with that of the wretched new daughter-in-law?

I learnt of these sessions much later, through Geeta, whom Hari-kaka had also tried to convert. By then, there was nothing left to do.

Initially, Hari-kaka rebelled against the change in small ways. First, he declined tea and conversation, then his timings turned erratic. Some evenings he didn't show up at all, and a few times, he even refrained from offering any explanations. He looked through Vani, addressing his statements to Ma or me. He continued listing the number of pants, shirts, t-shirts, salwars and the rest even if Vani hadn't finished writing the number for the previous item. And if she asked him to slow down or repeat, he obliged with a show of annoyance.

Now for the third time, he was demanding yet more money.

"What is this, Hari-kaka?" Vani looked up from her ironing-account book. "Again?"

He turned and addressed my mother-in-law. "Memsahib, majboori aahe."

"What compulsion?" she asked. "Are you increasing everyone's rates like this? And no-one is complaining?"

Hari-kaka didn't answer.

Vani offered, in a soft tone, "Is there a problem?"

He gave no response.

Finally, Ma said, "But this is not acceptable! We cannot just continue this way…"

He began some token pleading about rising costs but soon came to the point. "Memsahib… you are right. Yes, you find someone else, memsahib. It will be best for everyone!"

"Why are you suddenly talking like this, Hari? Are you in need of money?"

"By the grace of God, we are all well. I pray to Ram to extend the same to your family…"

Ma stopped him. "Listen, I'll give you your Diwali bonus in advance. Take ₹1,000 today and forget about this whole increase in price. Vanita, note it down. Come now, let's end this."

"Memsahib, you are very generous but I cannot take the money from you. It is best you find another dhobi."

"What has happened?"

Cautiously, he began a meandering explanation. As unsuspectingly as it started, I had a premonition; before long, Vani would figure.

"Memsahib, for years our grain has been indebted to this family. You got my children into an angrezi school, you paid for the TB treatment of my…"

"Get to the point, Hari!"

"My little ones, Kedar and Munnu both look … looked up to Purushottam sahib. They wanted to become businessmen like him. Have a big office and rise and work with computers…"

"So?"

"Now, they ask questions, memsahib. I have no answers to give. The ones I would look up to are no longer…"

"What are you trying to say?"

"I may be just a poor dhobi, memsahib, but I am still a Brahmin. I have always upheld the values that were so dear to our ancestors. I had so many such talks with Motthe-sahib's father also. Those were different days ..." His voice trailed away but soon found itself. "This family has changed, memsahib, but I am too old to change with it. You must allow an old man this little indulgence and find someone else."

He placed our bundle of clothes back on the sofa. A couple of clothes slid off. My eyes fell on Vani's pink and orange sari. I picked it up. Immediately, the dhobi averted his gaze while Ma peered at it through her glasses.

I stepped in. "You are insulting the daughter-in-law of this family?"

"Not you, memsahib, never you."

"Then it is worse."

His hands were shaking, I saw, but his head stood firm. As I spoke, he got up and made a move to exit.

"Namaskar," he bent low.

"Where are you going?"Ma asked.

"You are big people – you can do all these things, but I ... I cannot take a chance."

He bowed again, turned around and started walking, until he bumped into Puru and Shree, standing at the door.

My husband took a big step forward, forcing Hari-kaka to lean back. He towered over the dhobi.

"After everything we've done for you, this is the gratitude you show?"

Hari-kaka was smart enough to remain silent.

"Kaka, pick up those clothes immediately and continue your work as usual. What difference does it make to you?"

Hari-kaka didn't budge.

"Who are you to preach to us?"

Shree started rolling up his sleeves. "Pick up the clothes, Hari-kaka!"

The man was either very terrified or incredibly brave, for despite my husband's large frame and booming voice, he didn't move an inch.

Puru walked up to Shree. "Hari-kaka, will you come here after a month? Let it be for a while. Come next month."

He moved away, allowing the dhobi to nod and walk away. Puru patted my husband twice on the shoulder and whispered, "It is okay." He went into his bedroom. I heard the click of the latch and then the heavy footsteps of my husband storming into our room.

Obviously, Geeta had forgotten to switch off the aamti and it was reduced to a pitiful stock. But at the dinner table, no one seemed to notice.

When they announced their decision to move out, we weren't surprised. Mournful, yes, even devastated, but it was the death of a sinking geriatric. Puru busied himself with practical considerations, while Vani fussed around him, leaving us nervous and anxious. Ma fasted and prayed, not talking to us for days, weeping without warning and locking her bedroom. All visitors were discouraged; even Roopali-kaku remained out of sight.

If they were to move, just shifting to another house or even another city wouldn't do. The break had to be large and wide and deep for its effects to be felt.

"But where will you go?" Ma shouted in exasperation one evening.

"We cannot be in any place that will embarrass the family any more. We have to cut off from all such connections."

"Why didn't you think of all this before you married her?" Ma frowned.

"Ma! How can you say that?" Puru walked up to her and held her shoulders. "After they pointed fingers at me – that I had gone around taking advantage of Vani's…"

"But see, everything is coming true. You're in the middle of it, Puru!" she shouted.

"It's not Vani's fault – it is everyone around that has caused this. It's like they have taken it in their hands to play out our fate!"

"Let us consult an astrologer. See the options…" Now there were tears in her eyes and she swallowed back her sobs.

Puru sat down and held her hand. "Ma, we need to move away from everyone. That is the best remedy, at least for a while."

My husband stood silently in a corner, hugging himself, as if he were afraid of falling apart. In just a few weeks, he had lost several kilos. He barely ate and when he did, it was only to gain strength to argue against Puru's decision. I stepped forward to speak for my husband. "Puru, maybe it isn't so bad. We don't have to do anything drastic. A few more months and..."

"Plus, we have family and business almost everywhere in India." Shree walked towards me and added, "You can't cut yourself off just like that!"

Vani put her hand on my shoulder. "Umi, you remember Chacha-Chachi? Naresh-chacha?"

"Dubai?"

"We have been talking to them the past few weeks. The visas need to be..."

"Puru!" Ma buckled on the sofa. "Puru, you're moving to another country?"

All this while, my father-in-law sat silently on his bed, the door ajar, allowing him to hear us and yet staying away from our feverish pitch.

"It's the best option for now, Ma. We cannot have people talking like this to you and Papa, and about my wife."

"But won't they talk even more now?" I asked. "They'll have even more cause to gossip!"

"For a while, maybe, but then all this will be forgotten." Puru said, looking at Ma. "Chhotu will take over the responsibilities and Umi-vahini will keep our traditions alive, look after you…"

"And what will you do there?" my husband paced around the room.

"He must have planned that also," Ma retorted and shuffled towards her bedroom. "Don't you see how good he is at planning? Doesn't once consider what we will feel! Forget the world! Why is my son so bothered about what the world thinks and says? What about his mother and her feelings?"

She slammed the door behind her and we heard her cane rattle on the floor.

"Naresh-chacha is looking for some work," Vani ventured. "He said he can fix up some interviews in a few construction companies."

"I don't see the point of all this talk!" my husband raised his voice. "You can't go! It's impossible! All this will fizzle out, I'm sure. Let's just end it now!"

That night, my husband slept fitfully. In the morning, routine was abandoned. The men stayed home and no one mentioned appointments or meetings. Vani and Puru's phones rang frequently and they spoke with an urgency that unsettled my husband.

That whole week, Shree began spending evenings holed inside their bedroom, deliberating in a constant drone. Some days, he woke up close to noon, while on others, he stepped out of the house before sunrise, citing increased workload in office. I faded even further beyond the periphery of his thoughts and when he did speak to me, it was always an inconclusive rant about an unjust world and a righteous man.

Vani must have been packing at night for I never saw the suitcases being filled. They simply stood arranged by the door. She held a large shoulder bag and Puru fidgeted with the locks of the suitcases.

"Naresh-chacha's address is near the telephone, but we should have our own accommodation soon." Puru said.

"If you leave, then I am coming too!" my husband lifted one of the suitcases and took it back to their bedroom. "You can't just move out of our lives like this!"

Puru walked up to the suitcase and brought it back. "In some time, all this will settle down."

"I'm coming too!"

"Don't be silly. The business is in your hands now. And what about Ma and Papa? Someone needs to stay with them."

"Urmila can look after them!" My husband pointed.

All eyes turned towards me.

"Won't she want to be with you?" Once again, Puru said my words.

"What we want doesn't always happen, does it?"

"But Chhotu, if you come, then the point is lost. The family will be more divided than ever." He began loading the suitcases in the taxi waiting outside.

"How can brothers be parted like this? Tell him, Umi! Tell him, Papa!"

My husband strode around our circle and shook me by the shoulder. "How can you let your sister go like this? Won't you stop her?"

"I... I tried..."

"But they're still going! So try again. Stop her till they stop!"

"Let Urmila be, Chhotu." Ma's voice was soft but cold. "It is *that* woman who is determined to break this house."

Vani looked away.

"Nothing good has ever come with her presence. Maybe her absence will bring peace to this house."

"Ma, at least you don't talk like this," Puru remarked softly. He took her hand in his. "No one meant this to happen."

"You are so smitten that you don't see her plans!" she spat out. "A woman who separates a mother from her son will never know happiness from her children!"

"It was my decision! It had nothing to do with Vanita."

"That's what she wants you to believe! Tell him, Urmila! Tell him the ways of women."

"But Ma, Vani doesn't..."

"That woman was born this way. But what have I done to see this day?"

"My brother will not leave!"

"My wife cannot keep justifying…"

"This house is falling apart!"

"Will my son work as a mere contractor in a foreign country?"

"We will call when we reach," Vani muttered to whoever cared to listen, and shuffled into the taxi.

～❧

Eight years and counting.

The years have swept past since I last glimpsed my husband, but he is woven into everything I see. The man walking down the street has his head tilted to the angle at which Shree would hold his. The slightly ajar door of the room beside mine is open at the same angle as ours had been just before he strode out forever. A briefcase in an auto rickshaw might resemble the one in which he carried his clothes – but no photographs – as he tried to steal away.

If I carefully chose details from every single frame I have ever seen, I could easily piece together that event. I could choose a table from here, a mirror from that shop, a doorknob from this house and a man from an elevator and paint *Desertion*. Maybe in the next canvas, I'll really get down to it, etch out the moment of my rejection.

It had been an uneasy evening. Vani and Puru had been gone for three weeks, but that hadn't brought the respite I had expected. The large house was silent but for the sighs that fell on my ears, breathed by no one in particular. My husband was even more distant than usual, and I continued my botched attempts to crack his shell. Dinner was punctuated only by the clang of metal on metal as everyone fidgeted with the flavourless food, hitting their spoons louder on the plate to compensate for the missing conversation. And two missing people.

Although Puru and Vani's calls were brief and unemotional, I sensed the relief in their voices – Vani's freedom in an environment that could forget her history and Puru's lightness on being able to shed the coat of privilege. In Dubai, he had to start from scratch. It didn't matter what his surname was; he earned every meal, struggled for every reward and deserved every treat that chance brought him.

Sometimes he spoke about his job – as a middleman in a construction contract firm – and the newness of his relative poverty, but it was always with awe, with delight even. It was a romance he nurtured and needed. This outward struggle put to rest the battles that had waged inside. Puru, who had walked hesitantly among the grand buildings the Karmarkars constructed, would finally be able to own the streets of his new, harsh world.

I imagined the two of them labouring earnestly like the loveable heroes and heroines of films with trigger-happy villains. Imagined them sharing a single plate of food, huddling under a single blanket, working in the light of a single candle.

While I conjured up scenes of their difficult happiness, my husband only saw their dismissal and exile. Each day, he dreamt up new hurdles and sufferings, each night he called out to Puru under his breath.

One night, about a month after they had left, I remained awake long after the house turned dark. I sensed my husband twitching and edgy on the other side of the bed, but continued my pretence at sleep, knowing he wouldn't appreciate any show of concern. Even when the tap in the bathroom gurgled and I heard the cupboard groan, I didn't turn to look. It was only when I heard something swish under his side of the bed that I tensed.

The movement stopped for a second. When I didn't stir, it began again. The object must have been very heavy, because Shree was unable to lift it off the ground. A trunk of photograph albums? A collection of marbles, guns and board games that they played together as children?

Certain to my marrow that the object being moved was directly associated with Puru, I waited – for a light in the living room to switch on or at least the glare of a cell phone to reflect. Only darkness. With each passing second, my hunch strengthened. A heaviness settled over me as I battled my dread and sat up on the bed. Shree was not in the room. I walked into the hallway. Just in time.

"What are you doing?"

At 3 AM, with all the lights out, my husband was standing beside a suitcase, toying with the locks on the main door. He was fully dressed. He even had a cardigan thrown on.

He jumped and almost yelped. "Shhh!" He placed a finger to his lips. "They'll wake up!"

Foolishly, I started whispering. "Where are you going?"

He stared at the ground and pinched his forehead. "I should have been more careful."

An icy fist settled in my heart. "What is… all this?" I pointed to the suitcase.

He hesitated before blurting out. "I cannot take it anymore. The way everyone treats… treated Dada and Vahini is disgraceful!"

"But what are you doing?"

"I cannot stay here anymore. Where there is no place for Dada, there is no place for me."

"You're… leaving?"

It was dark; only the penumbra of a streetlight hit the back of his head.

He nodded. "I'm going to them."

His short hair stood up in spikes and I noticed that it hadn't been brushed. A stray beam illuminated his earlobe but not much else. I remember itching to turn him around to face the light. I yearned for the look in his eyes as he stole away from me. I almost walked up to him to rotate him by thirty degrees, but I stopped.

My feet shifted between confusion and clarity. One instant, I couldn't believe how this crossroads had come to be, and the next, I knew that it couldn't be otherwise. Everything led up to this and yet, nothing added up. My previous question had been incomplete and this was the only chance I had.

"You're leaving me?"

This time, he didn't nod. He simply turned and started fidgeting with the locks again.

"Stop!" Thankfully, I had forgotten to whisper.

He swivelled back. "Shhh!"

"I don't care who wakes…"

"Urmila, whether anyone wakes up or not, I can't stay here. I have to do this for Dada and for… myself. Maybe if I also go Ma-Papa will realize their mistake and…" he shrugged.

I wished I could shake him up and force him to face the facts – he lived in the shadow of his older brother, and secretly preferred it that way. He was fixated with Puru in a manner that everyone else labelled 'adulatory' or 'devotional', but I saw through the euphemism. In truth, it was baggage – a parasitic attachment. The filial blood didn't just hold them together. It walled my husband from others. In his private universe, Puru dominated the core, while others, particularly the unsettling ones like me, spotted the margins.

A shrink would need a lifetime to get this concept past my husband's defensive reverence. I only had a minute. I ached to tear through his claustrophobic attachment to Puru, to show him how blissful our world could be if we could just be us. But these would be futile, an alien tongue that he didn't speak. Only two approaches held meaning for him – one was Puru, the other practicality. In a last, desperate attempt, I turned to logic.

"Why are you going at this time of the night? Why didn't you tell…?"

"I told you so many times. You never took it seriously. It was always 'they'll come back' or 'we can't leave Ma-Papa' or some other excuse!"

"So you've been planning this all along? On the sly?"

"The flight is in two hours. You wouldn't have let me go if you knew."

"Now I know."

"It's too late."

"There must be another way! What will I do? What will you do? What about the business?"

"Sell it! I don't care! Everyone should have thought of this when they watched Dada and Vahini walk out of this house!"

"Listen, this is madness!" I took a step closer to him and he inched further towards the door. I held back tears. I would have all the time for them later. "Listen, I will talk to Ma-Papa again, make them reason… I promise they will understand!"

"Words won't work with them now."

"They will! I promise."

"I know my parents."

"Please give me one chance! I'll talk to them and…"

"No, don't! You'll make it worse."

I threw my arms up in the air. "Fine! You're right. Okay? Everything's wrong, agreed. The whole world has conspired against them, agreed. You feel terrible about it, fine. You're going to them, fine. What about *me*?"

He remained silent.

Of course, it was a foolish expectation. Shree's father had recently suffered a paralytic stroke and his mother hadn't smiled for months, but he was sneaking out. If he could leave them behind, how did I matter? A year ago, I hadn't featured in his life at all, and I existed only marginally after we were married; how was I to influence his actions in any way?

He broke through my thoughts. "Ma-Papa need you."

What I should have said then was, "And you? Do you need me?" What I actually stuttered in anger was, "And you? Don't they need you?"

"I'm sure you will fill the gap and care for them like a daughter."

"And who will fill the gap and care for me like a husband? Have you allotted someone for that too?"

Statements like these annoyed my husband the most – crude, smutty, unabashed. But he wouldn't let me provoke him.

I now wonder whether at least some of my outbursts were more his doing than mine. I deliberately used a vulgar expression instead of a delicate one, perhaps to inspect the new colour in his cheek or watch his eyes hit the floor in embarrassment, to gauge whether he could feel something for me other than a cool acceptance. Even if the emotion I provoked was shock, displeasure or anger, at least for those moments, I was more than a piece of furniture.

Once more, I was disappointed. His voice revealed no emotion. "Urmila, consider the words you speak. They do not suit a woman of this household."

Then, I heard for the first time, the sentiment that would plague me for years – "Vahini would never talk like that."

"What do you know about Vani? I have lived with her for…"

"I know enough! She is not brash and indecent."

Shree's conviction about Vani's virtues was based on an irrefutable logic – she was attached to Puru, and hence embodied an extension of all his goodness. When Ravi had spilled the beans on the relationship between Vani and Puru, Shree did not care about its inappropriateness. He only registered that Puru had chosen her, and so she was blameless.

The higher she floated towards the realms of goodness, the more I was pushed down in Shree's perception. I didn't lower my eyes when I spoke to his parents, didn't pass the rice nervously at the dining table, didn't serve him before anyone else, didn't know how every single member of the household preferred their tea (ginger/milky/green/masala) and fuss over the various beverages for an hour each morning.

"Just because she speaks in whispers and takes care of the breakfast doesn't mean that I am not…"

"She understands where a woman's dignity lies."

"Really? And where is that?"

"In the way she carries herself, in her speech and her gestures. For once, stop thinking of yourself and be there for another person, Urmila."

"And where does your dignity lie? In sneaking out of the house, leaving behind your wife in the middle of the night?"

"I had to resort to this because of you! You wouldn't have let me go otherwise! You fought with me every time I brought it up."

"Did you join hands and walk around the fire with your *brother*? Did you pledge vows to him? Did you place a mangalsutra around his neck?"

"We are bound by blood! My commitment to him dates far before I ever saw you."

"Then you shouldn't have married! You weren't yours to pledge."

For the first time, a change – his stoic posture dropped, his hand fell from the doorknob. My victory was my defeat; my fears stood confirmed. How could he be mine if he wasn't his first? Wasn't he as helpless as I was? In complete submission to the throes of love, in deference to its sacrifices.

I wished for that moment to stretch on, the one moment when we stood without pretences, in full sight of the baggage we carried – the instant when we had stripped ourselves and gazed at the sorrowful nakedness of our minds. We were victims, both, and inflicted stings on each other to forget our own attachments.

Our brief intimacy was pierced by a cry. "Chhotu? Are you awake?"

"Urmila?"

The first question had been thrown by Papa, the second by Ma, whom I could hear tottering towards us.

My husband turned his back to me and resumed the battle with the latch. It seemed to be stuck – my only ally. I struggled to find a way to hold him until his mother reached us.

"At least tell Ma! Don't run off like that."

"You tell her in the morning. Just explain away this noise somehow. Let them spend the night peacefully." My husband's efforts with the locks intensified.

"I'm not going to…"

"Urmila, just promise me. Please!"

"But what sense does it make? They'll know anyway. She's near her bedroom. Just tell Ma everything you told me and…"

"I don't want another scene."

Of course he didn't. My husband not only hated scenes, he hated every little fragment that went into them – dialogue, expressions, people, repartee, issues, groups, banter, questions. He would go to extremes to avoid a confrontation, even if it did nothing but intensify the heat. A master at ignoring and playing down, he could stretch a discussion for years, simply because he would never get down to it in earnest.

Shree loved backdrops; he could merge effortlessly in any setting until he was as unremarkable as a potted plant. His one active pursuit was to appear as passive as possible, never mind that to create such an appearance, he often had to take the most vigorous route possible.

This was one such example. Planning for days, coordinating endlessly this escape that no one would see, though everyone would know. He'd do everything he wanted to; he just didn't want it watched.

Perhaps my inability to picture my husband's face is not because of me, but him. He could camouflage like a shadow. He would blend with the sofa, disappear through a mesh of plants or hide behind food. His expressions were always fleeting, his mind restless, his body missing from crucial scenes, because he preferred it that way. Perhaps even now, through the years that separate us, he still holds command over how he is perceived. Even if I sketch till I run dry, his face dodges out of sight.

His last instructions to me were clear. "Tell them tomorrow. Don't do anything rash. Wait for us to come back – all of us."

The door swerved open and the streetlight outside outlined my husband's receding form. He stooped to pick up his bag and looked in my direction one last time. Then he sped away. As he turned, I caught a glimpse of his cheek. Was that a teardrop or a bead of sweat or just a play of light?

I stood with the door open until Ma reached me. "Urmila? What happened?"

What could I say? The rejection I dreaded had crept up while the world slept. I whispered to his absent figure, "My husband is not in love with me." Trembling, I inched closer towards the door. "He does not love me." I couldn't bear to look away from his direction. Nothing else mattered.

"Why is the door open? Who were you talking to?"

I battled with myself for an answer.

"He has left to follow Puru and Vani."

"Hai Ram!"

Both her hands went up to her mouth and her cane clanked to the floor. She followed the stick, sinking in a heap. I rushed to support her head before it could fall limp. I crouched near her, cradling her head. From his room, my father-in-law moaned and pelted questions that no one answered.

For a long time, we sat huddled together against the wall, breathing in each other's distress. The door remained open and the streetlight washed over us along with the chill of a breeze. We sobbed intermittently but were mostly silent, only our chests heaving. As the hours ticked away and dawn erupted, neither could bear to shut the door. What if his flight was cancelled? Or a rainstorm hit the airport? Or his passport was suddenly declared invalid? What if in the taxi my face clouded his vision? What if?

∞

For the first few weeks after my husband left, Ma searched for me every morning. She peeked into the kitchen, the balcony and the bathroom, not stopping until she found me. She searched me for signs of packing, grew anxious when I made three different pickles together – "What is the need for that? You'll be here to make more, nahi?" – and kept reiterating that Shree would be back – "If you are here, at least he'll have one more reason to come sooner…"

Several sonless horizons later, she changed her mind. "Go Umi. Go to him."

I threw my head on her tiny lap. "I don't know."

"Maybe you can create a relationship yet. It is selfish to keep you here. Because of us…"

"No, Ma. I don't want to go."

"What? Why?"

"So he can come to me."

Slowly, my colours transformed. Dubai. I dreamed of deserts, dry and sandy, ravaged by winds and ignored by clouds, of dunes and domes, brown and feverish, burning my skin.

With each day, the hopelessness sunk deeper. My rejection burned brighter, clearer, more final. Soon, my body gave up the pretence. I struggled to perform the most ordinary responsibilities. Once, I was chewing on toast when suddenly, I didn't want to feed this body, couldn't imagine nourishing it to face the life that stretched ahead. I spat the food on my plate and returned to the canvases and paints scattered in the bedroom. The next day, Geeta forced juice down my throat.

I began to hate loud sounds first; then, I couldn't tolerate movement. Soon, I could barely bring myself to speak. I'd ignore the phone, the doorbell, the questions. I'd respond with a shake of the head or broken, hanging sentences.

"At least talk to me!" Aai would plead with me each time she came over. "Come back home to us."

I'd point towards Ma and Papa's room and shake my head.

"They're also getting worried about you."

I'd nod. I knew. "What is there to…." I'd start and stop.

"Don't keep it bottled inside you, Umi. Does he call?"

I shut my eyes.

"Have you painted anything… new?"

"I'm tired."

One day, Aai brought a strange notebook. It had a spiral binding and every page was in a different colour. Each page also had a different shape – a cloud, a ball, a river; and some self-print – raindrops, footsteps, sand.

"I saw this and thought of you," she said. "Maybe you can write in it."

I shook my head; I couldn't write.

"Since you're too tired to paint, the pages have painted themselves. Put a few words down, you'll feel better."

At first, I just stared at the notebook, playing with the pages, flipping them and watching new colours emerge. It didn't really have a start or an end or a front or a back. It didn't even have a right side up. The book was crazy in a reassuring way.

I don't remember the day I started writing, but I recall the effort of each page. I needed several days to bring myself to hold that book. Sometimes, weeks passed before I could try again. I chose irregular pages each time, leaving many blank sheets, going back and forth, squeezing all the words into the sheet of my colour instead of letting them spill onto the next shade. I'm surprised that I remembered to number my sheets even in the whirlpool of hurt, anger and misery. The colours chose my words and urged them out, coaxing my pencil, breathing life into the tips of my fingers.

2: *Peach*

I wake up with the sudden, sharp realization that there is another day to face. I cannot get out of bed. I wish I had some long, terrible illness so I could just lie here and no one would say a thing. But I look normal – whatever that's supposed to look like – so I force my feet to shuffle out of our bedroom. I wish I could exchange my mind with another, any other, instead of this muddled, throbbing pain.

9: *Blue*

Shree, I give up. I'm broken. I'll do it. The clothes, the hair, the silence, the duties – I'll become the woman you can love. I cannot continue without you. I'll take your anger, your brother, become another you. In any case, every morning, some part of me slips away, as if it had never woken up.

3: *Red*

Send me a message, Shree. Ask me to come. Stop with the polite enquiries. How am I? What do you think? What do you want me to say? I cry every time I see the front door. When I see your shirts, I cannot breathe. If they say your name, I weep; if they don't, I ache.

11: Yellow

My goal is so small and seems so large. My mind keeps buzzing, 'If I can get through today, if I can get through today, if I can get through today...' but I don't know what will happen tomorrow. It's silly, it's awful. Each moment is a battle. Geeta said, "What has happened to you, Umi-tai?" and she started sobbing. I wanted to hold her and cry but I didn't have the strength. Then Geeta washed my hair.

8: White

Shree, I bought sleeping pills, five large bottles from five different chemists. How peaceful this sleep will be! For the first time, your desire and your rejection won't mix my dreams and my nightmares. I won't, I can't wake up to your absence again.

6: Pink

They're giving me something, I know. Ma pretends they are supplements or painkillers for the headaches, but they never show me the names of the tablets. Geeta keeps them locked in colour-coded boxes, and doles them out thrice a day. I don't know whether I mind this. I can't seem to muster enough strength for an opinion.

13: Green

I've started keeping lists. Where once I noted desires, now I keep track of my achievements. They are remarkably small and extremely important. Today I added two new triumphs: went for a movie with Aai and watered the plants. These activities remind me that I am not all chaos. I am more than the hurt that envelops me, soaks my soul, squeezes at every fading memory of joy. I live in an invisible prison and for a few moments of the day, I am able to forget the misery.

7: Purple

Maybe everyone's wondering why I can't snap out of it. I am a burden. I just can't seem to cheer up and I hate myself for that. Aai comes over often. Baba sits in the living room while Aai lies next to me on my bed. She does that so that I don't feel too terrible about not getting up. Sometimes, I don't even open my eyes when we speak. Later, Baba walks me to the living room and starts a game of chess. He makes sure I play black so I don't have to make the first move. I move a pawn. I move another pawn. Then I forget the game and keep looking at the board. Baba waits and sometimes he plays my moves too.

1: Grey

They tell me it will get better. They mean well, I know. But it just sounds hollow, a lie. I'm not sad. Sadness is too small, too clear, too easy. There's only a bottomless, hopeless despair. I have no will to move or think. Even when I try to imagine you, Shree, I am exhausted. Sometimes I feel like my mind is shutting down because it needs to save me. I cannot live with myself.

5: Orange

Early mornings are the worst. I can barely sleep at night and the sunlight brings with it people, questions and the compulsion of getting dressed and trying to eat. I make an attempt to be cheerful, just so that they can look at each other and think, 'It's working, she's better.'

When I can manage the chaos of colour, I paint, otherwise, I sketch with one of the many abandoned pencils that lie on the bed. I insist that the pencils and paper remain beside me, even when I sleep. And this notebook too. I pick random sheets on which I try to remember your face. In those pictures, you smile. I see that unconcerned, careless smile and I shiver.

12: Pink, orange, florescent

My fingers have lost control, my colours have turned wild. I'm scared, Shree. This morning, I tried a cloud but the canvas just mocked me. My colours are psychedelic and loud, tripping quickly over one another, cackling as they laugh. They rise and fall, tumble and slip, swish and thunder, merged and break apart as if they are putting up a fireworks show. They aren't tied down by lines; they aren't slaves to harmony. Yet, in their abandon, they find coherence and music. Maybe we can only know true freedom in complete madness.

4: Brown

Shree, for every month that you've been gone, I've wisened a year. That's a lot of wisdom so far. Today I realized this – you wouldn't miss me if I were gone. Gone forever, I mean. Maybe it's a relief to be so immaterial, so unloved. Now I only have to untangle my end of the thread. It's a mess, but it's mine alone. The days I pined for you and still do, the furious strokes of my brush trying to find your eyes, the empty pillow beside me, they're all mine alone. And I can live with them on my own terms, answerable to no one.

10: Maroon

Now, they are open about the pills. They've reduced the dosage too and Aai and I go for walks most evenings. I don't know what is more tiring – *fighting the urge to sit every few minutes or battling the questions that everyone cannot hold back. I wish I could just stay indoors, but among other things, I am deficient in Vitamin D. I don't know how Ma and Papa are managing. You wanted me to look after them, Shree, but you should have at least left me in a condition to carry out this instruction. They seem to have aged suddenly, but Geeta doesn't offer them any pills. Maybe they are spared the dark clouds that abruptly descend and engulf me.*

14: *Beige*

I often dream of deserts, the dry, relentless heat and the unforgiving stretches of loneliness, obstinate miles of sand in every direction, with not even the kiss of a breeze on my parched lips.

But lately, magically, droplets appear on the horizon. Teasing at first, they sink into the sand, rounded by their full laughter. They fall relentlessly, their play taking on urgent notes. I toss on my bed. Soon, they are lashing in earnest and flailing as they hit the thirsty landscape. Curtains of blue wash over all the brown and the grains soak in the colour, becoming rich and dark. In time, the sand is saturated and gives out tiny fissures of burps and sighs. The drizzle begins to taper and a film of water spreads over the dark brown. My breath is cool. Lately, for a few moments, my body submits to the mirage of the dream, to the dream of a touch.

Eleven years and counting.

Around me, the world wore a cloak of change and normalcy. Geeta celebrated the birth of a grandson, Ma leaned further on her stick, Papa's glasses got thicker and my canvases covered the floor of our – my – bedroom.

The men called infrequently; Vani called regularly. The men spoke to Ma; Vani spoke to me. Through these convoluted systems, we kept abreast of the general trajectory of each other's paths.

After all these years, Vani openly admitted fertility issues – "Neelam-chachi taught me a three-hour prayer that I must say twice a day so my seed doesn't keep getting wasted" – and Ma silently accepted the event of a truncated family tree.

Yet a couple of times it tumbled out in sighs, "But if you had got pregnant before Chhotu left…"

Of course, she held Purushottam accountable for her sonless, grandchildren-less state more than she did Shree. When Shree had followed his older brother, in a sense, he stuck to the script that he had grown up with. Puru had left them for an outsider.

Once, I suggested that perhaps Shree was more to blame than his brother.

"Why would you say that?" she stared intently at me.

"Purushottam left behind two people – you and Papa."

"So?"

"Shree left behind a wife too."

She reeled just a bit and looked away.

"Umi... Chhotu was always foolish."

"He decided to follow his brother, Ma, but in truth, he did just the opposite."

"Manje? Why do you say that?"

"Purushottam left everything to be with his wife, for her dignity and happiness. If Shree really respected Puru so much, he would have followed his example, not his footsteps."

She crossed her hands over her chest and her lips thinned out. "When they were children, we always encouraged their affection. What do you know? So many big families crumble because the brothers fight. And here there is so much property... we didn't want partitions and court cases!"

I left it at that, but something changed that day. She looked at me differently, a little more wary of my opinions, conscious of whether she met my approval or not. When she realized that I was suspicious about judgements – even my own – some of her caginess ebbed. Over time, the traditional power balance that had largely weighed in her favour, sometimes tipped towards me. We stood together; after all, we were both women in a long-drawn camouflaged mourning, having placed our happiness in hands that we could no longer hold.

Each time Vani called me about a new fertility treatment, I reassured her that yes, surely, this one was bound to help. Ma, who heard all her news but did not initiate a conversation, observed my expressions as I held the phone.

"They are trying again," I'd explain.

Sometimes, she'd read my tone and pat my head. "It's better to have no children at all than children who break your heart."

I wouldn't ask but she'd answer, "I don't know the emptiness you feel. But trust me, where you are bare, I only feel pain. And I pray for my hurt to just vanish and leave me with nothing."

Yet, I found myself drawn to infants. Their elbows. Their shoes. Their cribs. Their bottles. I stopped changing channels when ads flashed, hoping for one of the famous Johnson's variations. I gazed at early photographs of Shree and Puru, trying to discern the features of my unconceived child. Shree, as always, could never outstare the flash of a camera; his photographs emitted a distorted, uncomfortable quality. If one image had a missing ear, another didn't have a cheek: if I caught a glimpse of a tooth, the forehead was cut off; if a picture captured a dimple on his chin, his eyes appeared askew and misaligned. I could sense the photographer's desperate urgency with an infant who attempted to run into, hide from or warp each frame, determined to evade every attempt at being caught and archived. Didn't he do the same with my paintings?

As long as their health permitted, my in-laws kept alive a medley of curious friendships. The men and women of assorted coteries often shared anxious spite with each other, and we had to bend over backwards to avoid confrontations. Sunanda could not bump into Vishal Ranpise since his uncle had swindled her cousin in a land deal. Prachi Desai who owned the beauty parlour must never know that we have anything to do with the Galas since they had rejected her marriage proposal in favour of a girl who once happened to be Prachi's closest friend. And despite the builder-lobby's famed thick skin, Sharad-kaka would have staged a walkout the moment he spotted even the ends of the hair of Ketan Kale's head.

We weren't the only ones walking on eggshells; my in-laws' guests demonstrated tightrope stunts as well. They were fretfully particular about steering away from all talk of grandchildren – even their own. Yet, with a secret thrill, I looked forward to their lapses. An apology for turning up late – Sona hadn't allowed anyone to sleep all night. A short description of a first word, initiated by an uneasy slipup, wrapped up in a hurry. An account of the new kinds of toys available in the market. A discovery of a toddler's talent for singing or mimicry – or wonders – art.

Bhishis were the most fertile ground for baby chronicles, and if the variables were in place, the afternoons would smell of milk and burps, elongating like a fresh piece of chewing gum. They were punctuated by Gayatri-kaku's horror at her grandson's innocent queries, Sangeeta-kaku's delight at her granddaughter being accepted at the same school she had once studied at, and Latika's thinly veiled smugness on the birth of a son after three daughters.

My in-laws always encouraged such discussions, determined to prove that they had no cause for discomfort. However, invariably, such accounts required Ma to make an important phone call, scamper into the kitchen for more water or reprimand Geeta for forgetting to offer kothimbir wadis. Only I listened wordlessly, wishing they wouldn't stop, that someone else would remember a related incident, maybe even repeat an old memory – anything to keep the gurgling images alive.

The vow of children and progeny is a clever one; it binds all the other promises together. On that fateful day I had made this vow with his hand in mine, and I cannot bear to break it. However, I walk this path alone.

The fertility clinic is a string of contrasts held together by various forms of desperation. I am greeted by fumes of disinfectant rising from freshly scrubbed floors. Just where the vapours disappear, babies smile at me from posters, each with more dimples than hair. The whiff of their milky breaths and floral lotions is almost tangible, mixing with the odours of the disinfectant.

The woman at the reception notices my anxious, darting eyes and offers a practised smile. "Hi, I'm Monica."

"Urmila."

"What can I do for you, Urmila?"

"Actually I'm not sure. I wanted to check… make some enquiries…"

She nods as if she knows exactly what I mean.

"Alright, you fill up this form and then we'll talk again."

She hands over an elaborate questionnaire clipped to a writing board with a pen attached to it. "Take as long as you like." She points to a sofa behind me.

I haven't even got past the biographical details before I am lost. Age, sex, gender and contact numbers were straightforward but "marital status"? Should I stick to the legal status or the practical one?

After struggling with the form, I wait for the visitors at her desk to leave. On seeing my piecemeal answers, she leads me to an empty cubicle and asks me to wait for Dr Belsare. Everything in that space is a monochrome shade of white. The table, chairs, floor, walls, ceiling, even the paper in my hand all merge into one another like they have been carved from one single block. Only posters of infants in various moods and tempers break the singularity of the whiteness. I doodle behind the form, the black ink streaking across the page like a polluted river.

It takes her over 20 minutes to rush into the cubicle, but when Dr Belsare sits, she exudes the comfort of a plump, sweaty matronly woman who is deeply concerned, even if slightly inefficient. I pour out the facts – separated from my husband for over a decade, considering artificial insemination, entirely unsure. Grateful that she doesn't wear a mask of professional inexpression, I take longer than I had intended. She raises her eyebrows at my story, frowns at the mention of Shree and pats my hand encouragingly when I happen to glance at a dimpled brown baby posted above her head.

Soon, a bundle of brochures emerge from a white drawer I hadn't noticed. "You are a brave woman, Urmila," she offers, before clearing her throat and taking me through the process methodically. Was there any particular age group, ethnicity or background that I preferred? They had a database of over 3,000 active straws.

"Semen is delivered in a thin, 0.5 ml, high-security case called a straw."

I nod. Fortunately, she doesn't seem to be in a hurry and I

find that the more she talks, the better I feel about the process. Strangely soothing, smooth like the buttocks of the poster-babies – a far cry from how I imagined making a baby, but the procedure is truer to my life than any other course. A straw would suffice.

The conversation takes a route I haven't really accounted for – expenditure, medical tests, time frames, and percentages of successful insemination. Then she mentions the likelihood of twins or triplets. I smile. Perhaps it is time for such a bonus to enter my life.

PART VI

Shadru Thubhyaha - Vishnuthva - Anvethu

With this sixth vow of Saptapadi, as your wife, I promise you Ritu: togetherness and compatibility in all times.

Ten years and counting.

The house grew accustomed to our games. My father-in-law oscillated between moments of agonizing lucidity and nagging amnesia. He hadn't seen his sons for over a decade, but his declining memory did not allow him the relief of time. His mind often swallowed the years in between, and he longed for the men with an urgency that broke my heart. He cried for his sons one day and then spent the rest of the week asking when they'd return from office. I massaged his feet with eucalyptus oil and shouted bhajans in his one good ear. I confirmed that Purushottam had, in fact, walked in just as Papa had fallen asleep, that the water running in the bathroom was the sound of one of them bathing, or that they had called an hour ago, that very big projects required them to stay out until late. On days when he felt well enough to be wheeled into the living room, I set two extra plates at the dining table – Vani didn't figure in his fantasies – while Geeta visibly ironed the missing men's shirts.

Ma refrained from actively participating in this charade, but didn't contradict my pretences. Initially, I drummed up more enthusiasm, indulging the old man. Soon, however, I was offended by my husband's farcical presence in the life I had etched without him.

I needed the respite of my dawn rendezvous on the canvas, but I couldn't let Papa suspect. Although I painted with a renewed, painful zeal, I was cautious, letting Papa believe that I was indulging in flowerpots, fruit baskets or clusters of Victorian women lounging on Kashmiri upholstery. The smell of turpentine put him off ("It feels like we have a petrol pump in the house."), so I would mask it with cans of deodorant, reminding me of another lifetime when Vani ran after Baba, obliterating evidence of his sessions in the bathroom.

Stillness made its way into the house. When there was movement, it was sudden and jerky, much like Papa's spasms. A stream of doctors and nurses punctuated our lives, waltzing in and out of the fumes of disinfectant, turpentine and deodorant.

For a while, we drowned the silence through TV, but privately we were deaf to its rising and falling pitch. Gradually, we gave up our pretence and the TV became a relic, archaic and cold to our needs. It joined the list of objects whose meaning was lost to us, along with holiday photographs and the men's gym equipment.

One afternoon, Papa just wouldn't be appeased and I had to build on my performance. To convince him of his sons' presence, I prepared their favourite meal – misal – knowing that no one would eat it; Papa was on a liquid diet, I couldn't bear the spicy, oily gravy and Ma fasted on Thursdays.

The farce over, the misal wasted, Papa pacified, I fell asleep to block out the day. I was woken up by a damp, cold sensation on my feet. Ma sat at the edge of my bed, bending over me, sobbing silently.

"Ma! What happened?"

She just shook her head, still bent.

I jumped out of bed and put on my slippers. "What happened? Is Papa okay? Has he said anything?"

"Nahi Umi…" She whispered through sobs.

"Kaay nahi, Ma? He isn't okay?"

Finally, she looked up. "He's sleeping."

"Then why are you crying?" I sat beside her and straightened her back, rubbing it. The old woman joined her palms under her chin and bent her head.

"Why are you doing so much? And that ungrateful son of mine…"

I cradled her head.

"Even after he left you here alone. Why?"

"Ma, our relationship is not just about him, is it? After all these years?"

She shook her head. Then she placed both her palms on my head for a few seconds.

"Sukhi raha… God bless you."

She picked up her cane and tottered away. I slept again, surrounded by the paraphernalia of my canvases.

The last six months of Papa's life were the longest. I woke up twice every night to administer medicines. I washed away his groans and laboured under his weight, turning him so he wouldn't get bedsores. On days when the pain got too much and forced lucidity into him, he whispered to me, "Don't worry, it's not time yet. I have to at least see my sons' faces."

Yet, he died. The sons never came.

His breath escaped sneakily while we slept. Ma lay dozing beside him and woke up only because the silence was too unnatural for rest. She had grown accustomed to her husband's nocturnal wheezing, his moans and muttering. When they stopped, she looked at his peaceful face and suppressed a scream. She didn't even touch him, afraid of what she'd confirm.

When she reached me, I was already up, preparing the next dose of medicine and pouring out water. Ma stared at me through eyes thick with uncertainty, her face already white and cold.

"Stay here, Ma."

The smells hit me before I reached the room – sweat, shit and urine. I confirmed his pulseless wrist and tried to adjust the awkward angle of my father-in-law's body, which had suddenly become heavier. After throwing open the windows and cranking up the fan, I returned to my room.

I nodded. Ma stared at me. I stared back, scrutinizing every movement, every dart of the eyes, the twitch of her lips. I held her hand, shook my head again and waited for her to respond – for the flood of tears to wash over her face, the wails and sobs to ring through the house, laments and grief to shroud her body. They never came.

"Mala phone de."

Ma started dialling. I plonked on the armchair beside the bed, willing myself a few minutes of rest before I tackled the mountain that stared us in the face.

"Yes, sit for a while, Umi."

"Ma, we have to first look…"

"Ho – hello? Veena? Kaivalya bolte…" She whispered into the phone gently, conscious of the hour and the silence we were wrapped in.

Soon the house was bustling with white, murmuring figures. A group of neighbours took over informing the police and getting the death certificate; the nephews called the ambulance and arranged for the body to be taken to the funeral pyre. Someone took over the kitchen and made tea; another had prepared pohe and emphatically spooned some in our mouths. Women from the building brought flowers and carried homemade ghee for the puja. They set up the living room with their own silver diyas, kandils and samayees, not bothering to wait until Geeta brought the family receptacles down from the loft.

The druva weed, the incense, the priests, white sheets and new clothes for the corpse – every little arrangement fell into place by hands I hardly registered. The body was cleaned, wrapped and placed near the door with the head facing south.

"Better to keep it on the ground instead of the cot," one woman whispered to me. "He's returning to the lap of Mother Earth."

Then she sat near the head and chanted *Om Namo Narayana* in Papa's ear, right up to the moment the priests came and began their prayers. A lamp was kept burning near the head and jasmine agarbattis were placed all around the body to keep away the smell. All the mirrors of the house were covered so the departing soul wouldn't look into them and get enticed by reflections of family and wealth. A group of women disinfected the bedroom, threw away the dirty linen and even got maids to scrub the bathroom. Ma removed her mangalsutra and tied it around the neck of her deceased husband, asking him to choose her for a wife in his next birth as well.

Ma had not informed Roopali-kaku – their closeness having taken an icy turn after the men left – but she came anyway. Roopali-kaku still made her presence felt at common bhishis but was kept out of the more intimate gatherings. Sometimes, her footsteps didn't find our door for several months at a stretch. This morning, however, she dominated a corner of the living room and sobbed and wailed until a larger group surrounded her than the new widow.

Pradeep-kaka, Papa's former secretary, informed the mourners that Papa had discussed his last rites with him and desired a traditional wooden cremation instead of the electric one. This didn't surprise us – though Baba mumbled something about the wastage and the environment – the bigger problem was that the ghat would be available only by afternoon.

All morning, the body lay on the verandah as carloads of people from Satara, Pune and Phaltan poured in, jostling for space amidst the khaki-safari-suit clad clique of senior builders and junior politicians. The kitchen was cramped with high-octave whispers and over-helping. As a result, two diyas were lit where one would have sufficed, four heaps of marigolds were placed on a thali that required only a symbolic presence of the flowers and I was forced to down three cups of tea made by alternating groups of women. I stuck to Ma's side and kept a distance from Roopali-kaku's camp and her saga of memories and laments.

When we reached the ghat, I was unprepared for the fuss that would follow. At least 20 men believed that they were entitled to light the funeral pyre, considering the absence of sons. They argued as decently as the occasion warranted, until Pradeep-kaka broke up their frantic whispers.

Pradeep Godbole, Papa's secretary, had been in Papa's employment for all the years that the man had been mobile. When his boss suffered a paralytic stroke, Pradeep-kaka had also retired; Papa helped his sons set up a departmental store. Pradeep-kaka was one of those unobtrusive people who visited Papa every month, without once drawing attention to his loyalty. He looked into all the clerical needs of the family and was a witness to Papa's will. Now in his 70s, Pradeep-kaka carried about him an air of smug, entitled wisdom.

"Dada," he said, taking in all the men at one glance. "Karmarkar-sahib has left a will."

"That will come later."

"It's about his desires regarding his cremation formalities, Dada."

The men shuffled awkwardly at first and then eagerly launched into waves of relief.

"Then that will settle it!"

"That man thought about everything, didn't he?"

"He hadn't lost his mind to the degree that everyone believed."

Pradeep Godbole reached into his pocket and fished out a folded white envelope. It contained a single sheet of paper.

Namaskar,

I wish to thank you for all the affection and kindness that you have showered upon me, and for the assistance I know you are now extending to my family. The past few months have been quite stressful and I look forward to joining our Parmeshwar and freeing myself of this weak, disabled body. I am certain that I shall be in a better place soon.

I have tried to be as meticulous in my death as I have been in my life. Pradeep, bless him, is aware of all the details and shall carry them out at the correct time. However, there is something you need to know on an urgent basis, in fact, in the hour that I die.

I wish for Urmila to light my funeral pyre – unless she doesn't want to. I know it is customary for a son to carry out this act and every father desires a son for a moment like this. But my sons are pardesis and my daughter-in-law has fulfilled the role of both son and daughter to me. She has cared for me as my own offspring have not. I shall leave this abode in peace knowing that she has released this mitti and merged it with our Mother Earth.

I trust that Urmila and everyone else shall find themselves capable of carrying out this man's last desire.

Vishwas M Karmarkar

As Pradeep Godbole finished reading, a restless silence enveloped the group.

"Urmila?" One of the men eventually turned to me. "You want to?"

Before I could reply, another interjected, "What does that matter? This is highly irregular!"

"Dada wasn't himself in the last few years… Puru and Chhotu have hurt him too much."

"He seemed fine when he gave me the letter," Pradeep-kaka stated, placing the sheet carefully in its envelope again.

Another shuffled ahead, "Beti, you know that a woman can't…"

"Even your presence here is actually a big thing," someone else offered.

As if to balance this perspective, a third voice added, "But that much is okay, we're not saying about that. Now modern family girls come to…"

"Arre? Look at the other families! Where are the girls?"

I cleared my throat. "Kaka, Dada, you would want to respect Papa's last wishes?"

My question brought out hesitant smirks from the smarter members of the party. Anyone who dared to challenge the note would be disrespecting the former patriarch. Of course, lighting the funeral pyre in the absence of the dead man's sons was a matter of prestige, especially in the case of a man as influential as Papa. But the cleverer of the men realized that it would be more advantageous to follow the letter. One group conferred with the manager of the cremation ground, another spoke to a couple of priests and a third went out on bikes in search of what they called a 'modern' pundit.

Of course, detractors for the sake of religious practice were many but I did not dwell on their criticisms. In fact, I stayed away from the debate as much as I could. All I saw were animated heads debating in earnest. The groups warred it out between themselves while I stood ready, taking in the fragments that drifted towards me:

"That one will take money."

"Have they even informed the sons?"

"…for the first time…"

"Is it, you know, that time of the month?"

"Hai Sri Ram! I hadn't taken him to be the modern kind."

"…made him lose his mind…"

"Who is interested in contesting this?"

"I have my son's admission today."

"The cash is in the car."

While we waited, some of the women began strolling the grounds in groups. Many wrapped their dupattas about their heads and decided to accompany me if I did manage to light the pyre.

It took an hour but finally a willing priest was found, the protesters pacified, the mantras chanted and the green signal given. The body was carried thrice around the pyre anticlockwise and then placed over the logs. The pundit gave me a thick branch of kusa grass, which I dipped into the eternal fire of the doms who attend to funerals. The flame rose and flashed immediately – an auspicious sign – and some of the hostility towards me melted. A clay pot filled with water was placed on my shoulder and I was instructed to hold the flaming grass behind my back. Baba helped me pull my pallu tight over my mouth as the hot embers and fumes wafted over my face and into my mouth.

"Move anticlockwise," the priest explained. "In death, everything is reversed. Use your left hand."

I tried to tell him that I was already left-handed and but the smoke caught in my mouth and the calls to Yama got louder. The men zealously invited him to take away the soul of their dear friend and release him from his ties.

"The sacred flames will push his soul towards the heavens," the priest clarified. "The body will disintegrate and return to its elements."

Yet, as I walked, the heat of the flames paled in comparison to the glare of the group. They lapped the spectacle eagerly, their eyes taking in my tired, lonely body. They'd relish the discussion of this sight later too. The family that couldn't, wouldn't accept the inevitable, now reduced to ash. The woman who held on when the rest of the world had learnt newer pains.

With each round of the body, Baba knocked a hole in the water pot, symbolizing the oozing out of life. After three such cracks, the pundit instructed, "Now drop the pot and move away. Don't turn back to look at the body."

I let the pot slip and crash. The chants intensified and the crackle of the fire grew sharper. Soon, the smell of burning flesh singed my nostrils. There was no denying it now. My husband would never return. He hadn't come on Papa's deathbed; he wouldn't come on mine.

Suddenly, the realization fell heavily upon me. I stumbled. "Umi!" Several hands reached out. I sunk to the ground. They tried to haul me up, but I wouldn't oblige. I wanted to melt into the ground, to dissolve in the air, to disappear.

"She was very close to her father-in-law," I heard someone explain. Tears streamed down my face. "He's in a better place now," a woman patted my head. I shook my head as if to explain but the effort drained me further. I couldn't keep my eyes open.

"Here, drink this water."

"Someone get a chair!"

I fought the hands that tried to steady me. My mouth lost its will to speak. A weight pushed down on me and I had no fight left. I was alone, and I would always be. My fingers groped clusters of hot, wet earth. I yearned to sink lower into the ground, to lie in its rough and damp embrace.

A familiar hand weighed down my cheek. I looked up. "Ma!" I cried and fell again, sobbing so hard I ran out of breath.

"It's… it's over." I whispered. "He's gone for good."

She nodded and held me close. Then pushing my shoulders away, she looked at me intently. My gaze sought comfort in the hard ground with its smooth pebbles.

"You're burning!" she touched my forehead.

"I'm over," I muttered, through parched lips. "There's nothing left."

But there was. A short while later, I had to perform kapalakriya – cracking the skull to release the soul.

The others rallied around me and volunteered to take over.

"The real cremation is over now…"

"This is an add-on, a second part."

"If it doesn't break in the first instance, the soul suffers."

"Then you have to do the shanti puja for fourteen days."

"And offer food to the crows of this ghat. Only if the crows accept the food immediately is it clear that the soul has been liberated…"

"But if the dead person has any unfulfilled wishes, then also the soul will remain in limbo."

"Yes! Then too the crows won't accept the pinda… the food."

It was getting a little out of hand and to quieten them if nothing else, I reached for the bamboo with which I needed to tackle the skull. A hush fell over the group. I brought the bamboo down, leaning all my weight on it. The skull cracked. A faint cry of jubilation erupted but stopped midway. I dropped the stick. Ma huddled towards me.

"I broke it."

She nodded. "You broke it."

My head spun and I was glad for her arm tight around my shoulders. "Nothing more to do," I whispered.

We reached the car and locked ourselves in, glad to be left alone. I shut my eyes. Slowly, like in a dream, her sobs flitted towards me. They yanked me back to her pain.

"Ma…" I reached for her hand.

"Thank god you are here, Umi."

"I'm here, Ma."

"It's just us now."

"Yes," I whispered, looking away.

For a long time, we didn't speak – two women staring vacantly into the distance, reeling under the blow of cold loneliness. She had lost her husband, and mine had forsaken me again – a new, final rebuff. Our mouths mute, our hearts screamed for the man who was lost to one and the husband who had walked away from the other; for one man's desertion in death and another's absence at the time of his duty. I sobbed for the sons who had left her and the ones I had not birthed.

∽✍

The death of the only man in the house brought home the finality of our fate. Like unwilling survivors of a war, we shuffled about, uncertain of our role. We no longer needed to pretend for Papa, but we had fallen into the pattern. It would be too jarring to abandon our role-play and face our empty identities.

Each year, we mourned the anniversary of my husband's departure in a secret, silent ceremony – the watching of the door. We played out this rite without ever mentioning it, keeping up the charade of observing the rain or simply staring into space with a cup of tea, but we couldn't bear to miss it.

Although the family had dissolved irrevocably, and it was futile to wish otherwise, Vani wouldn't lose hope. She was determined to hold her child, never mind all the failed pregnancies and her increasingly frail health. Even the damning prophecies of her horoscope wouldn't deter her. She tried one remedy after another, one soothsayer too many, and fussed over three different herbal treatments a day. She reached out to anyone who would listen, and anyone who wouldn't.

One afternoon, as Ma and I were cradling our second cup of tea, the phone rang.

"Hello?"

"Umi!"

"Yes!"

My mother-in-law sat just three feet away. I attempted to display enough enthusiasm for Vani's satisfaction and adequate disinterest for Ma's.

"It's me!"

"How are you? All of you?"

"Shree-dada is fine. Puru also. How is Ma? Did she ask about us?"

"She's good. Of course! Don't worry."

"Good, good…"

She paused.

"Is everything all right?"

Ma gave up her pretence with the newspaper and leaned in.

"Yes, nothing to unnecessarily be concerned about."

"Then?"

"Umi, you have been to America na?"

"No. Why?"

"Oh, I thought you had gone for your painting work."

"No, I haven't. Why?"

"Actually Umi," her voice dropped, "I have been taking many medicines. Even the prayers and three sacred amulets…"

"Hmm. You told me."

"For the fourth time, the child fell, Umi."

"Oh!"

I never knew about the pregnancies, only the miscarriages. It was inauspicious to announce a pregnancy before the first trimester; the mother or child could be affected by an ill gaze, a jealous look or a potent curse. Widows and childless women in particular were usually the last to be informed.

"Puru is more devastated than me," Vani continued. "And Shree-dada is lost because of our grief. Sometimes I think maybe I should just accept my fate."

"Oh Vani, maybe it is best if…"

"That's why I was asking if you are going to America. They are quite ahead in these things, no? Maybe there are some advanced options. But don't tell Puru I am asking you this, he doesn't want so much tension."

"Vani, I haven't spoken to him for more than 10 years!"

"I know. I know… it's just… don't tell him. Okay?"

As the conversation continued, Ma moved closer and stood directly in front of me.

"Fine, I won't. But I don't think the America idea will help so much. There are so many good places in India. People come from all over the world…"

"Umi, I don't know about India. Puru gets upset when the talk comes up."

"Even if it is for treatment?"

On hearing this last sentence, Ma tapped my hand and frowned. I shook my head and smiled, indicating that there was no problem. I patted Ma's shoulder and turned away.

"For anything!" Vani was saying. "They couldn't bring themselves to come when Papa… they cried and mourned the whole month but they didn't… How much I told them, Umi, you won't believe. But we are married to stubborn men."

Vani had a way of making me feel married – that the attachment was not just imaginary, that there really was a man in my life. For this, I would always love her.

When I disconnected the phone, Ma was waiting, hands across her chest.

"That was Vani. She wants more fertility treatment."

Ma knew about the miscarriages but not always through me. Usually, Vani just spoke to whichever woman answered the phone. Ma received all news with a show of equanimity and she rarely asked questions. Whenever Ma answered Vani's call, she made it clear that less was more, often handing the phone over to me as soon as the first decent enquiries were completed. However, in unguarded moments, she reached out to me, replaying the conversation, adding footnotes and speculating on all the unspoken messages.

Vani accepted this distance with warmth and grace, never once straying from her stance of steadfast enthusiasm. I knew that this was another reason why my husband venerated the woman – this and her overt humility, her irrational generosity, her ability to toe the line, her clear acceptance of her place among all things feminine, but never feminist. If anyone ever painted or sculpted Vani, her form would be perfectly proportional and beautiful, her skin translucent, her eyes luminescent, her hair unravelled. And despite this perfection, men would only look at her with adulation, not desire.

"How much we run after things that only want to slip away from us!" Ma was muttering. "After so many years, hasn't she had enough?"

"She was wondering if there are any good fertility options in America," I ventured.

"America! Humph! We roam the world for children that elude us."

I remained silent. Perhaps Ma was glad. Maybe she was secretly thrilled with the bizarre tit-for-tat situation she and Vani were caught in. However, none of us had to think too long about Vani's medical tour to America, for within a handful of months, Vani placed another high-strung call.

She was five months pregnant. The foetus was holding on. "This is it, Umi!" she squealed. "I can feel it in every bone! This one will stay, it must!"

"Vani! Congratulations!"

I managed a feeble smile but Vani was animated enough for us all.

"You're going to become a mausi!" Her voice was breaking with excitement.

"Please Umi, do the nazar utarna for us. I can't let anything happen to this one!"

"You need to be here for that, na?"

"Use some photographs for now..."

The only photographs I had of Vani were her wedding pictures – our wedding pictures. I hadn't touched the album for years. It was enough to live the marriage day after day; I had no desire to relive the wedding.

Five months later, a letter reached us, with a photograph. On the back, Vani had scribbled, 'God is indeed with those who are patient.'

The child was bald, wrapped in white, eyes bulging and curious, lips slightly parted. The photograph contained movement. It was apparent that he had been squirming a moment before the picture was taken and an instant later. A fist stuck out of the cloth at an awkward angle, its skin wrinkled and pink. The bright multi-coloured wrappings did nothing for him and yet I suppressed a gasp. His eyes were dark and intense. They looked right at me.

The child lay on a woman's lap, a dress with a floral yellow print, and a hand on the knee, but there was no way to ascertain if it was Vani's knee. I was no longer familiar with her wardrobe or her proportions. I did however, have my husband's perspective to view Vani; if he idolized her, she probably smelt of cloves, coriander or lemon, her angles had taken on a maternal roundness, her garments flowed, but her hair remain tied.

And then I felt the heaviness on my shoulder. "What is that?" I passed the photograph to Ma.

"Is it…?"

I nodded.

"Oh my God!" Her hand went to her mouth and stayed there until she shivered with sobs.

"Come Ma, sit down…"

"That's my grandchild?"

"Yes, your grandson."

"Oh Ram! Look at that face!"

"I know… he's beautiful. Here, wrap your shawl."

"Will I die without seeing that face?"

"Don't talk such things now."

"The milk is on the gas… Oh my grandson!"

I rushed to attend to the overflowing milk and when I returned, she was reclining with the photograph clasped to her chest, her eyes shut, her breathing heavy.

"Have they chosen a name?" she whispered.

"I don't think so, Ma. Vani hasn't mentioned anything about the name."

The old woman sat up and straightened her nightgown. "Vanita – is she all right?"

I smiled; this was a day of firsts. "Yes, she's fine. She is very happy."

"I think I will go to the temple in the evening."

I attempted a feeble, teasing nudge. "Your grandson, Ma! How does it feel?"

Ma noticed my open longing and shook her head. "Grandchildren are good, Umi. It's wonderful. But children – they are overrated."

We chuckled and turned again towards the photograph. Surely, after all these years, if we could still want the men, this baby would certainly be very easy to fall in love with.

As the photograph sat beside us during tea and then through most of dinner, I sensed that a decision was on its way. I was ready. This time I needed a new canvas to sketch a new blueprint. Colours wouldn't do anymore; this time I'd use the throbs of my body, the blood of my womb. It was time to make another visit to the clinic.

PART VII

Sapth Sapthabhyaha - Vishnuthva - Anvethu

With this seventh vow of Saptapadi, as your wife, I promise you Sakha: to be faithful and provide lifelong companionship.

It is too soon to be morning but I am bombarded by music. I pry my eyes open; the room is fuzzy. The ringing of a phone cuts through my grogginess. The room is shaky like a watercolour and nothing looks familiar. My purse rests at the foot of the sofa-bed while a dupatta hangs over the chair. My immediate sensation is that of a headache.

"Urmila! Is that yours?" Aai's voice tears through my sleep. I remember; I am at my parents' house. I have come to spend a week with them. I am also washed under a few sleeping pills.

My hands are too limp to reach for the phone. The familiar melody stops ringing and then starts again. It is not even light outside. I stumble towards the writing desk and see the light of the phone flicking on and off.

"Umi! Your phone!" Now Baba screams.

I have no time to put on my reading glasses and check the number. "Hello?"

"Umi!"

"Ma? What happened?"

"Umi! I've been calling for so long! Why weren't you answering?" I hold the phone an inch away from my ear and cringe, her shrieks breaking through the haze of my sleep.

"It is what … the middle of the night! I think …"

Beyond the curtains, I see an inky sky with the fringes of dawn. Streetlights and a couple of headlights throw themselves against the glass of my window.

Suddenly my head clears and a surge of panic erupts from toe to head. My fingertips tingle. I cannot ask my questions fast enough.

"Ma? What happened? Are you all right? Did Geeta stay the night?"

"Geeta? She's here, making tea."

"Tea, now? Did she give you your medicines? Are you okay?"

"Arre Umi! Forget all that … my God! How do I tell you?"

"Tell what?" A dread freezes me. Ma sobs at the other end of the line, as I stand paralyzed.

"Puru and Chhotu …"

"What happened to them? Oh God, what is it? Why are you crying?"

"Oh Umi! My sons are back!"

By now, Aai is standing beside me, frowning, inching her ear close to the phone.

I find that I can barely whisper. "What?"

"They're here! In the next room… They came an hour ago. Just imagine!"

She is bawling into the phone, her speech disjointed and garbled.

"My sons! And… Vanita also. You should see the child, Umi! Just like Puru. They didn't want to bring him up in a foreign country… wanted the love of a full family. She fell at my feet, the poor girl, said that the grandmother always names the grandchild. Oh! I want to take her hand and kiss it. Umi, I shall now die in peace."

I slump on the bed and will myself to keep holding the phone against my ear. My mother has already stuck her face to the other side of the instrument. I struggle to speak, to string together some words. I mumble something faint and slurred, but she is not listening.

"After so many years… I'll have a son to light my pyre, Umi. At least the pain that Vishwas had to bear has not fallen on me!"

It does not make sense – this sudden change, this return. My words are slow and measured. "Why did they come? I don't understand."

"What should I explain over the phone, Umi? You come here and see everything. Even I don't know it all. They have been talking since they came, but I can hardly listen to a word! My sons are back! I just keep running my hands over their faces… Umi? One minute."

I can hear the phone rustle as she cups it with both hands. Someone else is talking to her. It is a man's voice. The sounds are muffled, but even through the disturbance, the authority of his tone falls on my ears.

"Umi?" My mother-in-law is back on the line. "Chhotu wants to talk to you."

I take a sharp breath and hold it, afraid to miss the moment of his voice. This isn't how I had anticipated it. I am suddenly not sure if I want to hear him. What if he has an icy edge or sounds unbearably casual or asks me something unforgivable like… like – how are you?

The phone rustles again as it changes hands. A few seconds pass in silence. Then, "Urmila." He is deep and silky, mouthing my name with the roundness of a caress.

"Urmila."

The sound envelops me and then opens up to let me slip away. I sink further into the mattress. The tremors begin in my stomach and travel to my mouth. Between silent sobs, I manage a few sharp intakes of breath.

"Urmila, we're here. Please don't cry."

That only brings on the moans more rapidly. I have to cover the phone while tears run down my cheeks and into my mouth. Aai is now holding me, her face also wet and sticky.

"We had been thinking about it for some time, but didn't want to say anything because nothing was sure… After the child was born, Puru-dada was eager to come back. A child needs to be with his own people. So many years have passed; things have changed. Sometimes, it is foolish to stay where you are when the world has moved on."

Once again, I am at the receiving end of the trio's plans. His words echo in my ears – *Sometimes, it is foolish to stay where you are when the world has moved on.*

His voice continues, glossy and detached in its calm, a slow relaxed tenor, self-assured, polished. "Vahini kept telling us that Ma would let go of everything that happened. Day and night, she would say 'I now know what a mother's heart is.' And Puru-dada wanted his little one – we have not named him yet – to know our culture, our way of life."

I haven't spoken yet. He doesn't know my sound. He probably hasn't spent nights ruminating over the pitch of my vowels or the curve of my whispers. His words don't need me to probe them on. They flow easily, filling me in, cramming me with the highlights of his return.

"We waited a few months because otherwise the travel would get too strenuous for the baby. But even then, we were never sure. Vahini wanted to write to you… we kept telling her to wait till everything was certain… Urmila? Say something. When will you come back? Every night, we had discussions. Sometimes, we went to sleep feeling sure that we would return and sometimes I thought that it was impossible. The 14 years in Dubai…"

As he speaks, I realize that for me it is still 14 years ago. The clock and calendar have deceived once again. I have insulated myself from the pricks that would rupture the world I had built so painstakingly. And now, finally a stab has caught me off guard, forcing me to face a reality that I had refused to internalize.

"Urmila? I know you are there… Why aren't you saying anything? Can you hear me? Ma… ti theek aahes ka?"

The lump at the back of my throat subsides for a moment and I believe I shall be able to speak without breaking down.

I take a deep breath and whisper, "Shree."

Only the sound of shuffling greets me. "Shree?"

"Umi!" It is Ma again, loud and rapid, forcing me to place the phone away from my ear again.

"Umi! Umi? Hello? Chhotu, has the line got cut?"

I no longer want to make the effort to hold the instrument. I bring my hand down on the bed. The phone now sits over two feet away from my ear, but I can still hear her voice.

"What was the last thing she said? Did she say when she's coming back?"

I hide my head in my mother's lap, aware again of the intense spasms that run through my forehead. The cold metal of her bangles emphasizes the heat of my face. I am flushed and shaking. I wrap my arms around her waist and break into tiny sobs.

"Shhh, Umi, my child." She holds my hair away from my face and pats my forehead.

Her whispers are accompanied by the cacophony at the other end of the line. I can hear a child wailing, my mother-in-law rambling and the distortions of movement.

I reach for the phone, and placing a finger on the red button, cut out the din.

"He's come back," I whisper into Aai's nightgown.

"Yes, Umi. I know."

"What should I do?"

"Do you want to go there now? We'll all come."

"No, no," I plead quickly. "No. Not now."

The phone belts out its tune again. This time I put on my glasses and look at the screen. A single word flashes – *Home*. I am drained and have no desire to answer it. I cut the call and switch off the phone. Stumbling towards the bathroom, I declare, "I'm going to wash up."

"Okay, I'll put on some tea. Your Baba is also awake."

I switch on the yellow light and vigorously splash water on my face. The mirror reflects old eyes without any laughter-lines branching out. The lower half of my face is distorted and a little lopsided. My mouth forms something like a sneer but the eyes are curious, almost bewildered.

I have seen that look before and it has always made me flinch. But this is the first time I have noticed it on myself.

The peculiar expression has been thrust upon me at a variety of social occasions. It is a combination of pity, wonder and confusion, a concoction of sympathies, panic and bafflement. The expression asks one question – *Why hasn't she left yet?*

Is this the current that will sweep away my cobwebs – this frown in this mirror in this house? Perhaps I have been waiting for this singular moment when he calls me from his house, and I cut the line.

I find myself exhausted. But I am unable to tear myself away from the mirror. I eventually resort to switching the light off and engulfing myself in blackness. Once the image is indistinct and grey, I step out of the bathroom and climb into bed, sinking into the mattress of my childhood. When I shut my eyes, my eyelids are heavy with silence – only for the first time, the silence is peaceful.

⁊⁊

It has been three months now that I have been staying with Aai and Baba; the longest in 14 years. I see that they are glad that I am here, although they would never express it.

It is ironical that I cannot bear to see the face that I sought for so many years. Perhaps what we covet and what we despise are two sides of the same coin, and I have flipped my fate.

It is movement, yes, but it is not progress.

I haven't been able to step into that house even to take my bags and leave. I still subsist on the few clothes Vani insisted on packing and sending my way. Aai and I wear almost the same size and though I am sometimes contemptuous of her garish colours, I love the feel of her clothes against my skin. It reminds me of warm afternoons when I would parade in her finery while Vani swore that my catwalk was better than that of Miss Universe models.

The little house is cramped now, but it wears a genial cosiness. Aai and Baba are careful with their words. They know that I am sore and I love them for their quiet affection that hasn't yet crossed the line into fussiness.

I am afraid of breaking the news about my visits to the fertility clinic, and I delay the revelation for as long as I can. Eventually, on a carefully planned evening, after Baba is saturated with mint tea and Aai has returned with two new saris, I blurt it out, faltering over every detail.

"Aai, Baba, I've been thinking of having a child."

"But you were so sure you didn't want to go back to that house!" My mother is equally keen that I stay away from my husband.

"No… not that way."

"Adoption?" my father demands. "Is that legally sound, given your situation? It seems very…"

"Is this because of Vanita's baby?" Aai places a hand on my head. "You need to break away from all that, you know. What happens in that house should stay…"

"Aai, I had decided long before they returned. These are the brochures and forms the clinic gave me and…"

"Clinic?" Baba doesn't take the papers.

"Artificially assisted pregnancy? You'll choose a stranger's ... help? And Umi, you're 36! What about the risk?" my mother starts pacing the room, twisting the end of her dupatta. "And what will we tell people? What about the Karmarkars? And Umi, there are anyway so many orphaned children, so many who need love and care. Why don't we ..."

"Please Aai. I need this."

"These decisions are not reversible, you know," Baba walks up to my mother and sits her down. "You need to take some time. Wait a little longer."

"Baba, the risk will increase as we wait. As it is, it may take many months for the pregnancy to actually..."

"But do you really want to bring up a child like this? No father? No proper income?"

"The paintings have been doing so well."

"But that is unsteady."

"I have some money and investments. You know." The conversation is going all over the place and I find myself unable to steer it towards the points that matter. Finally, I offer, "I am visiting the clinic tomorrow. You should both come and see for yourself. Then we'll talk."

They either believe that the visit to the clinic will change my mind or theirs, because the rest of the evening passes cordially.

The next afternoon, they sit silently as I discuss options with the doctors, take them through forms, point out the formalities and nominate my father in case any emergency intervention is required. They offer small smiles to those I interact with and rarely move beyond a slight nod. I am certain that I have another battle waiting in the evening.

On the way back home, squirming in the heat in the auto-rickshaw, I blurt out, "I was really hoping that you would be more..."

"Ek minute idhar rooko." My father taps the driver's shoulder.

"Why have you stopped here, Baba?" Without answering, he gets off, trots to a shop and returns carrying a box of sweets.

"We cannot discuss our first grandchild without sweetening our mouths first, can we?"

Tears well in my eyes and I find myself struggling to swallow the laddoo that he stuffs in my mouth.

Aai and Baba take turns asking questions, assuaging my fears and emphasizing their joy. Aai starts an elaborate discussion on a ceremony needed to ward off the evil eye and by the time we reach the house, we have moved on to baby names.

I realize then that I have remained oblivious of their intense desire for a grandchild. Yet, they wish me a child more for my sake than theirs. They may have reconciled to the lack of titters and shrieks falling on their aging ears, but they have never stopped stewing about how the future would find me. This promise of a sturdy pair of hands, however assisted-in-creation, eases some of the worry lines on their foreheads.

Their enthusiasm is significantly lower when I announce my second piece of news. I'll move into my own house.

"Isn't this your house, Umi? Why take on all the additional expense of rent and all? As it is, with a child, your bills…"

"It's not just about the money! Don't declare that we are going to have a grandchild and then take it away from us like this."

"Aai, I'll stay very close by, promise. It's just that all my life I have stayed in… I just need some space of my own."

"You are used to that big house. You feel cramped here."

"No, Baba! This house has accommodated all of me – every desire, every dream, every decision. What could be bigger?" I smile.

"Then what? Is it some new modern fad? First the baby and now this?"

"I don't want to oscillate from my parents' house to my husband's house and back! Please Baba, I'm finally… with myself. I need this!" My voice shakes a little and I plonk heavily on the sofa, sighing.

Their gloved approach towards me ensures that the discussion ends quickly and cordially. Baba even mentions that he knows an agent who specializes in brokering properties around that area. He extracts a worn brown diary and begins flipping pages.

"Ah! Here it is. Bandekar."

"Bandekar? That huge man?" Aai peeps in from the kitchen.

"He has a thyroid problem. Anyway, he is a very decent man. A little talkative but that's okay. Will have good contacts also. Umi, should I call him over tomorrow? Discuss our situation?"

'Our situation' refers to the fact that a single woman seeks accommodation in a respectable part of Mumbai – a statement riddled with contradictions. It doesn't help that a fatherless child will soon follow, and perhaps a divorce notice as well. However, Baba assures me that Mr Bandekar will work around the difficulties and hand me the keys to a fabulous apartment just down the street.

The next morning, when the gentleman enters our living room, he doesn't inspire the same confidence. He launches into an animated gossip session with Baba, spilling out juicy yarns of people whom I suspect Baba doesn't know. Aai rustles up some pohe for him and I excuse myself on the pretext of making tea.

When Aai and I re-enter the living room, our arms laden with trays of food and tea, we find the two men leaning towards each other, discussing in grave tones.

"Ah Umi-beta! What was the need for all this formality?" he asks, picking up a laddoo.

"Come, sit," he says to Aai while he sits on her sofa. "We were just discussing an important principle of success. Success in life, mind you, not that money-money kind of success. Have you heard of the carrot, the egg and the teabag?"

I exchange a look with Aai who immediately becomes busy with the pohe.

"No. I don't think I have," I offer, finally.

"Then I must tell you. It is extremely important and useful ... particularly in light of this big step you are taking with your life."

I hand him a plate of food but he places it on the centre table and continues talking.

"You see, beta, your whole life, you must try to be like a teabag."

Unsure of how to deal with this suggestion, I keep a straight face.

"I'll tell you why. See, there are three types of people in the world – carrots, eggs and teabags."

Mr Bandekar turns by a few degrees to look directly at Baba. "Now, Joshi-sahib, if you put the carrot in boiling water, what happens?"

"It gets cooked ... err soft, boiled."

"Exactly! The carrot becomes squishy and soft. These people are the weak ones; they cannot withstand the pressures of life. They get squashed and beaten up, become pulp."

"Hmmm ... I'm sure you know enough people of that kind!" Baba chuckles.

"Uff! More than I would like to! So rich most of them are, roaming in fancy cars and all. And a little nail chips here and there and they start sobbing and wailing. Anyway, then comes the egg. When we put an egg in boiling water, what happens?"

He looks at all of us for effect and then grits his teeth.

"The egg becomes hard, kadak! These people become bitter with life's problems. They hate everyone and everything – blame the government, the climate, the boss for everything that's wrong with them."

"You should start giving talks at those management colleges, Bandekar-sahib!" Baba says while handing the man his plate of pohe again. "What insight you have!"

"You are too kind, Joshi-sahib, but all these things need influence. Where is one able to get into anything good without some pull?"

"Very true… So you were saying about the egg."

"Yes! The egg becomes hard. Then we put the teabag. When a teabag is put into boiling water, what happens?"

"What happens?" my mother asked, mindful that so far Baba has taken on the onus of keeping the man's mood buoyant, and has been unable to eat a bite.

"Vahini, it changes the flavour of the water! Its taste passes on and what was once a scalding pot of plain water becomes a refreshing beverage." His eyes open wide in amazement.

"Ah! That's a very good point." Aai holds up our guest's teacup, taking the chance to remind him of his drink.

He takes it from her hand and continues, "The teabag doesn't change; it changes the water!"

Aai and Baba keep Mr Bandekar busy as he brushes aside their suggestions of starting what they term 'Management for Life and Work'. There is much discussion about the waywardness of young people and I realize that they can confer over the topic so freely because they do not see me as part of the subject. It is a long morning, marked by lukewarm tea, dry pohe and drier discussions. Worse, he takes no notes on my preferences or options and nods vacantly when I manage to get a meaningful dialogue in. I worry that he is going to assume that my tastes match his, and send me on a wild goose chase around stoical housing societies with aging populations.

The meeting concludes on very vague terms; I am not sure if he really deals in the kind of apartment I want and can afford. It is very difficult to get a straight reply out of him, but Baba assures us that realtors tend to be either imprecise or overpromising and the former is always more reliable.

Yet, when he thinks I'm busy in the kitchen, he unearths his diary again and begins marking out more names.

The weeks that follow are too crammed for anything to register in isolation. I make visits to the clinic almost every alternate day, going through a battery of tests, and spend my nights wading through files of donors. Aai and Baba probe a few times about Shree's reaction to my decision. When they find that I am indifferent to it, I sense a lightness in their faces and a grin in their words, but I am too dazed and sleepless to trust my perceptions.

Every few days, I ride with Baba at 20 km/h, sit through hours of broker babble, and explore everything within a five-kilometre radius of my parents' house. While Baba ferries me to realtors and apartments without once mentioning the cost of petrol, Aai insists on accompanying me to the clinic despite my pleas otherwise. The first few times, I squirm when she places a cold hand over mine as we wait in the reception area. But as we move from one step to the next, my aloof façade slips away, while my head finds her shoulder, sometimes her lap.

"Remember, the procedure comes with no guarantees, but we will continue the attempts," the doctor states each time she hands me a home pregnancy test kit.

"What is best will happen," Aai insists. "You don't know what has been planned for you."

I soon realize the truth behind her words. While Baba and I cruise all over the neighbourhood with the broker, a flat becomes available just a few buildings away.

By this time however, my ankles are heavy and thick. My kurta stretches over my stomach, forming a neat semicircle in the middle of my length.

The apartment is one of 30 dusty ones fitted into three grey buildings. If Aai and Baba peer out of their bathroom window, they get a glimpse of the topmost floor of my building. The comfort of this proximity is what makes them relent to me moving out in the middle of my pregnancy. This, and my promises to engage a full-time maid within a month, and to move back at the slightest hint of a complication.

They still don't approve, I know. But with each passing day, they resign themselves to my decision. Watching their quiet support, I get glimpses of what parenthood will demand of me.

The landlady, an aging widow who lives with her son in Goa most of the time, remains near the gate, while Baba and I take the staircase with high wooden planks, and check the place. The two-storey climb is too much for her and she clearly feels sorry to see me walk up. She stands beside her car, squinting at us.

The apartment has a single bedroom, a large living room, a spacious kitchen and a long balcony. It is one of those curious constructions that was originally meant to be a comfortable 1 BHK and then converted to a 2 BHK by an owner with an expanding family. Accordingly, one section of the living room and balcony is partitioned to make a small chamber. This room is the ideal size for a studio.

I picture a swing on the other half of the balcony and potted plants along the perimeter of the railing. The sight of the activity just beyond the gate will abate some of the isolation, I tell myself. Plus, Aai and Baba will be over every day. And in any case, in just a few months, I'll have company. The kitchen will need some woodwork, though the wardrobe in the bedroom will suffice temporarily. A few carpets, some curios and a bookshelf will dispel the cold, damp air of the house.

The broker promises a fresh coat of paint and Mrs D'Silva says I can choose the colour. She pulls me aside and whispers, "But how will you climb up? Right now, it is okay, but in the later months?"

"I don't have much choice. I don't want to stay too much into the suburbs. I take art classes at Dadar..."

"Are you an artist?"

I smile. "Yes."

"Like sceneries and flowers and all?"

"Err no, actually I do… people."

"People, eh?"

"The bathroom and flush and all are functional right? I didn't check."

"Listen, will you do a Madonna for me? In oil paint? I want a large one for my bedroom in Goa."

"Actually I…"

"Everyone has the prints and the plastic. I want a real painting, with the baby, of course. I'll cut your deposit by half, and give you a 10 percent discount on the rent."

I remain silent, unsure about the strange offer. She has never seen my work and I have always struggled with realism portraits.

"And when the house is being touched up, you can get a couple of walls of that special textured paint. It'll really cheer up the rooms. And maybe my next tenant will also like it. I'll tell them it was chosen by an artist-interior-decorator. Okay?"

Baba, who has walked up to us and has been standing a few feet away, nudges me in the back.

"All right, but it'll take some time." I place my hand on my belly.

"I'm not going anywhere," she winks and hobbles towards her car.

The realtor – a reference twice removed from Mr Bandekar – grows suspicious of our conversation and is clearly taken aback by the discount offer. His fee consists of a month's rent from each, the tenant and the owner, and Mrs D'Silva's generosity has cost him a pay cut. She asserts that I'd be providing her with a "world-class" painting instead and emphasizes, "What is money, eh? Maybe she can make one for you also…"

However, that doesn't impress him in the least. The realtor haggles through a forced smile until the old lady chides him for making a pregnant woman and two senior citizens stand and suffer in the heat while all of Bandra East looks on, all for "a few extra pennies!"

A week later, Baba takes upon himself the onus of moving my things. He coordinates with Vani, who packs my clothes, books and paintings into cartons, all the while stating how much she hates it. Baba hires a tempo to carry the boxes and hauls 17 cartons up to the second floor.

Meanwhile, I sweep and mop the house, scrub the bathrooms, clean the grills and spray deodorant all over to mask the smell of paint. I hear the tempo drive into the gate and walk down to meet Baba.

Instead, standing beside the driver, offering the man a tip, is Vani. She turns to face me and lets out a shriek. "Umi!"

Vani scurries to me and holds me in a tight embrace, all the while speaking in my ear. "Umi! Why didn't you come home? At least once? At least to see me?"

Baba stands a little distance away and shrugs. "Vanita insisted on coming and meeting you. She wouldn't listen to…"

"Of course I would insist!" She releases me and peers at my face. "You haven't changed at all… look at me!"

She pulls at her slight double chin and smiles."Of course, that is discounting this little mountain here." She touches my stomach lightly. "It's a little too big for the fourth month, na?"

I struggle to take in all she says and does and how she looks. I realize that she sports a few greys, as I do, and wonder at the sweep that drove us from childhood companions to middle-aged strangers, dissolving all the years in between. The strain of four miscarriages flickers on her face, but most of the time, she camouflages it with a broad grin.

"I can't believe I'm seeing you, Umi. And it's all thanks to me! If I had left it up to you…"

"Come up. It's not set up at all…"

"And that's why I'm here. I'll help you set all this up!"

I am not sure how well that will work out. "I'll manage, don't worry."

"Oh Umi! It's so good to see you! I never thought this day would come. And certainly never thought it would be… this way."

I manage a feeble smile and move to lift a carton.

"No, no," Vani interrupts. "You can't do all that, not in this condition. That's why I'm here, na? Here, you can hold this for me." She hands me her purse, lifts a box and begins walking up the stairs.

Of course, I would have run into one of them someday, perhaps at a movie theatre or in a mall. But I hadn't expected Vani to simply hop into the tempo with Baba and announce herself, not after I had categorically refused to meet them or even enter the house to collect my things. I just wasn't comfortable, I explained to Ma repeatedly. Her sons had taken 14 years to return home; surely I could be cut a little slack.

Initially, they believed I'd come around and called every evening. When I informed my mother-in-law about the trip to the fertility clinic, she exclaimed, "But now Shree is here!" Unable to respond immediately, I only remained silent while she whispered tenderly, "Give it some time, Umi. It will all work out."

Until I announced the pregnancy, everyone seemed to believe that the time-will-mend route was the best. After the pregnancy, the phone didn't flash their number and when it did, for the first time, the word 'divorce' found its way into our conversation. It was a very tentative expression, a let's-gauge-her-response or shock-her-back-to-reality kind of exploration. When I worked around the word with a quiet calm, Shree knew that change was in order.

A woman moving back into her parents' house is a situation that can be repaired; a woman taking up a place of her own has a finality about it. My search for a new home did more to convey the state of our marriage than any divorce paper could. After all these years of being entwined with others, I needed to set up my own place, even if it was temporary, even if it was difficult. In fact, it was a very welcome inconvenience.

Soon enough, my husband stopped offering his token reconciliation, though he did once – on Puru's suggestion – mention that if I chose to return, he would be happy to accept the child on the condition that no one knew that he wasn't really the biological father.

The opportunity for this complex situation is far from arriving – he has failed me for too long and there is no way I can trust him with the life shaping inside my womb. Yet, true to his style, he maintains our ambiguous relationship. After the initial passing reference to a divorce, he hasn't broached the subject. I wonder how he answers all the anxious queries from relatives, and further, how he will reconcile with our status as my pregnancy becomes more apparent.

I should have known, however, that Vani would establish an independent relationship with me. She is determined to extricate a path through whatever muddled liaison I maintain with the rest of them. We go back too far for anything to matter anymore, and it isn't like Vani to let go.

This isn't the only aspect of the old Vani that I recognize as we sift through the cartons together; she is just as talkative, anxious and over-obliging. Yet, I am comforted by her presence. As we thaw, I find that I can choose my memories of her, leaving behind anything that pricks.

Soon, she unpacks a large carton and emerges with a saucepan and a strainer.

"Vani, you packed vessels? But these are not mine. They're…"

"They're yours. You've lived in that house so long… and

actually half of everything is yours. Tell me how were you going to make tea for your sister if I hadn't packed this?"

She laughs and displays, some cups, plates, spoons, bowls, pans, knives, jars, a chopping board and even a pressure cooker. From a large cloth bag, she fishes out sugar, coffee, tea, rice, dal, milk, potatoes, bread, onions and eggs.

"Vani had kept this bag of groceries ready." Baba mumbles while inspecting the contents of the rest of the boxes.

While Vani fusses over tea, Baba creates a makeshift table using one of the cartons and plates up some biscuits. She sustains a constant babble about how wonderful my paintings are – she has wrapped them – and how she wishes she had some talents too.

By the time we settle down to ginger tea – yes, she carried ginger too – I find myself slipping effortlessly into Vani's chatter. In some ways, it is like the years in between have never happened. Once again, she is the sister I love so dearly, the companion I have always wanted. Our banter reminds me of two little girls sitting under a blanket, a torch in hand, flipping through film magazines.

Vani tries to imitate Arab women, recounts how terrified she was on the plane back when it encountered turbulence and describes the houses they had lived in in Dubai.

"You see that box there, Umi? From there to this wall, that's it! That was the whole kitchen. If two people stood in it, one would fall into the cooking pot! Shree-dada had to cut the vegetables in the living room and pass them to me."

Baba's gaze falls on me at the mention of his name, but

my smile remains unwavering. Better still, I find I am quiet within.

Shree – it is like any other word: book, chair, tree, bus, face.

We sip tea on the balcony and our gaze falls on the activity outside. With office hours coming to an end, a cacophony of car honks and the drone of buses have replaced the gentle hum that had prevailed earlier.

The shadows of the boxes grow longer. The cream paint on the wall bears a richer finish when lighted by the dull gold that floods through the window. Baba gets up and rinses our cups. He then busies himself with stacking the paintings carefully in the studio.

Vani touches my hand and whispers, "Don't you want to meet him, Umi?"

I look down at where our skin meets.

"It's been so many months now and you haven't seen Shree-dada once. You don't even call him!"

"Did he send you here?"

Vani reels back, shocked. "No! Of course not!"

"What is the point of seeing him, Vani? It'll be like looking at that man driving that blue car or like going and seeing what my neighbour looks like."

"He's your husband!"

"He's a stranger. He doesn't know anything about me… I don't know anything about him! You know more."

"You care about him … and I know he cares about you."

I shake my head. "Then why did he leave me? What compulsion did he have to follow you and Puru? A marriage is not formed by walking around a fire and tying a thread! Did he ever live the marriage? I entered that house and fulfilled my responsibilities. *I* was a dutiful daughter, *I* did everything I could to please him, I was good to you and Puru…"

"Of course, but…"

"He may have held my hand and walked around the fire, but he failed its test, Vani."

The room suddenly seems a lot smaller. I wish Baba would leave the paintings and join me. "I don't want to live in that limbo anymore."

Baba appears behind me and places a hand on my shoulder. "Umi, I'm going to get some nuts and screws. We need to fix that mirror in the bathroom. I'll also drill the hook behind the door. That rod for the napkin is also slightly loose…"

I nod and he walks away, still speaking as he makes his way down the stairs. "Don't worry, I won't be long. Saw a shop in that lane near the temple. It should be open…"

Once his voice disappears, Vani joins me at the ledge of the balcony and turns me around to face her. "Now that you've done all this, are you happy?"

"I've stopped waiting for someone to perform a miracle. I have taken charge my life… so maybe I am happy."

She smiles. "Umi, look at what you've become! We have been

talking for two hours and you haven't once asked about your nephew. You didn't even come for the naming ceremony!"

I slap my palm on my forehead. "Gosh, I'm sorry Vani… how is little Sunny? I wanted to tell you that Sunil is a lovely name. His photos are very cute and…"

"He's all right, enjoying being pampered by everyone!" She guides me back to our makeshift dining arrangement and gestures for me to sit.

"How did you manage to leave Sunny alone and come?"

"Puru is home, taking care of him, and Ma and Shree-dada too. There's an entire army at his service!"

"He looks adorable in that photograph you sent."

Vani reaches for my hand. "Won't you come to see him at least? What has *he* done to you?"

I nod and smile. "I know… it's just that I've been so busy dealing with all the people who featured in my past that I have no time left for the present. But that's going to change," I affirm. "It'll no longer be about what was."

I place a hand on my belly and make little loops on it.

"You'll bring Sunny here, won't you? The little ones can play together."

Vani slips from the stool and sits on the floor. She leans towards my stomach and places her ear next to it. I bend and smell the coconut oil in her hair. As she encircles my waist with both arms, I find myself hugging her from the shoulders.

We remain that way, rocking slightly, making tearstains on each other's clothes, the room getting more orange by the second, and our shadows growing thinner and longer, until they are stretched, irregular beams on the floor.

⌒⌖

I wonder when I will stop feeling surprised at my happiness.

The morning is a taut one, threatening to erupt. I have missed such mornings for too long and find myself eager to embrace the tiny, domestic issues that face me.

Last week, Naina took her first step. Rhea is still to take hers. If they weren't both similar- sized bundles, no one would have guessed they were twins.

"It looks like a small step for Naina and a giant leap for Rhea!" Baba laughs as Aai frets once again about Rhea's milestones.

"Stop being mean about the baby. I'm really worried about her. You know… she's the elder one."

"Elder one! The doctor simply picked her up first from the large slit!"

The caesarean has left an unsightly mark along the circumference of my belly, but I touch it with fondness. *See this line?* I'll tell my daughters one day. *You came out from here.*

Aai sits on the floor beside Naina and claps animatedly. "Waah! Nainu has become a big girl now! You won't need mummy to take you everywhere now… huh?" She tickles my daughter's stomach and they both chortle. "Then you'll come to meet me? On your own… even when your busy mummy doesn't bring you, huh?"

A little distance away, Rhea amuses herself with the pattern on the tile, a pool of sunlight bathing her face. She is a quiet child, content in an old way. I suspect that joy will always come to her in constant, optimal measures. Naina, on the other hand, already displays signs of getting high on the yoyo of life. She breaks into an impulsive walk, laughing animatedly, waving her hands in abandon. The next moment she lands with a thud and sends a heart-wrenching bawl across the room.

Aai immediately starts beating the spot where Naina fell. "Bad floor!" she says, patting Naina alternately. "Why did you hurt my little darling?"

I watch as she wipes my daughter's tears, and whispers, "See, I hit it. Now it won't hurt you again. Okay?"

She takes Naina on her lap and rocks her. It takes only a few moments for Naina to erupt into wild chuckles again. But the safety of her grandmother's lap is turned on its head when she reaches out and pulls a hairpin from Aai's bun. Naina eyes the object a little too intently and the pin is an inch short of her cheek when I snatch it from her hand.

"Uff, Naina!" I pick her up and she begins screaming again. I set her down near Rhea. "Now be a good girl and play with your sister."

Rhea observes the new presence with the same steady smile, even as Naina moves from hollering to sobbing to giggling to throwing soft toys in every direction.

While the children amuse themselves, I set out three plates and plonk a pot with sprouts cooked in an onion and coconut gravy on the table. I place a packet of bread beside the food. Aai's lectures on healthy food have intensified and I have finally caved in to her pestering. At least once a month, I am subjected to a do-it-for-your-children-if-not-for-yourself sermon, always concluding with, "You're not so young anymore!"

They visit us almost every day and I ensure that I rustle up something that will not invite a torrent of fresh censure. I keep my fingers crossed and hope she'll love the curry enough to ignore the bread. I've been too busy mastering the girls' Cerelac and mashed potato concoctions to put my rusty roti-making skills into practice. I can manage vegetables and gravies but don't have enough practice for rotis – for the first half of my life, Vani had ruled the kitchen and in the second, Geeta had taken over.

They are both due to visit us for tea this afternoon. Vani pops in every two or three months and has apparently been spreading the news of how adorable the twins are. She has managed to entice Geeta into making a tentative visit this afternoon. However, I am sure Geeta has already begun feigning a headache to get out of it.

I don't blame the poor woman; it is a complicated situation. While Puru and my mother-in-law are unsure about what to do with my surgically assisted family, Shree prefers – as always – to ignore the awkwardness entirely.

Different sets of people know different stories about our relationship. Extremely distant ones believe I am living with the Karmarkars, slightly closer ones think we are divorced, most of the extended family are told that we have separated "but nothing is formal", while only a handful of them are aware of Naina and Rhea. Vani tells me that they have ended up in a complicated web of versions, always worried about slipping up or the circles mingling with one another. Consequently, their social interactions have trickled down significantly. This, she says, gives her an excuse to visit me so frequently.

After the twins were born, she broke down in front of Puru one day. "You don't encourage anyone to come home. You don't go anywhere. I'll go mad…" she apparently sobbed into his chest. "This has become like a jail! At least let me visit Umi!"

Hence, her uncensored access to me. On the other hand, in the past year, I have seen my husband twice – once here and once at his house, both times surrounded by the paraphernalia of family and the pressure of a truce. He has been cordial and quiet on the most part, emphasizing only that there is no need to go down the divorce path. I sense that he is a believer of the "if you aren't going backward, you are going forward" school of thought. Only that can explain why he maintains the status quo and expects me to consider it a step towards reconciliation.

"See? He wants you," Vani never fails to tell me. "Otherwise why would he say no to a divorce? Even with the children and all… that's a lot for a man."

"It's not enough for me," I tell her each time. I suspect that it will never be enough.

When Vani strolls in later – without Geeta but with Sunny – the same tirade falls on my ears. "I don't know how you are managing all by yourself," she states. And then with a twinkle, asks, "Do artists really make so much money? Are you like MF Husain or something?"

I chuckle and roll my eyes. "God! No. But I get by… and then I conduct art classes too."

"But there was that big protest some years ago."

"You saw that?" I ask, surprised.

"No, Aai told us, after… after we got back. What was the problem?"

"No one is sure!" I chuckle. "Anyway, I don't think I'll be doing that kind of stuff any more."

"What kind?" she wants to know.

I almost begin to explain, but I check myself. Vani will not understand. I have not created a single half-decent canvas since their return from Dubai. A few times, I fought myself and forced out some sketches, but they were false from the start. The lines were awry and the colours forced. Worst of all were the eyes of the women I attempted. The eyes had stopped looking. They were opaque, no matter what strokes I used. No longer were they fiery and probing. No more did they force onlookers to avert their gaze. Their questions had stopped. Their story had emptied.

"The kind that asks questions," I say, and before she can probe, I add, "Anyway, I have my hands full for now."

"Yes, but you already have so many!" She tilts her head in the direction of the studio.

"Yes, that should last a while." The past few years, when my colours spewed forth with urgency, I had churned out paintings by the dozens. They were marked by eager, determined strokes – seeking, probing, screaming. Sometimes, in just a couple of days, I'd had to reach for yet another canvas, yet another hunt.

However, for several months now, the images have vanished and I find that colour has deserted me. The studio is stacked with paintings, but now they don't speak to me; they are just heaps of dye and tangles of strokes. At one time, the pictures implored me ahead, charted my desires, but now they are as quiet as a sunset.

"I'll take my time, Vani. I don't need to paint like I did earlier."

"That's because of the kids. How on earth can one have any peace of mind with two little infants? Why even my Sunny... Sunny, where have you disappeared?" She looks around and spots him under the dining table. "You naughty boy, have you given your mother a moment's peace, huh?" She smiles at him, eyebrows raised.

"Now where are Naina and Rhea?" she continues. "Why can't I see them? Naina..."

Vani pushes herself up from her armchair and walks towards the kitchen. I follow her.

"I have invested the money from the earlier paintings. And then there's all the wedding jewellery and all..."

"Each time those two think up new places to hide!"

"But it is not enough to live in a place like Mumbai."

She stops peering under the table. "You know, Umi, Shree-dada should be giving you something…"

"That is not what I'm saying."

"That's what I'm saying." Vani places her hands on her waist and looks straight at me. "Now the business has also restarted, right? It's not like he can't. And then technically, you are still his wife, so if you need…"

"Vani, technically I was still his wife when a lot of things happened. He doesn't make decisions based on such things. You know it. So why bind him to something he has never felt comfortable with?"

"How much you have changed, Umi!"

I smile. "Things are about to change a little bit more."

"What? Don't tell me another kid!"

"Vani!" I roll my eyes. "I've been thinking – it's too expensive to live in Mumbai. And bringing up two girls… do you know the kind of toys available these days? Plus, Aai and Baba want all of us to stay together. Anyway, maybe we should shift."

"Again! Where are you thinking of?"

"Maybe Kolhapur or Ahmednagar. You know… a smaller city, at least Pune."

"Umi! So far… How can you leave Mumbai? Everything you know, everyone…"

"Yes, but finally, it comes down to a handful of people who really matter. Aai has relatives in Kolhapur and Baba's cousins are in Ahmednagar. And everyone has people in Pune!"

I chuckle, but Vani's face remains serious. "Listen, if it's about money, I'll talk to Puru…"

"No, that won't do. Please don't say anything yet. I still have to sort it out in my head."

She slumps on the armchair. I sit beside her and pat her hand.

"I shouldn't have brought it up so soon. Maybe after I had finalized…."

"And shock me later! No, this is better," Vani shakes her head emphatically. "At least I can dissuade you now. I mean how does going to any of these places really help? What about their schooling? Mumbai has the best schools!"

"Aai and Baba are really keen that we stay together and their house is too tiny," I say. "In fact they suggested it. If we sell their house… gosh, the property rates! You know if we sell their tiny 1BHK, we can buy a bungalow in Pune!"

"Umi, that's it! I'll talk to Puru. We'll arrange something and then…"

From the next room, a wail interrupts Vani. We both rush towards the sound and find Naina sitting in a yellow puddle while Rhea inspects her with a curious frown. A little further, Sunny remains engrossed in a plastic mobile phone that emits high-pitched ringtones.

Vani lifts Naina and starts washing her in the only sink in the house. "What happened to my little girl?"

I gather some rags from near the gas cylinder and begin mopping up the mess. We take turns rinsing baby bottoms and dirty dusters under the low-pressure tap.

"See how it is here…" I begin while waiting for my turn. "And their house is also so old, so small. What's the point of living in such a congested city? It's not like I am tied to a job or a business. I can take paint, art classes anywhere."

"And me?" Vani opens a new packet of diapers. "How will we meet? And Sunny? How will he meet his sisters? And the girls – they don't have only one grandmother. And Puru, plus…"

"Vani," I rinse the dusters and begin helping her with the diaper. "Why fool ourselves? These girls are not part of the Karmarkar family. Pass me that powder from the shelf."

"That's because you're running away!"

"It's because I have been left behind. I'm only catching up."

Naina's eyes have been darting from my face to Vani's, unsure of what to make of our expressions.

"Why is my little darling so confused?" I rub noses with her and she breaks into giggles again.

Vani frowns. "You're just stepping from the frying pan into the fire!"

"I have already been through the fire, Vani. I have felt it

burn my cheeks and singe my hair. Enough of these agni pareekshas!"

Vani places a hand on my shoulder and half-embraces me. "No one meant for things to be this way. It's not like anyone purposely made you go through everything."

"That's true, but no one loved me purposely either. I was never important enough. I just got dragged through the decisions he made – his individual decisions, never us as a couple."

"So you're doing this to get back at him?"

"No." I laugh. "I'm doing this to get back *my* life. Aai and Baba said that we could sell the house, buy a nicer place in Pune – for half the money – and invest the rest. They have other investments too, I have investments, some of the paintings have done quite well. I will continue with my art, conduct classes. Omkar-kaka has been talking about this lovely 3 BHK garden flat, it's very close to the Mumbai-Pune expressway. Imagine a garden! The housing complex has a club house, a children's play area…"

I rattle off the amenities as if I'm reading from a brochure, and Vani's curious expression settles deeper on me. Her eyebrows are creased and her hand remains frozen on my shoulder. I suspect that for the first time, she realizes she won't be able to talk me out of it.

"There are some very good schools nearby. The connectivity to the major markets and all is also very good. And even for Aai-Baba, there's a meditation centre, a jogging track, a swimming pool. In Mumbai, where is it possible to get…?"

"Oh Umi!"

She holds me in a tense embrace. "I'll keep coming to visit you," her voice rings in my ear while we clasp each other. "I promise."

"I know you will," I pat her back. "You'll probably be the only one."

When we release each other, three pairs of inquiring eyes are looking up at us. Sunny stands with his toy phone in hand while Naina and Rhea are on all fours. We sweep the children within our fold and they erupt into titters and giggles. Rhea and Naina sit on my knees while I hold them by their buttery waists and rock away. On either side, their cheeks press against mine and I feel the chuckles in their muscles.

"Oh! You look so adorable like this – all three of you together!" Vani squeals. "Wait, wait. Hold it. I'll take a snap. Stay exactly like this."

She fishes a cell phone from her purse and grins. "Say cheese!"

Only I cry "Cheeeeeee!!!"

Rhea and Naina, both surprised by the uncharacteristic sound, turn to look at me. At that moment, Vani clicks.

She hands me the phone and smiles.

On that tiny screen, my face beams, gazing straight ahead. On either side, my daughters are observing my expression with amazement. I decide that such moments will occur more often.

I look at the image for a long time. My mouth no longer seems bitter. The lips are not thin with anger. The eyes do not seek; they are calm and clear. The face is not frayed with dejection; it is marked by a fullness that comes with purging every cause of every wrinkle.

Yes, it is fourteen years younger. And fourteen years lovelier.

Acknowledgements

I'd like to thank all the people who saw me through this book. Saket, who would battle the world, return home and ask me how my day was, only to hear, "I thought of a new scene", and then promptly prepare dinner, so I may continue that strange, invisible work. Ma, my first reader, Dadu, who once introduced me to a magical world in a dusty, cluttered by-lane of Grant Road: the lending library. Kshama, who is my sunbeam and Nitin, who is hers.

Thank you Sucharita Dutta-Asane for your feedback, Anil Menon for knowing when to offer a pat on the back and a kick on the backside, Kanishka Gupta for taking the manuscript to eyes-that-matter. Thank you Pheji Phalghunan, Sandhya Iyer, Akash Shah and the team at Jaico for making this your baby too.

Thank you Guruji Naushir for the unending faith.

And finally, a thank you to storytellers past and present, who have populated the world with their beautiful, flawed characters. They have been some of my closest friends. Because the urge to create comes not from perfection but from restlessness, from the itch to tell those stories again and again, until their voices harmonize with ours.